P9-DFO-663

D0002759

The Mammoth Cheese

Sheri Holman

Author of the bestselling *THE DRESS LODGER*

Praise for *The Mammoth Cheese*:

"Holman has put on seven-league boots to tread a wittily intricate dance step. . . . [*The Mammoth Cheese*] possesses, page by page, or bite by bite if you prefer, an intense, refined and lingering flavor. . . . [It] lofts global literary thoughts upon agile local activity. . . . I like and admire her novel a lot."   —Richard Eder, *The New York Times*

"Holman has fashioned a tale that is poignant and powerful and, like an award-winning cheese, surprisingly complex."
            —Chris Bohjalian, *The Washington Post Book World*

"Stunning . . . A Great American Novel par excellence . . . *The Mammoth Cheese* is as smooth, and often as surprising, as dreaming."
                  —Bethany Schneider, *Newsday*

"Holman's novel is brilliant, the characters deeply rendered, the philosophic underpinning astute, the touch sure. . . . Holman is one of those novelists whose world you trust completely. She's as adept as Barbara Kingsolver at tracing the political and intellectual life of small rural communities."   —Barbara Sjoholm, *The Seattle Times*

"[An] enjoyable slice of Americana . . . A panoramic social novel with a needle-sharp point of view sends up both small-town America and politics."   —Bella Stander, *People*

"An intriguing and gratifying read, a mélange of characters and situations rooted in contexts both historical and contemporary, conflicts both personal and political. Though humor resonates throughout the novel, the emotions it contains and evokes are quite real—often poignantly so."   —Jessica Treadway, *The Boston Globe*

"Lovely, disarming . . . Tough, sad and surprisingly sweet."
—Jennifer Reese, *The New York Times Book Review*

"Holman has written a robust, witty novel that captures the comedy and tragedy of the struggle for independence."
—Ron Charles, *The Christian Science Monitor*

"Sophisticated . . . Believability is one of the things that make [*The Mammoth Cheese*] such a wonderful book. . . . I heartily recommend it."   —Sharon Barrett, *Chicago Sun-Times*

"Ambitious . . . Holman's ability to constantly create sharply turned phrases, and the honestly earned humor that she instills in the story, helps balance the tragic elements and make this a memorable pastoral fable."   —David Hellman, *San Francisco Chronicle*

"Holman's latest imaginative sprawl of a novel explores quintessential American themes—independence, patriotism and politics—to great tragicomic effect. . . . A gifted writer, Sheri Holman has written a deft novel about duty and rebellion and the ways we seek to mend the wounds of history. . . . She paints a believable portrait of small-town America, with all its foibles and heartaches, dreams and guilt."   —Anita Shreve, *Book* magazine

"[*The Mammoth Cheese* is] a bighearted story that incorporates the plight of the small farmer with the caprice of modern politics in an utterly pleasing way. . . . Holman does such a satisfying job at weaving American history into her modern tale that readers owe it to themselves to take a nibble."
—Karen Sandstrom, *The Plain Dealer* (Cleveland)

"*The Mammoth Cheese* is a capacious book. Huge and amazing things happen within it."
                    —Julie Schumacher, *Star Tribune* (Minneapolis)

"An outstanding job . . . Holman weaves the stories together so well that it takes only a few chapters for the reader to feel like a native of Three Chimneys. After that, *The Mammoth Cheese* moves quickly and effortlessly toward its surprising and memorable climax. . . . *The Mammoth Cheese* is about politics, history, religion, love, money, excess and independence—in short, it's about all things American."
                    —Jay Pawlowski, *The Rocky Mountain News*

"Flawlessly plotted [and] satisfying."
                    —David Kirby, *The Atlanta Journal-Constitution*

"The denouement of Holman's sharp American satire could easily be a scene cut out of a Robert Altman movie. . . . Holman's intricately crafted look at family, religion and class in the rural South seamlessly blends the quotidian and the surreal."
                    —Barbara Aria, *Time Out New York*

"Holman's splendid title denotes a loopy homage to the historical past. . . . This is one of the richest American novels in years. Its abundance of character, plot and promising visuals make a feature film version all but inevitable."
                    . —Bruce Allen, *Hollywood Reporter*

"A story about modern culture and the punch it packs in all corners of America. Whether it's the excesses of politics, industrialization or relationships, Holman takes readers on a witty and satirical trip through Three Chimneys, Virginia."
                    —Amanda Davis, *St. Louis Post-Dispatch*

"*The Mammoth Cheese* is a brave book, daring to compare the good product of the title with the curdled failure of humanity to render our own backstory without malice."

—Neena Husid, *Austin American-Statesman*

"Written with charm, intelligence and a lot of nerve . . . As in *A Stolen Tongue* and *The Dress Lodger*, Holman shows what can happen when imagination and audacity collide."   —*The Arizona Republic*

"An ambitious creation from an inventive mind. One of Holman's gifts is the ability to bring to life the small details and social under-pinnings of human behavior so realistically that it seems almost effortless."   —Amy Rogers, *Creative Loafing*

"Wonderful . . . [Holman's] story is deep and compelling, populated by characters moving and thought-provoking, and her images are precise and surprising. . . . Any way you slice it, Holman is on her way to greatness."   —Susan Hall-Balduf, *Detroit Free Press*

"Engaging . . . The novel's farcical elements are deftly integrated, as are its many stories, by Holman's limber prose as she movingly captures life in a small American town where even its young are struggling with the wounds of time."

—Sherryl Connelly, *Daily News* (New York)

"Holman's well-written words of cheese and love are a balm for those seeking a solid story with fully developed, endearing characters and a fitting and satisfactory ending."

—Anita J. Firebaugh, *The Roanoke Times*

"Time and setting determine character and plot in Holman's novels in a way that's reminiscent of the best Dickens novels of the nineteenth century, and the best John Irving novels in ours."

—Nan Goldberg, *The Star-Ledger* (Newark)

"Pure Americana . . . Successful in mixing pageant, pop culture and unchained drama."   —Rob Neufeld, *Asheville Citizen-Times*

"Too well written and too much fun to miss."
                                        —Margaret Black, *Metroland*

"Dazzles with its combination of history, religion, political satire and tragedy. Every character here is a delicately nuanced, vivid creation. . . . Holman weaves a deft consideration of American history and political ideals into an exuberantly eccentric tale of small-town life."
                                        —*Publishers Weekly* (starred review)

"Modern and folksy."
                        —Rebecca Ascher-Walsh, *Entertainment Weekly*

"Holman virtuosically entangles two arresting plotlines . . . [into an] enthralling narrative. . . . Part Jon Hassler, part Robert Altman film— and all-around terrific."   —*Kirkus Reviews* (starred review)

"Engaging . . . explores big ideas with an off-kilter freshness and a genuine knowledge of human experience. . . . Holman is treading in Barbara Kingsolver country here, and she expertly navigates the terrain with similar unfussy prose and wry perception. . . . Sheri Holman has written a marvelous, entertaining novel with characters whose lives are as unabashedly untidy as America itself."
                                        —Robert Weibezahl, *Bookpage*

"A bravura performance!"   —*The Literary Guild Book Club*

"A sweeping, diverse, thought-provoking work."
                                        —Regis Behe, *Tribune-Review* (Pittsburgh)

"This big but nimble novel . . . is absolutely compelling in its swift satire, yet readers will also respond to its deep sympathies for 'well-foibled' individuals. . . . Human nature exposed at its rawest—and most entertaining."   —Brad Hooper, *Booklist*

"A wedge of pure Americana . . . Holman is a skillfully detailed writer whose prose blends the factual with the personal in a manner as straightforward as it is compelling. . . . Holman's characters are deftly drawn, flawed and earnest, corruptible and alight with brave dreams."
                    —Eliza Clark, *Toronto Globe & Mail*

"Wonderful . . . Holman made her debut with the grisly, remarkable *The Dress Lodger*. She is even more remarkable here. Her story is deep and compelling, populated by characters moving and thought-provoking, and her images are precise and surprising."
                    —Susan Hall Balduf, *The Philadelphia Inquirer*

THE
MAMMOTH
CHEESE

ALSO BY SHERI HOLMAN

A Stolen Tongue
The Dress Lodger

THE
MAMMOTH
CHEESE

a novel

Sheri Holman

Grove Press
New York

Copyright © 2003 by Sheri Holman

All rights reserved. No part of this book may be reproduced in any form or by any electronic or mechanical means, including information storage and retrieval systems, without permission in writing from the publisher, except by a reviewer, who may quote brief passages in a review. Any members of educational institutions wishing to photocopy part or all of the work for classroom use, or publishers who would like to obtain permission to include the work in an anthology, should send their inquiries to Grove/Atlantic, Inc., 841 Broadway, New York, NY 10003.

Published simultaneously in Canada
Printed in the United States of America

FIRST GROVE PRESS EDITION

Libarary of Congress Cataloging-in-Publication Data

Holman, Sheri.
The mammoth cheese : a novel / Sheri Holman.
p. cm
ISBN 0-8021-4135-8 (pbk.)
1. Historical reenactments—Fiction.   2. Presidents—Election—Fiction.   3. Mothers and daughters—Fiction.   4. Women dairy farmers—Fiction.   5. Rural families—Fiction.   6. Multiple birth—Fiction.   7. Cheesemakers—Fiction.   8. Cheesemaking—Fiction.   9. Virginia—Fiction.   I. Title.

PS3558.O35596M36   2003
813'.54—dc21   2003041796

Grove Press
841 Broadway
New York, NY   10003

04 05 06 07 08   10 9 8 7 6 5 4 3 2 1

To my daughter, Elizabeth Hanover Redmond, who allowed me to
see it from the other side

PROLOGUE

Like a dog unaware it was about to be put down, Manda Frank's cottage sat in the long shade of her new house. There was nothing wrong with the old place, from what the governor could see. It was built narrow in the shotgun style of the 1920s, with an asphalt roof and a mange of wavy gray asbestos shingles. Cinder blocks propped up its front porch, but at least it had a porch, which was more than his grandparents had had in the end; and the Depression glass windows, running floor to ceiling, let in as much light as an eastern exposure could. It had been big enough for Manda and Jake and their daughter Rose, with a shed to store the dogs' food and a two-acre run out back to start them on rabbits. Still, thought the governor, it was sure to go.

"Over here, sir."

Governor Brooke's press secretary, Sandy Jameson, led him away from the done-for shack and over to the new house on the same lot, a half-finished two-story colonial, pink and naked with exposed insulation. Construction had started the week after the news was announced, but Manda had gone into labor at thirty-two weeks, and even with men working around the clock, the place was still a mess of tenpenny nails and half-hung Tyvek, with scraps of stamped lumber littering the yard and rolls of roofing paper leaned up against the west wall of the old place. Sandy was directing him toward a man sweating in his too-tight button-down oxford shirt. His face was red from the heat and he looked ready for a beer. But then, weren't they all? It had to be ninety-five degrees outside.

"Right this way, Governor," said the man, whom Sandy informed him was Francis Marvel, the contractor on the house. "We've got great things planned with the donations we received."

Adams Brooke paused, waiting as he'd been taught for the cameras to catch up. Because of the special circumstances, there was easily five times the number of normal reporters today, most of whom, their not being assigned to the political beat, he had never met. As they walked toward the house, Francis Marvel unrolled a blueprint. Here was where he intended to put an entertainment center with surround-sound viewing, and there a Jacuzzi for the exhausted parents; right here would be double refrigerators and double ovens for all of Manda's extra cooking. You'll have to use your imagination, Francis Marvel was saying. He had laid out the rooms large and spacious with vaulted ceilings and intercoms and mood lighting and stain-resistant carpet, but it was clear from the tension in his jaw, he was beyond upset that they had gone ahead and delivered Manda's children before most of the Sheetrock was even in place.

Adams Brooke was about to step in behind the contractor when he felt the sudden draft of camera lights shifting away from him. Their suffocating heat had been the hardest thing to get used to on the campaign trail, but now, without them, the governor felt oddly chilled. He turned to see what had unseated him and discovered all of the fish-eyed lenses and trolling red lights trained on a small girl in the front yard. Summer-tanned and gangly, she looked to be about five years old, and, he could tell, was perfectly miserable in a dress. Her fizzy, erupting curls had been matted down with gel and barrettes by her grandmother, who stood behind her, beaming for the cameras in her fieriest red slacks suit.

Are you jealous? Can you love them? Are you worried about sharing your mommy and daddy? The reporters asked the little girl so many questions, which her Mamaw ordered her to answer politely, but Rose (the older daughter, Sandy whispered) didn't really know what to say. To her the babies were just a blur of cameras and light and tiny bald heads. Beside him, Brooke could hear the contractor describing futuristic bunk beds that would fold into the wall like those you see in European train cars, but he had stopped listening. The poor little girl in the yard was barely able to answer one question before another was fired at her.

. "Excuse me, please," he said to Francis, leaving the contractor in the doorway. He walked back to the crowd of reporters and gestured for them to let him through. The governor squatted so that he could look into her eyes. They were the golden-brown of autumn corn.

"Miss Rose," he said amiably. "There has been all this talk of babies, but I'm curious what you think we should know about *you*."

The little girl stood shyly with her hands behind her back, leaning into her grandmother's legs.

"Answer the governor, sweetie," urged her grandmother. "He's come all the way from Washington."

Rose Frank took the measure of Governor Brooke, to the delight of those filming, and then, after a thoughtful second, reached into the front pocket of her sundress and held out a small swatch of purple and sky blue carpet. "This goes in my room," she said. "I got to pick it out myself."

"Well, why don't you show me where it will go," suggested the governor gently, and reaching out, took her hand. With all the cameras trailing, Rose led him through the shell of a two-car garage covered by a blue tarpaulin, past the new donated car seats, navy blue and flocked with yellow ducklings, stacked next to a wall of donated disposable diapers. Rose Frank led the governor and reporters into the new house, through the raw, half-built hallway and up the stairs to a room that looked down over the red clay driveway and that was to be hers alone. The babies, all eleven of them, had to share three rooms, she told him in explanation of everything she felt, but she got one all to herself.

"Excuse me, Governor," said Sandy, glancing nervously at his watch. "But if we're going to get by the hospital and still make the university fund-raiser tonight, we need to get going."

"Thank you, Sandy," replied the governor. "Miss Rose, it has been a pleasure to meet you."

Rose ducked shyly as the cameras turned to follow Adams Brooke out of the house and into the chauffeured black Buick waiting out front. The secret service and white news trucks caravaned down the driveway and onto the dirt road that ran past the Franks'. Almost immediately, the rough road gentrified to pavement, and Adams Brooke rolled down his window. Having grown up without air-conditioning, he had never gotten used to the stale dead flatness of it. His press secretary elbowed him in time for the governor to spot a woman at the end of her driveway, wildly waving a *Brooke for President* poster. Behind her stretched a rolling farm, dotted with dairy cows. Jerseys, he correctly identified, just like those his grandparents kept. That seemed like a good omen, and he was looking for good omens anywhere he could find them with the election being so close. He gave the woman a hearty thumbs-up as they sped by. "Remember—Family Matters!" he called.

"So tell me about the Franks," said the governor, settling back against the black leather seat. His secretary consulted his notes.

"They're young," he said. "Twenty-three. He collects recycling—paper, tin; she raises hunting dogs. They've beaten the record by three. From what the locals have told me, they had their daughter in high school, then five years went by with nothing. The husband wanted a son. Watch out, though—there's talk of revoking her fertility doctor's medical license."

Adams Brooke scowled. "It's an American's God-given right to have as many children as she likes. I can't support a woman's right to choose if I don't support her right to choose this."

Sandy Jameson nodded slowly, as he did whenever he disagreed with the governor, and turned his attention to the landscape passing outside. Being a Chicago kid, he was fascinated by the imperialist aspirations of Southern kudzu and marveled at the way it grew through the canopy of trees along the route, dropping down to smother an abandoned car or to claim for itself the entirety of a broken-down pole barn.

A few miles out, winding Snakehill Road straightened into School Street, and the convoy slowed toward town. *Now Entering Three Chimneys, Virginia*, they read. *Population 781*. The sign stood just before a spire of red bricks set back from the road, the oldest of the town's eponymous chimneys, and all that remained of an eighteenth-century way station between Staunton and Richmond. Technically, it belonged to St. Barnabas Episcopal Church, but sentimentally, it was the property of the church's pastor, Leland Vaughn, who with his wife and grown son inhabited the rectory next door. Just past the simple Colonial-era church, Three Chimneys began in earnest, and Adams Brooke was treated to as charming a small town as he'd encountered on his long and arduous campaign. Twenty-four great spreading oaks, donated in 1896 by the First Baptist Ladies Horticultural Society, and representing each president of the United States— excluding Abraham Lincoln—had been planted as a colonnade at the corners of School and each intersecting block for the length of the town. Wrapped in white lights like snow princesses, these trees greeted Baby Jesus each December; girt with wide yellow ribbons, they fretted over hostages and mourned missing veterans. Now that the entire country—the entire world, for that matter—was trained on Three Chimneys, the oaks wore pink and blue sashes for the Frank Eleven, with rattles hung from their boughs like polystyrene icicles.

More satellite vans crowded the two-lane street, parked with their wheels on the sidewalk so that traffic might flow. As the governor's car inched through town, he recognized all the familiar hallmarks of a small Southern hamlet. Snow White Tea Room, with its greasy windows and patched screened door. Mercer's Hardware. Tinton's Grocery, where neighbors were still allowed to buy on credit. A white clapboard Community Center sat off the town square, beside its accompanying marble obelisk War Memorial, carved with the names of the glorious Confederate dead. Adams Brooke had grown up in a town nearly identical to this one in eastern North Carolina. That town now had four super stores five miles in any direction, and chain businesses had long ago uprooted the locals. It cheered him to see holdouts like Three Chimneys, and it was for towns exactly like this that he vowed to take back the White House.

"Marvin, if I might trouble you." He leaned forward and entreated his driver to pull over. Sandy looked anxiously at his watch, but knew better than to rush the governor at moments like this. His employer was not a religious man, but he did believe in destiny—at least of the manifest sort. If he could take one person at a time, in one small town at a time, he could eventually take the entire nation.

Governor Brooke stepped out of his sedan and walked to the green, where the town entrepreneurs were hawking T-shirts to raise money for the babies' college funds. Before she became the most famous mother in America, few of her neighbors even knew Manda Frank by sight. If they knew anything about her, it was that she had once pulled her hunting rifle on a teacher who gave her a bad grade. (The gun wasn't loaded, the charges were magnanimously dropped, and the arrest never appeared on her permanent record.) Beyond this, Manda Frank, with her long, dark hair and hard, boyish features, was a mystery. She might be spotted, in the early spring and late fall, wandering the woods in her bright orange vest, following her dogs with a brace of fresh-skinned rabbit slung over her shoulder. Manda was perhaps the last person in Three Chimneys anyone expected to become famous, and certainly not after the fashion in which she did.

Now her neighbors thrilled as Governor Brooke bought a T-shirt and pulled it over his long-sleeved pinstriped shirt. The T-shirt sported silk-screened portraits of Manda's eleven babies, and below were written the words: "Three Chimneys' Small Miracles."

"Who is the gifted artist responsible for this?" asked the governor. A trim woman with hair like powdered sugar reluctantly stepped forward to take credit. She was introduced as Mrs. Leland Vaughn, wife of the local Episcopal priest.

"This is some town you have here," he said.

"We try to give help where it's needed," answered Mrs. Vaughn.

Adams Brooke smiled at the kindly woman and bought two cups of pink lemonade to benefit the Frank Fund. He took them back to Sandy and his chauffeur. It was awfully hot to be driving with no air-conditioning.

"Okay," he said, climbing in. "Let's go to the hospital."

At first, she was hidden from him by Mylar balloons and the jungle of flowers that crowded her small, private room. The sprays—roses and gardenias and birds-of-paradise—were magnificent, practically every florist in Charlottesville, and even a few as far away as Richmond, having been cleaned out. The governor's eyes landed on a card attached to one especially opulent bouquet: the prime minister of England. On the muted television that nodded beatifically from a corner of her room, he noticed the featured story was about her and the children. "Welcome Frank Eleven," read the caption.

Downstairs, in the University of Virginia Hospital parking lot, he had fought his way through a sea of well-wishers and curiosity-seekers and a handful of protestors, picketing the irresponsible use of fertility drugs. Three Chimneys Elementary's fourth-grade class had arrived by school bus to serenade the Franks on their recorders, but not allowed onto the maternity floor, they settled for entertaining those below with "Go Tell Aunt Rhody" and "Ode to Joy." The media was even thicker here than back in her hometown, and much of it attached itself to Governor Brooke as he made his way upstairs. The cameramen, too, were barred from her room, though when the floor nurse wasn't looking, one managed to wedge his lens inside.

When he finally saw her, Manda Frank lay enormous and pale against her white cotton sheets. She was probably not an unattractive woman under normal circumstances, he guessed, but now she was horribly bloated from the pregnancy and green from a bad reaction to anesthesia. Her long, Indian black hair fell limply on either side of her heavy face, and her eyes were closed behind glasses pearled with thumbprints no one had thought to wipe away for her. Governor Brooke longed to reach out and clean them on his shirttail, but he knew that would strike them all as too familiar.

"So where are you hiding them?" he asked jovially. "Where are you hiding Three Chimneys' newest Democrats?"

The two men sitting on either side of her rushed over to pump the governor's hand.

"I can't tell you how honored we are that you would come all this way," Jake Frank, the babies' father, stammered. He was as skinny as his wife was large, with a prominent Adam's apple and a scant brown mustache.

"And you must be Reverend Vaughn." Brooke turned to a silver-haired older man wearing a cleric's collar. "I understand we have you to thank for these little ones. You bucked the doctors when they said it couldn't be done."

"*Pastor* Vaughn, please. It's friendlier," said the priest, whom Adams Brooke placed at about sixty-five. "You don't play eeny-meeny-miney-moe with your family's future," he continued. "It was in God's hands."

"Is she sleeping?" asked the governor.

"In and out."

"Don't wake her," said the governor. "She looks like she's had a rough go."

Manda Frank had been on mandatory bed rest for over six months, spending the last few weeks almost upside down to ease her overworked heart, and taking her food intravenously so that the babies would have more room. The terbutaline pump they stuck in her leg to forestall premature labor made her heart race and her skin crawl with fire ants; the magnesium they alternated with it kept her dizzy and nauseated and her jaw so slack she couldn't even spit out her toothpaste. Her contractions had started around week twenty anyway, as many as twelve an hour, even with the pump. Manda's uterus went about its appointed duties, working away like an inmate with a pickax, with only the medicine and her sheer will holding the babies inside. At twenty-two weeks, they sewed up her cervix. When finally the babies were so crowded the stitches started to snap, the doctors gave her a shot of Celestone to help develop their lungs, said a prayer, and delivered them the next morning. When she woke, a nurse was handing her a blurry Polaroid of her eleven children, their eyes and mouths taped as for a kidnapping, their chests and arms growing tubes like eyes on a potato.

"Where are the little ones?" asked the governor. "They are all doing well?"

"So far, so good," said Pastor Vaughn. "They're in the NICU. We can take you down there, if you'd like."

"I can't believe I'm standing next to the man who might be the next president of the United States," gushed Jake. "Pastor Vaughn, will you take our picture?"

All the time the men were talking, through all the white teeth and pop of flashbulbs, Manda Frank had a slow itch building inside her head. It was an image not of the eleven red new potatoes laying immobilized in the NICU. Nor that of her husband saying, We're naming the eldest after you, Governor: Adams Frank. Jake Junior, he's number two. Nor the loud guffawing when the bedside phone rang again a few minutes later and Pastor Vaughn answered it, stammering, Yes, oh thank you yes, Mr. President, she's doing quite well, and the governor reaching over and taking the phone good-naturedly from her minister's hand, saying, I'm sorry, you're too late, Mr. President, I'm right here with her. And if you lose by eleven votes (winking at Jake), we'll know who to thank! No, the image she had in her head was of old brown and black Turbo, the first hunting dog she ever raised, when she was fourteen, who got pregnant three weeks after Manda bought her. She waited and waited for that dog to lay down those puppies; she brought her extra food, massaged her swollen belly, rubbed liniment on her hard red nipples. But the puppies never came. Finally months past when she should have been due, Manda took the dog to the vet. The doctor examined her closely, took blood, tested the milk leaking from the distended teats, and shook his head. I don't know what to tell you, Manda. This dog's no more pregnant than you or I.

"Did you remember to feed the dogs?" Manda looked up abruptly, speaking for the first time since the visit had began. The whole room turned to stare at her. But why? she wondered. It was a perfectly reasonable question. If the dogs weren't fed, they'd tear each other up. Her husband sat down worriedly and took her hand, Adams Brooke broke off the fine speech he was extemporizing on the American family and the Franks' exalted place in it. Everyone from the lurking cameraman to the nurse who came to take her blood pressure to Pastor Vaughn looked embarrassed at Manda's question, and the governor took the ensuing silence as his cue to leave.

I

THE ELECTION

"Politics [is] a subject I never loved and now hate."

—Thomas Jefferson to John Adams, 1796

CHAPTER ONE

It was a long walk to the end of the driveway. Margaret Prickett saw the sun glint off Mr. Kelly's U.S. Post Office truck, nearly airborne from the pink and blue balloons tied to his side-view mirrors in cheerful disregard of government regulation. He loved kids, probably because he had none of his own, and kids loved him. When her daughter Polly was a little girl, she used to leave wax paper cups of Pepsi inside the mailbox, the red flag raised so that he wouldn't drive past thirsty. And though by the time he opened the little black oven the cola was flat and fatty with melted wax, in gratitude he would always leave her a rubber band. It was a splendid economy.

Mr. Kelly got out of his truck only when there was something to sign for, yet to Margaret's eyes, that morning he stepped out seemingly empty-handed. Two days ago, she had ordered some flour from King Arthur's, but that couldn't be here so soon, could it? She waved to him, a big hearty arm-sweep, as if to say, Great to see you. Got something good? He waved back, an unenthusiastic little shake from the wrist which could only mean, Registered letter.

Sure enough, she spotted it on his clipboard, the little square of serious pale green. She stopped about fifty yards away from him, suddenly overwhelmed by the mid-afternoon heat of the day. She felt drowsy from the narcotic tangle of honeysuckle and wild morning glories that overgrew the fence beside the gravel driveway, and nearly deafened by the lawn mower whir of dog-day cicadas. Maybe she could just turn around and calmly walk back to the cheese house. Lock herself in and make August deal with Mr. Kelly. Maybe she could just stand here until he disappeared like the mirage he looked to be in the heat, a postal spectre no more valid than a canceled stamp.

Margaret saw his eyes go from the letter to the house behind her, and some primal protective instinct took over. She pulled herself together and made herself be polite.

"Just give me your John Hancock right here," Mr. Kelly said, trying not to look at Margaret directly when she reached him. As the mailman, he probably knew more town secrets than the expatriate shrink, Andrew Friedman. "Been to see Manda yet?"

"Can't get through the crowds," Margaret answered, happy to have something else to talk about. "We'll take some food over when she gets home. Polly's dying to see the babies."

"You can't imagine the mountain of letters she's been getting," he said, taking back his pen and tearing off the little green indictment. Couldn't say it got lost in the mail. Couldn't claim to have never seen it. "And stuffed animals out the ying-yang. Even a full-sized purple gorilla like you'd win at the fair."

"Amazing," replied Margaret, taking the letter.

"Well, give my best to the young one." He tipped his hat as he climbed back into the truck. "Tell her things are mighty parched out on the trail without her."

"Will do." Margaret smiled and watched him pull away. She turned back to her hundred acres, imagining the entire parcel yellow and blighted, the barn incinerated, the house blasted to its foundation by the bad news she would release when she opened this envelope. The entire history of Prickett Farm seemed to stand between Margaret and breaking the seal. She slowly started back up the driveway.

Like the Vaughns, the Pricketts, too, could claim one of the town's three chimneys. Margaret walked past the tower of bricks that sat up the hill by the path that led through the woods to the Franks' new house. Though a perfectly good shade tree grew not fifteen yards farther on, for as long as anyone could remember, the Pricketts' herd of buttery Jerseys had grazed their way across a rolling pasture of Potomac orchard grass to this chimney for their midday nap. The history of the cows' partiality could be read by all who had the eyes to see: the much-hoofed grass from barn to stream, the long detour from stream to woods (avoiding the horrible spot in the middle of the meadow where years before Tiberia's Queen had dropped a putrid calf, sending the whole herd leaping and bellowing about); the down-hill path back to the barn, hard-packed and nearly bald from hungry rushing. But afternoons always found the herd sidled up to the ruined chimney as it cast its long sundial shadow upon them and counted off the hours till evening milking. An old farming adage says that Holsteins will look for the filthiest place to lie down, while Jerseys search out the cleanest, and in some collective cow memory, these girls must have sensed the echo of solid oak floors and imported rugs be-neath their shaggy bellies; for back in the old planter days, when the county still sent a delegate to the House of Burgesses in Williamsburg, the cows' chimney had been attached to one of the wealthiest home-steads in Orange. It had heated Mr. and Mrs. Mandeville Prickett, their son, three daughters, and any number of hour-old infants that had been vainly warmed before they were on their way to the graveyard out front. It went on to thaw a second generation of red-cheeked Prickett children, plus the nieces and nephews, the half-frozen out-of-town guests, and even their distant neighbor, young James Madi-son, who once took shelter with them on his way back from Mr. Robertson's Boarding School, before the house burned down in 1779. It was the worst kind of fire, a ridiculous, careless fire, when the tallow Mrs. Randolph Prickett used for dipping candles flared and caught the drapes. The whole family and all their people fetched buckets of cold water from the spring that ran along the edge of the property, but to no avail. The wax caught the cloth and the cloth caught the wood and the wood caught the roof until all that re-mained were a few blackened studs, the iron door hinges, and the chimney. The family sent their indoor people to live with their field people, while they bedded at neighbors until a new house could be erected.

Now the cows served as its walls and the abandoned chimney looked down the hill on the second Prickett homestead, built lower on their property, nearby the stream: a whitewashed brick farmhouse in a stand of oak trees, far enough back from the water to weather flash flooding, but close enough for buckets to be passed hand to hand. Margaret took a long look at the new house (though it had been standing for two hundred years, no one referred to it as anything other than "the new house"). It was so familiar, she rarely observed it any more closely than she did her own tired face in the bathroom mirror each morning. Now, in light of the letter, she saw it as Mr. Kelly must have seen it driving up every day, as her neighbors must see it. Its old green tin roof had completely rusted out along the flashing, the verandah screens were squirrel-torn, the bricks in desperate need of repointing and a whitewash. Margaret had every intention of taking care of all those little things before they got worse, and yet, worse they got, year after year, as the money went to the more pressing disasters of crop failure and low production and drought.

She continued up the driveway toward the house, passing the geriatric tractor out in the alfalfa field, and the manure spreader, which she'd spent most of the morning trying to de-clog. With Francis gone, it was unlikely she and August would plant a crop after next year. It would make more sense to keep the pastures up and simply buy their winter feed until she could repopulate the herd. She felt traitorous even thinking such thoughts, for Margaret Abingdon Prickett was born into a proud family, a family that honored its history, that considered giving its child a middle name like Ann or Lynn or Sue as unthinkable as laying shag carpeting over hardwood floors or living out by the airport. Cows are not the only creatures of strong habits, and for many years after the fire, the Prickett sons were proud to live in the new house exactly as their fathers had in the old: planting tobacco, driving the hogsheads down the old rowling road to sell to traders in Fredericksburg, buying their furniture and throwing their barbecues on credit they carried from one crop to the next. When, after the War (and by "the War," everyone in town still meant the Civil War), the price of tobacco plummeted, and a collective feeling of urgent survivalism gripped farming communities all across the South, it seemed to the Pricketts that they must never allow themselves to become dependent again—if they could not smelt their own cannons, they could at least produce their own food. A great agricultural shift took place in Three Chimneys and the luxurious tobacco crop found itself eschewed in favor of pragmatic corn and peas; hogs for meat, oxen for labor. But of all the money borrowed during Reconstruction to coax a real farm from the brown stubble of Bright Leaf, they spent by far the most (neighbors shook their heads; far, far too much, they said) on their new state-of-the-art dairy: the dairy up ahead that, 140 years later, Margaret Prickett still used.

Omnis pecuniae pecus fundamentum.

The herd is the foundation of all wealth. It was a quote from the Roman historian Varro, and it was a clever lesson in etymology, for the Latin word for wealth, *pecunia*, comes from the word for cattle, *pecus*. It was the official motto of the American Jersey Cattle Club, and it was stenciled in strong black letters onto a sign that hung in the Prickett cheese house. Margaret's great-grandfather was even a member of the Jersey Scouts of America until 1919, when the moniker was dropped on protest by Boy Scouts of the same name. Jersey cattle were to restore the Prickett family fortune, and to that end, they borrowed heavily to raise a modern stanchion barn with new-fangled swinging headgates, and to build adjacent, over the running stream so that the icy water might cool the milk most efficiently, a cheese house, complete with floor-to-ceiling wooden shelves and ripening cave. No expense was spared on sowing the pastures and digging the trench silos, and a good thing, too, for the cows chosen to graze upon the Prickett clover and to populate the fine new outbuildings were, naturally, no common stock themselves, but descended from the First Families of Virginia dairy cattle. These mothers and daughters, sisters and aunts could trace their lineage back to the famed Tormentor family and the celebrated stud, Flying Fox. Sultana's Foxy Increase was true Jersey royalty—on one side the great-great-great-great-great-and so on-granddaughter of Flying Fox, while her distaff side wound back to Sultane, the acknowledged "mother" of all Jerseys in America. Compared with their cattle, the Pricketts joked, they were mere upstarts.

The herd is the foundation of all wealth. This motto was Margaret's inheritance. She knew it was only in the mysterious alchemy of those patrician stomachs working together to turn grass and grain and sunshine and water into the most sublime milk, hinting of fresh Piedmont air and summer's own roses, that the Prickett Dairy Farm had any prayer of survival. She would not abandon the motto—even if the herd upon which it was founded had dwindled to a mere twenty-two when, after her father died, she was forced to sell off three-quarters of the stock to recoup his bad investments, and even if the second house was collapsing around her. She was raised on homemade jonquil-colored Jersey butter and crumbly sharp Jersey cheese that her great-grandparents had given names like Manassas Gold and Wilderness Cheddar. She had been taught at her grandfather's knee how to preserve calves' stomachs at the dark of the moon and how to tell, almost by smell, the exact greenish moment that curd separates from whey, and if she'd become almost Confucian in her fealty to her ancestors' ways, then so be it. There were some things in life worth preserving.

Margaret shoved the letter deep into her pocket. Nothing so far had shaken her resolve to continue as her great-grandparents had a hundred years ago, not even when her soon-to-be ex-husband Francis Marvel packed his bags and moved out, nor when her daughter Polly wept that their life was getting so weird any minute PBS was going to show up and make a documentary about them. Registered letter be damned. At thirty-six, Margaret Prickett knew who she was and she knew what mattered. There was still a place in the world for those who did things the right way, the old-fashioned way. Sadly, for the aristocratic Jerseys napping at the old chimney, unaware they were about to go the way of all *anciens régimes*, First Virginia Savings and Loan did not agree.

At three-thirty in the afternoon, all was quiet in the barn except for the soft strains of Sinatra that Margaret left playing on the sound system for the girls. Over the years, she'd had success with Grieg and Joni Mitchell—it never mattered, classical or modern, so long as it was the same thing every day—but nothing soothed the girls like the sweet, swinging chauvinism of Frank. Their milk flowed freer when he crooned to them, they no longer kicked over their pails, but stood dreamily by like bobby-soxers, chewing their bright pink Bazooka cuds. The cows even had favorite songs. This summer it seemed to be the melancholic "It Was a Very Good Year."

Inside, she washed up and dressed for the cheese house, tying her wiry hair under a kerchief. Margaret used to be considered one of the most attractive girls in Three Chimneys, though she thought few were likely to confer the title on her now. She had no-nonsense brown eyes and a tall, vegetal figure; she wore her chestnut hair, grown long through missed salon appointments, in a single plait down her back. Margaret had devolved from attractive into that adjective farmers loved to use for thoroughbreds of any species—she was a "handsome" woman, and had become, like many of pure blood, utterly indifferent to what others thought of her. Now she pulled on her homemade white cotton shirt and pants, the scuffed white plastic boots that came to just below the knee, then tied on a white canvas apron. Before she headed over to the cheese house, she wanted to quickly check on Sultana, the only springer left this fall, since Jolly Chimney's Anna and Orange Frieda had already dropped their calves and none of the replacement heifers had gotten the job done. They were young yet, she reasoned, and might very well take next month when she got the loan of Franklin's stud again. Sultana was one of the best milkers Margaret had, so she'd give her a rest of sixty days or so after she laid down, and then bring the stud back in. They used to have a stud of their own, but with only Margaret and August to work the farm, he had become just too much of a handful.

Margaret followed a plaintive low to Sultana's straw-filled stall, where August had brought her in early from the pasture. Like an ungainly grasshopper, he crouched with his long legs drawn up around his ears, a big red one of which he had pressed against her belly.

"What's wrong?" Margaret asked.

"Thought I heard—probably nothing," he said, rubbing the taut caramel bulge. He was trying to convince himself he had not just heard what he thought he heard. A calf's heart beats twice as fast as its mother's and so there was always a double heartbeat inside the drum of a pregnant cow. He was not positive, but he thought he detected a faint syncopation. "Might be twins."

"Don't say that," she answered grimly. "Hasn't Manda had enough to last us all?"

"She's due in six weeks." August rose and checked the calendar on the Palm Pilot he carried in his overalls. "Probably time to dry her off."

"Let's take her off her concentrates."

She gave August directions on what succulents to cut out of Sultana's feed to help dry up her old milk so that her new milk could come down, and stenciled her rump with a big, purple D in indelible marker. When she leaned over, August noticed an envelope sticking out of her deep apron pocket. She saw his eyes go to it worriedly, but in perfect August fashion, he did not ask her about it.

"I'm going to the cheese house," she announced.

He nodded numbly, and electronically punched Sultana's new feed ratio into the spreadsheet he kept on each one of the girls. "Remember, I have my program tomorrow," he called as she headed toward the cheese house.

"What time will you be back?" she asked.

"By milking time."

Margaret hosed off her boots before entering the small stone building and dunked her arms, up to the elbow, in a bucket of disinfectant she kept by the door. The whitewashed antechamber, built over a cold, underground spring, was her favorite place on the farm, especially on hot early-September days like this. This morning's small-mouthed, hooded pails bobbed like stainless steel buoys in the spring-fed tank, and Margaret checked the thermometers she had in each. Through a low doorway, she could reach the main room, where her cheesemaking equipment hung over a thirty-year-old water-circulated double-walled vat, the only real upgrade her father had made, sick to death as he was of feeding the old woodstove. She kept her cultures in mason jars on the shelf, neatly labeled *Penicilium candidum,* and

Lactococcus lactis, and *Bacteria linens*. August had repaired the old Dutch press she used for the larger cheeses and Margaret tightened the screw on this morning's creamy almond Caerphilly.

She took the ten steps down to the cheese cave, dug out behind and half beneath the house above. Because of the spring, the cave had nearly ideal conditions for ripening. It was just humid enough and a constant fifty-five degrees, winter and summer. Upstairs, she sweltered over the stove and the curd vat, but below, the sweat dried on her forehead, her heart slowed, she could make the rounds of her wheels and plump pyramids and black waxed blocks of Yellow Tavern and Mattaponi Reserve.

She began this afternoon with her day-old ten-pound Cheshires. Margaret sniffed each swaddled bundle, gently unwrapped it, and rubbed a handful of coarse salt into its sticky rind, going over every inch of her cheese like a mother cat would over her young. These larger cheeses took longer to harden, and if she wasn't careful, she could lose them all in the early days to cracks and air pockets and all the wrong sorts of bacteria. There was nothing worse than to tend a cheese six months, reverently turning it to make sure it dried evenly, carefully waxing it, only to cut into a gassy bloat of ruined milk. It happened to Margaret from time to time and she never ceased taking it as a personal failure.

Down here in the cheese cave, it seemed safe to look at the letter. She didn't need to open it to know what it said: It was the emphatic end of the conversation she'd had last week with her extension agent, the same conversation they'd had every few months since her father died. Once more, he begged her to switch to Holsteins—which though giving a far less rich milk, gave in quantities far vaster than Jerseys. Barring that, would she not at least upgrade to milking machines? No one outside of a few crackpot Mennonites, he said, still milked by hand. But Margaret never expected to turn a profit on milk alone. No, in her soul, she was not a farmer; she was a cheesemaker. She had learned her ancestors' farmstead recipes and perfected them: milking by hand into the same seamless zinc pails her grandparents used; heating the milk in the same copper cauldron; cutting it with the same wire knives. She was obsessive in her quest to keep the recipes absolutely faithful, going so far as to culture her own molds from pumpernickel and rye breads she baked herself, just as her grandmother did. And Margaret's carefulness was finally paying off. Last July, she saw her sales spike when she was mentioned beside Duke's Mayonnaise and Hanover tomatoes in *Gourmet* magazine's Southern Culinary Hall Of Fame.

If she could just hold on two months more, she thought, turning the letter over but still not opening it. Two months to keep them at bay. Those eight weeks would make no real difference in the quality of her cheeses, nor in the farm's cash flow, but two months from today was the first Tuesday in November, and on that day, the one man who had the power to make this little slip of mint green go away would be in office.

Adams stands for Amnesty.

He spoke the word over and over, a banner waving above all those other fraught mn words like amnesia and amniocentesis, an unimpeachable mouthful, a rockets' red glare of eternal pardon and utter freedom.

Amnesty.

It was what Adams Brooke promised when he was elected. An abolition of the estate tax on small farms, but beyond that, a one-time government bailout of farms earning less than $250,000 a year. That simple, he repeated nearly every night on Margaret's black-and-white television. He was raised on a working dairy farm, he had watched his grandparents struggle, and he promised—no, he *vowed*, with his forefinger raised and his hair standing on end—to redress the wrongs of four decades' worth of uncaring administrations, to wipe the slate clean, to find a place at the table for those who grew the food that was eaten at it!

Forgiveness of her dairy's debt meant everything to Margaret, and not just for her sake, but for the memory of everyone who'd come before her. Amnesty today meant forgiveness at last for Mandeville Prickett who defaulted on his British creditors, and her great-great-great-grandfather Abingdon with his worthless box of Confederate bonds, and her father who speculated on Internet stocks when he didn't even own a computer. It meant grace for all the preceding generations who had brought her to this dark, gnawing place, so burdened with her family's mistakes and miscalculations that she would never get out from under it in her lifetime, and thus would be forced, like her father, and his father before him, to bequeath it to her daughter Polly. And did she hear him? Adams Brooke demanded on the Sunday morning talk shows. Not low-interest loans, or postponements, or debt restructuring, but free and clear absolution. This was what he vowed. This was why Margaret Prickett would never again have to sign for a registered letter.

Margaret put the envelope back in her pocket and unlocked the door to an even darker moonscape of a chamber, where in semitwilight her soft cheeses bloomed blue and green, three-inch silken hair nodding faintly as she entered, tasting the air around her. She settled each upon her palm, stroking them like sightless ocean creatures, easing their crine into a velvety softshell. It was not legal for her to sell these, her favorite, secret children, because they grew from raw, unpasteurized milk and were aged under two months. But a few chefs had ferreted out her contraband and were ordering it for the best restaurants in Charlottesville and Washington and as far away as New York City. Margaret didn't mind breaking the law over something like this. These cheeses were as old as humanity itself, they were as close as you might come to circulating the earth and ether of a place, your plot of land balanced on the tongue of a diplomat in Dupont Circle or a starlet in SoHo. Why suddenly now, in this cramped corner of the twenty-first century, should our government be proscribing the established methods of thousands of years?

Adams Brooke and her cheese. To August and Polly, the two who knew her best, it seemed she cared about nothing else these days. Some people in town thought that had she cared more about her husband, he wouldn't have needed to spend so much of his time down at Drafty's with Andrew Friedman. Many said her obsessiveness about Brooke had driven Francis to his affair—what man wouldn't be jealous

if his wife spent every night down at her self-styled Election Headquarters, running off flyers and phoning complete strangers in other
counties? But then there were others in town who said it was more a
chicken-or-egg sort of thing, that they never saw Margaret out late
stumping for Brooke until after the news about Francis and his secretary broke.

"Mom!"

Upstairs, she heard the screen door slam Polly home from school.
"Mom!"

Margaret set down her mermaid *Epoisse* and raced upstairs at the
sound of panic in Polly's voice. August had dropped the bag of rolled
oats and cottonseed meal he was measuring out for Sultana's dinner
and run outside to see what was the matter. Polly was halfway down
the long gravel driveway, pointing wildly to a caravan of cars churning a pillow of dust on the old dirt road that led from Manda and
Jake's house next door. There had been a ton of cars up and down
the dirt road since the news was announced—curiosity-seekers mostly,
the kind of people who park outside the houses of convicted mur-
derers or drive to the steep embankments off which school buses have
plunged, and wait, as if to feel some emanation of the event. But the
six black Buicks and two news vans that went flying down the road
looked far more official.

"Mom!" cried Polly, catching sight of the license plate. "It's
Governor Brooke!"

"Why didn't someone tell me he was coming?" Margaret Prickett
wailed, flinging off her apron, snatching up one of the many posters
she kept in the barn, and sprinting down the driveway to stand with
her daughter. August retrieved her apron with its mint green letter,
and carefully hung it behind the door before walking down to join
them. The three stood by the mailbox while six identical black cars
with tinted windows, two white vans impaled by corkscrewing satellite antennae, and the ten-year-old, two-toned banana Cadillac
driven by Mrs. Frank, Jake's mother, rumbled past them. Margaret
waved her sign like a madwoman, shouting out his name, jumping

up and down, until all that remained was a choking cloud of dust and the magnificat of cicadas.

The cows, when they were driven in for their afternoon milking, immediately felt the full force of her disappointment. They were used to hearing her sing along with Frank—"Summer Wind," "Forget Domani"—and nothing could make them forget the terror of having stepped in a gopher hole or being barked at by a big dog like coming in from the pasture to Margaret's sweet singing voice and soothing hands. But today she did not sing. And when she milked them (not even dry—their udders ached afterward) she leaned her head against their flanks as if it were too heavy for her to hold upright.

"A man like that," August said from his own milking stool, "he must be booked solid with appointments. He must be racing around all over the country."

But Margaret didn't want consolation. She left her pails for him to empty. She had to go turn the cheese.

That night, Margaret washed her hair with borax and an egg yolk, and while it dried, she kneaded two loaves of raisin bread for Polly's breakfast in the morning. Her kitchen was dark and quiet, with only one low-watt bulb in the ceiling fixture and a kerosene lamp on the counter. The lamp cast its flickering shadow on her coffee mill, still perfumed with home-roasted beans for tomorrow's percolator, and on the crank wooden butter churn, freshly washed with sweet cream and well water, which had just an hour before yielded its new butter to the icy shelf of her old white Hotpoint refrigerator, as heavy to open as a coffin. It was a large but homey kitchen, with patina-streaked copper pots hanging from the ceiling and a brick hearth big enough to roast a whole pig. Margaret sifted flour onto the worm-knotted farmer's table in the center of the room and slammed the bread down, punching and heeling the gluten to elasticity. Polly was tucked safely into bed. Margaret had laid out her one hundred per-cent cotton school clothes and was preparing a preservative-free breakfast: homemade yogurt and butter in the refrigerator, hand-canned peach jam in the pantry, fresh raisin bread. While she worked, the old black-and-white TV played the ten o'clock news soundlessly in the next room: scenes of Amanda Frank's stricken face against the white hospital pillow, of Jake and Pastor Vaughn standing by like boys waiting for a ballplayer's autograph, and of Adams Brooke—her good, honest Adams Brooke—straddling the hospital room threshold like a colossus. Margaret shaped the loaves, draped them with a damp cloth, and set them to the back of her old cast-iron gas stove, where the pilot light kept everything a little bit warmer. Another day of saving her daughter from pollution. Another day closer to amnesty. Margaret sat down at her floured kitchen table, buried her head in her hands, and waited for the bread to rise.

CHAPTER TWO

The Greeks, who among ancient peoples came relatively late to complex finance, had a unique way of describing the interest on a debt. They called that which comes due *tekon*, or "child," the same word they used to name their offspring. A child is to his parents as interest is to capital, both a descendant from and a magnification of the original investment. The *tekon* of Margaret Prickett and Francis Marvel lay dreaming in her bedroom, the fruit of an obligation she was utterly disinterested in repaying. She slept soundly in what had been her mother's room as a girl, surrounded by the same faded pink and yellow rose wallpaper, trellised from floorboard to ceiling, the frame for her feather bed resting upon wide-plank floors oiled with generations of young-girl footprints. Their samplers hung on her walls, quavery alphabets behind glass, stained with blood-rusty age spots; the rugs they hooked covered her floor, ragbag ice floes adrift in the moonlight. Asleep, Polly could be all that her mother imagined— an unspoiled, natural child, as wild and fresh as the pastures she walked, a slender little milkmaid who was living outside of history, as comfortable in the twenty-first century as she would have been in the nineteenth.

But just as interest delights when working for us, and strikes horror when we see it mounting in our creditor's favor, so Polly could turn on a dime. She had grown moody over the past year since her father left, and increasingly unpredictable. One day, she would throw her arms around her mother's neck, smothering her with kisses; the next she would barely grunt hello. And she was an equal-opportunity terror. Preying on her father's guilt for having "abandoned" her, she demanded fast food, and CDs, and synthetic fibers, all the things her mother forbid. The only time either parent might trust her completely was when

Polly was asleep. With her defenses down and her hormones in the
arms of Morpheus, she might at last become her honest self: a tired
thirteen-year-old child, suffering through a divorce.

When the sun rose through the curtainless windows, Polly was
already awake to greet it. Since classes had started this year, she found
herself practically vibrating out of bed, impatient to get her chores
over with and catch the bus to school. Her father thought it was about
damn time she started taking things seriously, her mother didn't
notice—but neither would have guessed that the reason Polly leapt
from bed each morning had a name, and a face, and a slight North-
ern accent.

In the bathroom, Polly pulled on her work clothes and vigor-
ously scrubbed her face with her mother's homemade soap, the first
batch of which had made her skin sizzle and blister. A little less lye
and a little more rose oil, and Polly could tolerate it, but she still
yearned for her lost sapphire chalice of snowy white Noxzema.

Red-eyed and nearsighted, Polly peered at herself in the mirror.
She had read a novel when she was a kid where the main character
started off at nine and then suddenly, through the magic of ellipses,
was fourteen and much wiser than her younger self. You knew she
was wiser because she'd lost her baby fat and her hair had grown long
enough to wear in two blonde braids, and she no longer felt the need
to torment those weaker than she. Polly would have given anything
to . . . away the past three years and flip the page to fourteen. Glasses
were cute on a six-year-old (purple plastic frames from Lenscrafters)
but on an eighth-grader even wire-rims were dreadful. Her hair, shining white in elementary school, had dulled to the color of wet hay,
and lost whatever natural curl it had once had. She had a straight
nose, hazel eyes, and a long, narrow body like her mother's. All in
all, she was a perfectly fine, perfectly plain girl, with nothing at all to
recommend her. Just face it, Polly thought glumly. He is never going
to love you for your looks.

Down in the kitchen, she lit the burner of the gas stove and put
coffee on to perk. Her mom had made more raisin bread, which she
liked, and she slathered it with their own butter before swallowing it

in two gulps. She fixed her coffee and started for the cow barn, stopping along the way to pet the narrow-ribbed, fat-pawed barn cats that tried to trip her. She sometimes squirted milk for them and they leapt high in the air to catch it in their pink mouths.

She was up so early, even August, usually the first one here, hadn't arrived. It made her feel grown-up and competent to slide back the door in the pink dawn light, everything so still and expectant. For a long moment Polly stood in the doorway, aware of her life unfolding inevitably in the way only a teenager can be. He would never love her, but she could bear it. Because she had this farm and these dear, dumb, dependent cows. She would go on for their sake. She would be alone, yes, but Joan of Arc was alone, and Queen Elizabeth. When one's people needed one, what else was one to do?

Polly flipped on the barn's sound system, and at the sound of Frank, all twenty-two cows scrambled to their feet in anticipation of being fed. And as if Polly had depressed the key marked EMPTY on an old Wurlitzer organ, together in church-choir unison, and with great seriousness of purpose, the cows collectively took a bombastic shit. It went on for a solid two minutes, the baritone splattering and tattoo of urine, twenty-two cows performing their morning's epic evacuation. It used to send Polly into fits of screaming laughter. She would hide her head in August's lap for the measure of this music and he would delight her with huge, wet mouth-farts of his own. Today, though, she merely sighed. "Love and Marriage." The irony was not lost upon her.

When they were done, Polly opened the gate on Chimney's Avis and led her to the milking station. She measured out her feed and the old girl went to work eating, while Polly stroked her flank and curried away the matted straw that clung to her velvety udder. It seemed like such old hat to her now, but she remembered when she'd first been taught to milk. As with everything else, her mom and dad fought over the best way to do it. Her mother was a careful milker, gently closing off the base of udder and using her whole hand to squeeze out the milk. On his parents' farm, her dad had been raised a stripper, which meant he used two fingers, pinching the milk down the teat forcefully. They'd each allowed the other their error, but neither would see it perpetuated in Polly. Polly would sit on the trilegged stool wanting desperately to do it both ways, to show them she could make the perfect compromise, and still fill her pail. Her father eventually walked away in disgust, her mother sat stony-faced, then roughly taught Polly the importance of gentleness with cattle.

"You're up early," August said, coming up behind her and making her jump. She hadn't even heard his truck pull in. He collected his pail and brought Tiberia's Queen over to the milking station. Like Polly, he measured her feed, then swung the old metal stanchion over her neck to keep her still while milking. They each had their own group of cows they milked in exact order every day. They'd once had four men working for them, but that was when the dairy was bigger, before Polly's grandpa died.

"Your mom okay?" he asked.

"If you call being a complete freak okay."

August smiled and settled down at his stool. He was a champion milker and could milk a girl dry in about seven minutes, while it took Polly closer to fifteen. They worked in silence, there was only Sinatra and the tinny syllables of milk hitting the pail. Polly strained the warm, frothy liquid into the taller hooded stainless steel canisters August would carry to the cheese house for cooling, and spilled a little out for the barn cats. She'd just settled down to Sultane Chimney's Surprise when her mother came in, looking like hell, Polly thought.

"I've got some flyers for you to take this afternoon," Margaret said. "I left them on the table."

Normally, Polly would argue, but her mother's swollen eyes made her hold her tongue. "I'll miss the bus," she said.

"I can give you a ride home," August chimed in, always listening, even when he seemed absorbed in something else. "I have my program today."

"Great," said Margaret, leading Orange Frieda around to her stanchion. She turned again to her daughter. "You never told me what your principal said about getting rid of the vending machines?"

"He said he'd think about it," answered Polly noncommittally.

"Because that's how it starts, you know," Margaret continued. "Put in a few soda machines in exchange for new band uniforms, then suddenly they're supplying textbooks, and the next thing you know, the school's being renamed Pepsi Junior High."

"I don't think they're changing the name to Pepsi Junior High." Polly sighed.

"Not if I can help it."

By seven, Polly was finished with her chores, showered, and stood waiting for the bus at the end of her long driveway. A tan Oldsmobile with Wisconsin plates drove slowly by, scanning the address on her mailbox, obviously looking for Manda's house. The whole country had gone crazy over these babies, but Polly didn't know what to think. Manda used to baby-sit her when she was little, but she had a hard time picturing her as the mother of twelve. She was used to Manda hiking deep into the woods with her fishing pole and her rifle, riding her three-wheeler down the abandoned railroad beds outside town, braving that whirlpool of snarling black and tan hunting dogs she and Jake raised, with a twenty-pound bag of Alpo over her shoulder and slop bucket held high overhead. Manda didn't seem made to stay in the house, wiping behinds and warming formula. She had strapped Rose onto the handlebars of her mountain bike and kept riding. How was she supposed to do that now?

Polly saw the grill of the bus with its flashing yellow lights cresting the hill, and behind it, a long line of cars choking on its dust, unable to pass on the narrow dirt road, trapped behind the lumbering tin can of screaming schoolkids. If she were able to see the license plates, she knew they would read like a road map of America: Delaware, Idaho, Kansas, Ohio. Hundreds of wise men bringing not frankincense and myrrh but used high chairs and fifty-dollars-exactly checks written out in glitter-gold indelible pen.

"The Earth belongs in usufruct to the living, that the dead have neither right nor power over it."—Thomas Jefferson, Mr. March chalked on the

board. Except in the window it looked like: ".ti revo rewop ron thgir rehtien evah daed eht taht, gnivil eht ot tcurfusu ni sgnoleb htraE ehT"

The last green-mossed eponymous chimney sat across the street from the middle school, perfectly framed in the window of Polly Marvel's seventh-period history class. The Marvel Family Chimney, as it was still called, was stripped of its house during the fires that ended the Battle of Wilderness in 1864, the same week the Marvel family lost four of its five sons. Reconstruction was to mean rebuilding, but by then Mr. Marvel hadn't the heart to lay any stone beyond the markers he'd set for his boys, so the town offered up its own tribute to his loss. The council voted unanimously to change the town's name from Vaughn's Tavern, as it had been called since its founding, to Marvel's Chimney, Virginia. The gesture set old Mr. Marvel to weeping, yet he would not hear of his family being singled out when so many had suffered, and so the mantle of martyrdom was cast over the other two chimneys as well. But when the county granted money for a school, Mr. Marvel donated the plot opposite *his* family's ghostly white chimney, so that the town's children, looking upon his ruined house, might forever appreciate the price of war.

To the casual observer, it certainly appeared that Polly was fulfilling her paternal great-great-grandfather's wishes. She stared out of the window, absorbed in the whole tragic story the whitewashed bricks had to tell. A nut brown wren gathered sticks to line its nest in the chimney's flue; dark clouds gathered over the fallow field, setting it in stark relief. And yet, there was nothing in the world Polly cared about less than her chimneous inheritance. She was, in matter of fact, studying a reflection in the darkened window, a safer way of watching him than gazing upon his splendor directly.

"Does anyone know what the word 'usufruct' means?" She saw him turn back and wipe his chalky hands on his pants.

It was last period, when most other eighth-graders had elected for study hall. But Polly and nine classmates—those who were at all serious about going on to college—had chosen instead to take Mr. March's honors history class. Polly had Mr. March twice: third-period American history, and this special seminar which was going to focus, he said, on precedents in U.S. history. Not presidents. Precedents.

"Anyone?"

Mr. March had been at Three Chimneys Junior High for ten years and was by far the most popular teacher in school. He wasn't so young anymore (thirty-three) and he was starting to lose a little hair in the back, and he was not overly tall. He looked like a spy in a submarine movie, Polly thought, the one dark-haired man who didn't fit in, who might at any minute lapse into another language, even though you could never detect an accent. Maybe it was the little round steel communist glasses he wore, or maybe it was his haircut, combed across his forehead at almost the Hitler angle. Her friend Bethany had heard that he was from New Jersey originally and that he had gone to Columbia University and that he'd been in Berlin the night they tore down the wall. He had a chunk of something spray-painted on his desk, so that part was probably true.

The thing about Mr. March was that he remembered what it was like to be young. He treated them like people, like people who might just have more on their minds than the Stamp Act. He was the sort of man you hesitated before saying "Yes, sir" to, though you had been taught to say it to anyone who looked to be ten years older than you, and you certainly said it to all the other teachers, but somehow saying it to him sounded sarcastic, like "Who are we kidding." And so you caught yourself swallowing the last part, so that all your affirmatives came out like "Yes, s——." "Yes, s——." Like a hiss.

"Miss Marvel? Do you know what 'usufruct' means?"

Polly cut her eyes quickly from the window and back to Mr. March incarnate.

"No, s——," she said. "I'm afraid I've never heard of it."

"Usufruct means the right to use and enjoy something, to draw from it all the profit and advantage it might produce, provided we don't alter the substance of the thing," he explained, without making her feel stupid. "It's how our third president thought we should look at government. Instead of me saying, This country is mine, and everyone after me must do as I did, I would have to say, This country is yours; it belongs to a future generation; I am only the custodian of your country. And you are allowed to disagree with how I set things up. In fact, you almost have a duty to overthrow me."

See, even in things like that, Polly thought, even explaining some boring point of history, Mr. March made it about *them*. None of the other teachers did that.

"*One generation of men does not have the right to bind another*." Up it went on the chalkboard.

It was really hot in the classroom and Polly found herself leaning her head against the cool pane of glass. Two nights before she'd had a dream where Mr. March invited her over to his house for dinner. Outside, the house looked just like the one she'd ridden past on her bike many times, but inside was cavelike, with stalactites dripping from the ceiling and stalagmites growing from the ground, so that there was no place to put a kitchen table, much less chairs, and they had to eat crossed-legged on the bed. She had just taken a bite of steak when he leaned in to kiss her, his glasses thick and luminous as polished moonstone. But she still had her fork in her mouth and it was embarrassing and they laughed and then she woke up. Since then, she hadn't been able to look at Mr. March directly without blushing.

"We're going to study this famous phrase of Jefferson's as it affected the infancy of the Republic," he continued, addressing the class, but looking at her directly. "How does a country create precedent when one of its very Founding Fathers favors periodic revolution?"

Mr. March had this way of holding Polly's gaze, even as his body turned back to the blackboard. She was a little embarrassed by his outfit today. Most people are not dumb enough to wear corduroy on the top and bottom. Especially when it was this hot out. Nonetheless, she liked noticing the difference between Mr. March in third period and Mr. March in seventh. How the sleeves rolled above the elbow had fallen to just below, how his shirt had come a little more untucked in back, how his pants had finally found the right relaxed placement around his hips.

Bethany passed her a note. "Eaten any good steak lately?"

Polly crumpled the note and shoved it in her backpack.

"Jefferson wrote: 'It may be so proved that no society can make a perpetual constitution, or even a perpetual law.' Do you understand what that means?" Mr. March asked, when there were no gasps of surprise forthcoming. "It means every generation has the right, almost the obligation, to create new precedent, even if that means overthrowing the existing government. Isn't that exciting?"

The class nodded blankly.

Mr. March looked about the room in disgust. "What's happened to you? Kids in my day were constantly looking for ways to rebel. This would have sent us running out into the street to smash things. Christ, by the time I was your age, I'd stolen my first car. How many of you have stolen a car?

No hands went up.

"Figures." Mr. March sighed, "We are a county founded by traitors, ladies and gentlemen. Back in 1776, we were smart-ass kids running away from home because our parents wouldn't let us do what we wanted. Then suddenly, with the stroke of a pen and a simple declaration, we recast ourselves in the role of parents. The traitors—the rebels—became the Founding Fathers; we were no longer the bad sons. Now we had to behave. But still, that rebelliousness lingers in each and every one of us. In third period, we'll study everything the State of Virginia requires for you to move onto ninth grade, but here, we're going to question. Do you understand?"

Yes, sir, they said, a little stunned by his free use of the a-word.

"The problem with you kids is that you have no personal investment in politics. Why should I be surprised you're not getting this? How often do you question your government? How many of you have even been following the election?"

Drew Powell raised his hand.

"Who do you favor, Mr. Powell?"

"The president, sir."

"And why is that?"

"Because he's most likely to win."

"A pragmatist. Anyone else?"

Shyly, Polly raised her hand.

"And who do you favor, Miss Marvel?"

"Governor Brooke, s———."

"Can you state your reason?"

"My mother says he supports the small farmer. He looks after the little man. She says it's time for a change."

"'Change.' That beloved word of every politician." Mr. March whirled to the blackboard and scrawled it like a gang tag. "Is not Change merely the watered-down version of Jefferson's generational rebellion? He proposed that every nineteen years we should sweep away the old laws and rethink them for ourselves. Now we talk about Change as if it's some radical concept, when it is only the weakest reflection of Jeffersonian radicalism."

Polly sat up a little straighter at her desk. He was so passionate. Why had she never thought of things this way? Before she knew what she was saying, she interrupted.

"But what can we do about it?" she asked. "We're not even old enough to vote."

"You are never too young to have an opinion, Miss Marvel," he retorted. "And to see things for how they really are. If you see hypocrisy and injustice, you owe it to your country and yourself to speak out. If some Northwestern University journalism students could get a man released from death row, why shouldn't an eighth-grader affect the outcome of a presidential election? It makes about as much sense, doesn't it?"

The bell rang and Mr. March stalked out of the classroom, followed swiftly by the students. Polly remained in her seat, still transfixed by Mr. March's words, issued like a challenge. Did he really believe an eighth-grader could make a difference? If so, he was the most unique adult she'd ever met.

"Come on, we'll miss the bus." Bethany tapped her on the shoulder. Polly looked down at her laden backpack, full of her mother's flyers. "I have to stay after and do something," she said with a sigh. "I'll call you tonight."

Polly waited until her friend had left, then slowly made her way down the pink halls, past the mural of her school's half-crazed mascot, the Three Chimneys Rebel: a squat, bearded cartoon infantryman in a gray slouch hat waving the Confederate flag. She passed the shut doors to the auditorium, where she knew August was playing to a handful of retired people, but she had time enough to be embarrassed by that later. Just outside the auditorium stood the cardboard boxes marked Franks Food Drive, filled with dented cans of last Thanksgiving's cranberry sauce and pumpkin pie filling, niblets, and two dusty boxes of Hamburger Helper. And beside that was the sign-up sheet for Franks Volunteer Baby-sitting Duty, only seventh- and eighth-graders allowed. Polly used the purple marker on a string to sign her name. So far, all the names were girls'.

Outside, the green sky promised a nasty storm. It was that way every September—the slow hot buildup like gas inside an oven, until the inevitable explosion in the late afternoon. The leaves showed their silvery bottoms now and the wind lifted her hair off her neck. Over by the parking lot, one of the hundreds of news trucks that had descended on Three Chimneys had navigated School Street all the way out to the actual school and was setting up a live feed. Polly recognized the weatherman from Channel 5 talking to the Pep Club members who had sponsored a Frank Eleven Car Wash. What do you think of having eleven new neighbors? the weatherman was asking, while the wind whipped his microphone cord. We think it's super! We hope to raise two hundred dollars today. Come on out!

Polly circled behind the news truck and crossed into the Arlington National Cemetery of neatly parked white cars and minivans. Everyone in town had seen the same report declaring white the safest color for driving at night, and like everyone else, Polly secretly thought that if a person were rash enough to purchase forest green or indigo, he might very well have only himself to blame should he be broadsided. Three-quarters of the white cars in the lot had "We ♥ the Frank Eleven" bumper stickers (a dollar each from the Glee Club), and many had guest passes in the front window, showing they were here for August's presentation. Her mother knew the lot would be full today, which was why she'd insisted Polly take the flyers this morning. She was even letting her come home late for milking, which was miraculous in itself and further confirmation for Polly that her mother had gone nuts.

Vote Adams Brooke, The Farmer's Friend.

Polly thought it made the governor sound like a hemorrhoid cream, but her mother was proud of the alliteration. Polly slipped a copy of the red, white, and blue flyer under each set of windshield wipers, the "least she could do" (again, her mother), since she wasn't old enough to vote. She felt like an idiot with the news van only yards away, as if she might get caught on tape doing something illegal like breaking her teachers' antennae or stealing the glass from their side-view mirrors. Quickly, she made her way up one row and down another, involuntarily noting whose inspection stickers were about to expire and whose windows needed washing. Mrs. Barker, the sixth-grade math teacher, had erected an altar to her Hawaiian vacation across her dashboard, with little hula dancers and a red plastic lei draped over her rearview mirror. Coach Emery, head of junior varsity football, had a stack of orange parking tickets on his. Each car Polly exhorted to vote for Governor Brooke, her mother's demigod, her mother's boyfriend. Polly was so sick of hearing about Governor Brooke, she could hardly wait for November.

Polly crammed another ten flyers under another ten windshield wipers, working quickly, as the wind was practically ripping them from her hand. When she came to one of the only nonwhite cars in the lot, she had raised the wiper before it registered just whose car she was about to indoctrinate. A rusted green Karmann Ghia. With no "We ♥ the Frank Eleven" bumper sticker. With a dimple in the passenger side door. With a paperback copy of *The Ugly American* and an open bag of Doritos on the backseat.

What made her test the handle? she would wonder later. Whatever possessed her, on learning it was unlocked, to open the door and

slip into the front seat? Inside, the car was hot and airless from having been closed up all day, and it smelled of gym clothes left for weeks
in the bag. But it was his car, and everything inside bespoke him. She
ran her fingers over the cracks in the fake leather dashboard, over
the lashed steering wheel cover, over the hot, black stick shift. Once,
when her father was really drunk, she drove him home from a Fourth
of July picnic at the Andersons'. She would never forget the terror
and excitement of her headlights cutting through the black tunnel
of trees, of mailboxes and road signs springing like wild animals out
of the darkness. She didn't know how to move the seat closer, so she
had to stretch almost diagonally to reach the pedals, and could barely
see over the dashboard. From the time she was eight, she had been
mentally preparing herself to drive. But the route she had memorized,
that she went over nightly before falling asleep, was the twisting drive
to the hospital in the event both her parents were felled by simulta-
neous heart attacks, not the half-mile home from the Andersons'.

A few fat raindrops hit the windshield and Polly knew she should
get out. This wasn't right. But then again, hadn't Mr. March encour-
aged them to break the rules? When was the last time she'd felt so
tinglingly treacherous?

She popped open the glove compartment to a miniature ava-
lanche of tape cases. Arlo Guthrie, Country Joe McDonald—Polly
didn't recognize any of them. He had papers, too. His pink auto
registration. Harvey D. March. David? Dagobert? Creased receipts
from Wendy's and Food Lion. A postcard of the Brandenburg Gate
(so it said on the back) written in German, but signed most un-
Germanically, Sandi. Under the seat, he had an unmarked videotape
in a plain blue case that was beyond tantalizing. Was it something
he recorded off TV? Was it a video postcard of Sandi kittenishly romping through the beer gardens of Berlin? Polly couldn't stand it.

Why was she doing this? She closed her eyes and leaned her head
against the seat. He wasn't so handsome. He teased her and made
her feel stupid. But time after time, since the first day of class, it had
been her he singled out. Her he raised up. Her he put down. Back

when she was a kid, she used to go over to Manda's house to play
with the hunting dogs. Manda would tell her, Be careful, don't con-
fuse them. To a dog any attention is good attention. Polly felt like
that now. Like Mr. March could slap her with a newspaper and she
would fetch his pipe.

It had begun to rain in earnest while she sat there—heavy curtains of water, a blinding flash, and then hail hammered the windshield. What was she going to do? Across the parking lot, the Channel
5 weatherman sprinted for his van, the Pep Club forsook its bristles
and squeegees and ran shrieking for cover. She opened the door a
crack, was instantly soaked with rain, and quickly shut it. But it was
too late. Water puddled on the floorboards, on the armrest, on the
seat. He was sure to know someone had been in his car. Frantically,
Polly mopped at the water with her extra flyers.

"I didn't realize my car theft story would be so inspirational."
Mr. March said flatly.

She felt the cool rush of air as the door flew open, then the surprise of rain on her skin. She traced him from his brown loafers up to
his black umbrella, hail bouncing off it in flying check marks. When
she made her way to his face, she saw first a flash of real dark anger,
then, in an instant, a return to his familiar expression of sardonic
impassivity.

"It started to pour and I just ducked in for a minute to get out of
the—oh God, you must think I'm some sort of criminal breaking and
entering. It was unlocked. I didn't mean—I was just putting these
flyers—." Polly thrust the curled, smeared mess at him. She was trying her best not to cry in sheer embarrassment and he wasn't helping
any by staring at her in that "There's a hair on my plate" way of his.
Rain streamed off his umbrella like a force field protecting him from
her, keeping her trapped in the car, staring up helplessly. Why was
he looking at her like that? Why wasn't he moving?

"Were you giving out these flyers because you believe in Governor Brooke or were you just doing it because your mother told you
to?" Mr. March asked at last. He had to shout over the rain battering
his umbrella, and at first Polly couldn't be sure she heard him right.

"Pardon?" she asked.

"If you believe in him, I'll forgive you, but if you're merely furthering someone else's crusade, I'll kindly ask you to take that off my car."

He took a step back, and Polly flew out to pluck the sopping flyer from his windshield. She stared at him pitifully for the briefest of seconds, then mashed all the remaining flyers. "I'm sorry," she whispered.

"I'm trying to teach you, all of you, to think for yourselves. I don't care that you wanted to snoop inside my car. At least you did that for you."

He climbed into the spot in which she'd just sat, pulled the door shut, and rolled down the window. "Do you need a ride?" he asked, and she answered miserably that she had one. "Here, take this." He passed her his umbrella, and if he'd handed her a lit stick of dynamite, she would have taken it. "You don't always have to do what your mother tells you, Polly. Remember, we're a nation of traitors."

She clenched the shiny lacquered handle of his black umbrella, her fingerprints pressed to the echo of his warm fingerprints, and watched him pull away. She'd never been so mortified in her life, and yet she couldn't stop smiling.

Almost without trying, they'd forged a new precedent. He had called her Polly.

CHAPTER THREE

"It is July Fourth, 1826, exactly fifty years after the signing of the Declaration, and I am dead."

The large room was dark and still. Even after nearly two hours, the tall, weather-beaten man who spoke had not found comfort with his voice, never made for public speaking in the first place, which came out whistle-thin, as if someone had siphoned off half of it before it reached his lips. He had an unconscious habit when thinking of bringing his callused fingers to his mouth, lightly pinching to shape the next word out. But though his thoughts were grand, no amount of manipulating could make the voice that conveyed them larger than it was. He spoke from his Windsor chair, attired in elegantly simple period costume: white hose, homespun knee breeches, an embroidered vest over a white cotton blouse, a French blue silk jacket with deep cuffs. On his head he wore a barely powdered auburn wig. Around his neck, he wore a loosely knotted cravat.

"I died not knowing my rival John Adams was to expire only hours later with my name in his mouth," he said. "Like me, he had clung to life, desirous only of achieving that final, fateful anniversary. I left this world surrounded by faithful servants and my family, but saddened to realize they could not go on living here after me, for I was dying deeply in debt. As I closed my eyes on Martha and the grandchildren, it seemed to me I saw the twin seraphim of my beloved Patty and youngest daughter Maria, bathed in light, their arms outstretched to receive me. Lay down your life as a public man and take up your eternity as an insubstantial ghost, they seemed to say. You are safe from fame here. And even as they spoke, it seemed I heard another voice from across the same divide. I heard my rival's wife calling out to summon him with words that might have applied to us

both. 'I am more and more convinced that man is a dangerous creature,' the great, wise Abigail Adams was saying, 'that power, whether
vested in many or a few, is ever grasping, and, like the grave, cries
"Give, give."'

"Give, give," repeated the man in soft tones, leaning over the
single candle at his side. "I gave to my country and now it is time I
give to God."

"Good-bye, my fellow patriots. Good-bye."

The candle guttered at the touch of his breath, and the room
dropped into darkness. He would shortly be revived, he knew, with
the applause that inevitably followed, but he liked, for that long
hushed moment, to surrender to the undertow of his own death. The
cold rush swept him off the hilltop of Monticello, back through
swampy Washington, intoxicating Paris, back inside the hollow stomach of Independence Hall, where he paused with a quill in his hand
before he was pulled back to Patty's bed, lay once more upon his own
hard cot at the College of William and Mary, stared into the fire on
his mother's rug at Shadwell, then curled back into the purple warmth
of the womb. Viewed from there, a man could forget the daily struggle,
the pain endured forging an important life. Would it not be a cosmic
kindness, he thought, to let us return to the womb upon our deaths
and see that each stage of our hard-fought lives was inevitable, like
God the valet had merely been holding open successively larger coats
for us to slip into?

But soon enough the lights came up and the applause called him
back to life. He was once more in the middle school auditorium, where
rows A through N were filled with balding men in brightly colored
trousers, accompanied by patient wives, their white heads cocked in
polite interest.

Thomas Jefferson gave them a deep, heartfelt bow. "That con-
cludes my little talk, 'The Patriot in Repose,'" he said. "Now, if my
kind friends have any questions for me, I would gladly entertain
them." This crowd was not shy. Fifteen hands immediately shot up.

He knew the sort of questions they would pose, before they even
pursed their lips to ask. How did it feel to pen the Declaration of Inde-

pendence, Mr. President? How could you have written "all men are created equal" and yet still have kept slaves? Mr. President, if you had been alive at the dawn of the Civil War, would you have supported the succession of Virginia? Often he would get the amateur historian, dandruffed and bespectacled, who aspired to stump him with some bit of arcana. More often, it was men and women who had read the latest *New York Times* best-selling paperback on Lewis and Clark and were full of desire for more detail. The most painful question he ever had to answer was from a young black honor student, who addressed him politely as "sir." "Sir," she said, with the low-voiced force of a thousand lashes, "do you believe I have no right to exist?"

But he never got tired of answering their questions, even ones he'd answered a thousand times, even ones that hurt. What was old to him was new to them, and his audiences showed their enthusiasm in their endless fascination with his wine collection, with his nail factory, with the influence of John Locke on his writing. They wanted his opinion on television and the welfare state and the New Deal. They wanted to know if he thought America had lost its way.

August could never pinpoint the exact moment when his hobby had crossed over into a lifestyle, but the likeliest candidate would have to be the week, ten years ago, when the Chautauquans came to town. They set up a large tent and loudspeakers, chairs, and a concession stand on the lawn by the War Memorial, and his first thought was that a Pentecostal revival had gotten terribly, terribly lost here in Episcopalian country. But he soon learned from the public librarian that they had been invited here from out west, that they were not Do-You-See-the-Light evangelists, but living historians presenting a humanities program meant to edify and entertain. Over the course of seven nights, in period costume, and without breaking character, each Chautauquan presented a life of an eminent American: Alexander Hamilton, Harriet Beecher Stowe, W. E. B. DuBois, Jane Addams. Each began with a monologue, then moved to questions from the audience, and finally ended with a return to the self—not the historic, exalted self, but the slightly lonely, overly bookish Oklahoman or South Dakotan, who gave their reasons for why they spend a goodly portion of their lives as someone else. Teddy Roosevelt had called the Chautauquan tent shows that traveled during his time "the Most American thing in America," and August was spellbound. In his family, that which passed away was hallowed and tended and carefully maintained. But for these people, it seemed, what was dead was dead, and an identity was fair game for anyone who fit the clothes and learned the language. August left that revival—and "revival" it was for him, for he *had* seen the light—a changed man. He could not only study Jefferson, he could become him, at least for the edification and entertainment of others. What better way to learn history than to engage in a dialogue with it? Than to prod it and demand it explain itself? At first it felt almost sacrilegious to use the hallowed "I" in reference to his hero, to answer as Jefferson would have answered, to express opinions that others might very well take away as fact, and all without an advanced degree of any sort. But then, as he honed a monologue and bought his first powdered wig, it began to feel more natural. The kinship deepened until, ten years later, he had, without even trying, created a union, and a whole new filiation of self.

He called on a man in the third row, who pushed himself up and walked to the standing microphone in the left aisle.

"Mr. President, thank you so much for taking time away from your duties to speak to us this afternoon," the man began, tickled to play along. "We know what a busy schedule you must keep. My question for you is . . ."

How did it feel to write the Declaration of Independence? Hmm . . . The president turned the question over as if for the first time giving it any serious thought.

"You must remember, my friends," he began, "the question was not whether, by a Declaration of Independence, we should make ourselves what we were not, but whether we should declare a fact that already existed. As I wrote in my *Summary View* of 1774, 'The God who gave us life, gave us liberty at the same time: the hand of force may destroy, but cannot disjoin them.' We were already free men; we just needed Old King George to realize that.

"It would be difficult for you to imagine what we suffered before the Revolution, how we found ourselves emasculated and abused at every turn, by men we had never seen and could not vote out of office. You know about the paper taxes and the tea taxes, but did you know an American subject was forbidden even to make a hat for himself, though the fur was trapped on his own property? That we were forced to ship our raw iron, heavy and expensive as it was, for refinery in England so that they might sell it back to us? That a standing army was kept at our expense, so that they might with impunity take over our houses and eat us out of our winter provisions?"

No matter how many times he outlined the abuses of the British crown, he found himself still angry over the enforced infantilism of a great nation. He could hear his thin voice, calmly outlining dates and places, and yet, as in his death, he was somewhere else—alone in a close second-story room, staring at a sheet of blank parchment. They had petitioned the king over and over, like reasonable men, but the tyrant simply would not listen. And now he was forced to endure the pestilence of a summer in Philadelphia, while his wife languished at home near death. He stabbed his quill in his pot of ink. He wanted to retire from public life. This George must be made to understand. He wanted to go home.

He realized his fist was clenched deep in his pocket and that he had stopped talking.

"I'm sorry," he said. "Next question?"

A middle-aged woman in a denim jumper raised her hand. "I have a question, but I feel silly asking it," she said, blushing.

"I am your president, madame, here to answer whatever question you pose. Is that not the purpose of a democratic government? To answer to the people?"

"Well, then . . ." She screwed up her courage. "Are you by any chance related to the real Mr. Jefferson?" she asked sweetly. "You look surprisingly like the portraits I've seen." Next to her, her husband rolled his eyes in embarrassment.

"Am I related to myself, madame?" the president answered with a smile. Rule number one of the Chautauqua Living History School:

Never break character while in costume. "Who else should I resemble?"

That got a laugh.

"What made you say the Earth belongs in usufruct to the living?"

The president scanned the audience for the owner of that familiar voice, and found her in the back row, dripping wet, her eyes challenging behind her glasses. He hadn't even seen Polly slip in. She used to love his brocaded costume when she was younger and would beg to try it on, though the knee breeches came all the way to her ankles and the coat hung to her knees. Back then, she thought ponytails were just for girls, and she would snatch the lightly powdered wig from his head, and race around the stables shrieking, August is a girl! August is a girl! But since she turned thirteen—no, he could peg it even more exactly—since her father had left, Polly had been avoiding him. She seemed embarrassed by everything he did.

"The Earth belongs in usufruct to the living. . . ," he began, for she seemed to want a serious answer. "That is taken from a letter I wrote to my dear friend and protégé, James Madison, in 1789. In it I was trying to point out the inherent unfairness of one generation's forcing another to pay its debts. My wife's father, rest his soul, left me his land, his people, and his crippling encumbrances, and I spent the remainder of my life struggling with inherited debt. But I do not want to give a false impression—I was not the wisest steward of my money. I could have sold off more land to repay my loans, but I considered it beneath my dignity as a gentleman planter. I could have forgone the numerous changes to Monticello, I could have drunk less fine Bordeaux, I could have entertained fewer friends, but somehow I could not force myself to forgo these small indulgences."

He felt a stirring of the old chest-tightening panic even talking about how much money he owed, like the long bony hand of John Wayles was reaching up from the grave to rifle his pockets. He died owing over $100,000, which by today's reckoning would be several millions. It was not something he was proud of.

"When I wrote to Madison, I was thinking of the raging revolution in France and my own personal finances. What right did Louis XV have to strap a nation—or for that matter, what right did my father-in-law have to strap me—with a bill for extravagances enjoyed during his lifetime? Why should we toil and suffer to pay back money spent by men who gave no thought to us? Ten years later, when as president I became father to my countrymen, I applied this philosophy to reducing the national debt, so that generations after me would not be left in the same predicament. Unfortunately, those who followed me were not quite so conscientious."

"But I heard you wrote that no society could make a perpetual constitution or even a perpetual law because of this," she challenged him in her old sophist voice. Just like she used to quiz when she was little: Would you rather freeze to death or be burned to death? And you can't choose "neither."

What had gotten into Polly? Since when did she care about any of this? Well, he would play along. "What a good little history student you are . . . Miss Marvel, is it? Who has not entertained a youthful idealism they would rather forget?" he asked. "I did say that. And my friend, the wise Mr. Madison, quickly disabused me of the notion. How would anything get accomplished if we were constantly revising the laws? he wrote back. How soon would chaos reign? My friend had spent years of his life pushing through our nation's Constitution and Bill of Rights; I doubt he would have looked kindly on each new generation's wiping it clean. Perhaps in the end, he was right. We've done pretty well so far."

Polly sat down, seemingly satisfied, and August glanced at the clock over the last row to see it was nearly four o'clock. He needed to change and get over to Margaret's before evening milking. With great deliberation he loosened his cravat and removed his wig, setting it reverently on the chair behind him.

"Now, friends, it is time for me to relinquish office and don once more the humble mantle of August Vaughn, private citizen," the erstwhile president announced. "I hope you have enjoyed your time with Mr. Jefferson as much as I have enjoyed bringing him to you."

By the time the applause died and August had shaken hands all around, it was nearly four-fifteen and they were running late for milking. He and Polly walked wordlessly back to the parking lot, where the storm had passed on like every other summer squall, leaving the air sagging and nearly opaque. August plucked a soaked Adams Brooke flyer from beneath his windshield wiper.

"I think your mom can count on my vote," he said, but laid it flat to dry on his dashboard nonetheless.

"Since when did you become so interested in Jeffersonian finance?" August asked when they were halfway to the farm and Polly had not spoken. She had been staring out of the lowered pickup window, deeply engrossed in the gas-rainbowed puddles and cornfields flashing by.

"We were studying him in history today," she replied. "Mr. March thinks we've lost all our traitorous fire. He thinks we need a good rebellion every now and then."

"You know Jefferson was mostly thinking about his own personal debt when he wrote that letter. Don't let your history teacher twist his words around."

"Oh, you think you know everything," Polly cried, stung by his criticism. "You might wear his clothes, but you aren't really him, you know. You can't know what he thought."

Everything was a battle these days. Of course August couldn't know everything in Jefferson's head, just because he'd spent the last twenty years of his life studying every facet of the man. But he had a good idea he knew more than Polly's history teacher, whoever he was.

They pulled up the long driveway, sending gravel popping behind them. August had automatically pulled into the bald lane of grass beside the barn, where he usually parked, before he realized another truck was already there, blocking his way: Francis Marvel's navy blue pickup. For a moment after he cut the engine, both he and Polly hesitated with their hands on the door. Margaret was standing beside her husband, leaning on her pitchfork with that defeated slump August recognized as her Francis-stance, as if all her internal organs wanted to shrink as far away from him as possible. Francis waved to them, and Polly, because she was annoyed at her mother and August, decided she loved him today.

"Hey, Dad," she called, flinging her arms around her father's waist. He kissed the top of her head.

"Hey, Peanut," he replied. "How's it going?"

"Fine."

"Getting good grades?"

"Yes, sir."

"Eating right?"

"Yes, sir."

"Not pregnant yet?" He scowled at her.

"Not as far as I know."

"That's my girl." He patted her approvingly. "Your feet are younger than mine—run on inside and get your old man a glass of tea."

Polly dutifully trotted indoors, and Francis turned his attention to August.

"Hey, my friend. Finally getting that sex change you always wanted?" Francis nodded at the remnants of August's stage makeup.

"Nice to see you, Francis." August rubbed the edge of his sleeve over his cheek. "Love to chat, but I'm late bringing in the ladies."

"Don't apologize, man," Francis called to August's retreating back. "All the damn estrogen flying around this place, it's no wonder. I swear I was about ready to go into heat myself before I took off."

"We all just assumed you had, Francis." August smiled lazily over his shoulder.

"Damn if I didn't, man." Francis roared, always one to appreciate a joke at his own expense. "Damn if I didn't."

Margaret walked back to the haylage she was bailing into the girls' troughs, and her ex-husband followed her, picking up as if they hadn't been interrupted.

"So, anyway, I'm sorry. I thought you knew he was coming. I was just doing it for the publicity. Personally, I hope the cocksucker goes down in flames."

"Don't say that," Margaret snapped.

"Listen, who cares about politics?" said Francis. "Everyone saw the house on TV and the phone's been ringing off the hook. I've changed the name of the company to Chimney Eleven Contracting. I'm getting the signs printed up, and I just got the cards today. Here, take one." He thrust a white business card at her: Chimney Eleven Contracting, with nine little Monopoly-style houses running the border and two smaller ones dotting the i's. She slipped it in her pocket.

August pulled on his work boots and tried to not eavesdrop on their conversation. He had always hated the way Francis spoke to Margaret, as if she should be eternally interested in everything he had to say, no matter how painful it might be for her to hear. Her husband was still a good-looking man in his early forties, tall, with a sharp Roman nose and thick blond hair that didn't show a streak of gray (Polly, much to her mother's chagrin, had never been able to prove he was dyeing it). His complexion had the ruddy glow of outdoorsmanship or alcoholism—his burgeoning gut seem to imply the latter—and he had picked up in college that Richmond tic of wearing Docksiders without socks. August had known Francis as long as he'd known Margaret, and he'd disliked him almost as long.

"We're going to be fucking rolling pretty soon," he was telling her. "I've got a guy signing contracts tonight and I think I've finally given the zoning board enough damn money to put in the sewer line, but you know, with all the expansion, cash flow is just a little tight this month—"

"Don't." Margaret put up her hand to ward him off.

"It'll just be until next month, as soon as I finish Manda's house. Man, I couldn't have *bought* that kind of publicity."

"Francis," she warned.

"Goddamn, I said I'm gonna have it. What more do you want? I can't give you what I don't have myself."

"Your daughter needs school clothes. I can barely pay August as it is. And what are we supposed to do about college?"

"Why the hell are you talking about college?" Francis shouted. "She's in the damn eighth grade."

August wanted to jump in, to say, Don't think about me, I don't need the money. But he knew this would only put her in a worse position.

"I need to bring in the cows, Francis," Margaret said. "We have to talk about this later." She turned from him, only to nearly collide with Polly, who had appeared in the doorway holding a glass of tea.

"Bye, Peanut." Francis drained the glass and handed it back to her. "See you this weekend."

"Finish up what you're doing, Margaret," August offered as her husband stalked out. "I'll get the girls."

August followed Francis out to the driveway. He took a look back over his shoulder at Margaret, furiously forking hay into the rack, blinking back tears of rage. He reached out to put his hand on Francis's shoulder, but the other man's muscles, hard as ingot, jumped a sharp "Screw off" beneath his fingers.

"Listen, Francis. I know things are tight," August said once they were far enough away from the barn. "I've got plenty in the bank. Why don't I loan you some—you give it to Margaret and tell her it's from you. I don't need it right now."

"What the hell's wrong with you, man?" Francis narrowed his eyes. "You out to get a piece of my wife?"

August took a step back. "Francis, how can you—?"

"Aw, I'm just shitting you." Francis punched him lightly in the chest. "I can't take your money. Don't worry about Maggie. She's got more than she lets on—her dad played the stock market. They'll be fine this month, and I'll have it by next."

Francis opened the door to his new pickup, the driving-around-town not hauling-chicken-flats model, and climbed up behind the wheel. "Let me ask you." He motioned August closer. "When was the last time you took a vacation? Or even a day off?"

It had been nine years, but August didn't like to think about that. He didn't have anywhere he'd especially like to go. And besides, if Margaret didn't take off, he didn't feel he should.

"I worked a farm my entire life," Francis said. "First my daddy's, then Margaret's daddy's. I am finally free." Francis leaned in, and for the first time August could smell the hint of beer on his minty breath. "And, shit, if it took having everyone hate my guts, well, I'm sorry.

Get out while you can, man. There's no shame in buying your milk at the damn grocery store."

August pulled into the rectory at six forty-five, the same time as every evening, and parked next to the old chimney. The comforting rattle of his mother sorting heavy silverware, digging through the sideboard for summer's spindly handled ice tea spoons and flat-plated fish knives, greeted him as he walked toward the house. It was Friday, so she would have poached a salmon and made a cobbler. His favorite was blackberry, his father's was peach, but since today was the first Friday of the month, the calendar favored peach. His mother didn't have a preference; she loved all cobblers ecumenically. Inside, his father would be sitting in his recliner, reading and listening to the nightly news on NBC. He had watched no other news since the narrow-tie days of Huntley and Brinkley, though he sighed over the sharply chiseled, pretty-boy anchormen his network sported now. Throughout the broadcast, he would call out the headlines to August's mother, who would be tossing a salad or tasting the snaps for salt, and she would nod, though he couldn't see her, happy to have the world filtered through her husband. Almost everything she knew in life, from wars to peace processes to mass genocide, she had gotten from the next room.

August checked the mail and saw that the book he'd been expecting from the antique dealer in Ashfield, Massachusetts, had arrived. It was a rare monograph on crop rotation at Monticello. Not the book everyone else had, but a volume published privately in 1928, for a subscription of two hundred readers.

"How'd it go today, son?" his father called from the living room.

"We had a great turnout," he answered. "You?"

"I sat with Manda most of it. I'll tell you all about it after your shower."

"Dinner will be ready at seven," his mother said as she said every night. He would take a fifteen-minute shower. He would sit down

promptly at 7 P.M. smelling of tarry Head & Shoulders and Ivory soap.
He would have clean fingernails to look at when he bowed his head
for grace.

August hung his costume in the hall closet, behind the winter
coats so that his mother would not find it and wash it before he had
the chance to do so himself. An outsider would never have found
the closet door camouflaged on the Wall of Ancestors, as he cheekily
used to call it as a boy, a gauntlet of neatly hung oil paintings, tin-
types, and 1930s color-washed studio portraits that ran from the
front door to the kitchen. From the way his parents spoke, August
had grown up thinking himself little more than a jambalaya of these
men and women. He had his grandfather's eyes, his uncle Clement's
mouth. His mother's hair, his father's sense of humor. The similari-
ties were uncanny, they said, and more subtle ones revealed themselves as he grew: Great-grandmother Adele's kindness to animals,
Great-great-grandfather Burbidge's ability to do complicated sums
in his head. Any bête noire made him just like Great-uncle Robert, who swore he hated chocolate but loved M&M's, assiduously
picking out all the brown ones. Any tendency to shyness, he inherited from his mother's sister Susan, who would sit in the attic
for days at a time as a child, not even coming down for dinner. It
comforted him to have every angle accounted for, so that there was
very little of himself left over to ruin. The only thing no one in the
family could affix was this Jefferson eccentricity of his. Everyone
was kind to him about it, but in their heart of hearts, no one understood how a grown man could want to be anyone other than who
he was. There were no actors or even schizophrenics in the family.
There was just no precedent for it.

He opened the door off the hall that led to the finished basement, where he lived. The ceiling was low for such a tall man, but
that just meant the slouch he had been cultivating since high school
had finally come in handy. The room was equipped with the oak
bedroom set his father had owned as a boy: a narrow single bed, a
writing desk with a new computer, and a cane-backed chair. If the
pictures he had pasted all over the wall were of a woman, the police

would have carted him away for a stalker, but luckily for his sake, they were no lascivious glossies or Peeping Tom grainy snapshots. No, the broad forehead and furrowed brow, the cleft chin and eagle gray eyes belonged to one distinguished head, reproduced in color and in black and white, formally posed and cubistically scratched in crayon by a second-grade class. It was the same face as that on the shiny nickel, and if August had had merely a nickel for every face on his wall, he would have been a wealthy man, indeed.

The walls not covered with images of Jefferson were reserved for works about him. Floor-to-ceiling bookshelves housed Jeffersonia, arranged by their Library of Congress numbers. August had nearly everything published in English on the man and his times, with many more boxes of books in the attic. He put the new entry on crop rotation in its LoC slot and headed to the shower. Exactly fifteen minutes later, he came upstairs, where his father was telling a joke.

"Father Abraham wanted to upgrade his PC to Windows 2000," Leland was saying to his wife, who had never touched a computer in her life. "His son Isaac was incredulous.

"'Pop,'" said Isaac, "'you can't run Windows 2000 on your old, slow 386. Everyone knows that you need a Pentium with at least sixteen megs of memory for that!'

"But Abraham, the man of faith, gazed at Isaac calmly and replied, "'God will provide the RAM, my son.'"

August laughed loudly to cover his mother's smiling confusion and took his place between his parents.

"Well, son, another one under your belt," his father said.

"Yes, sir."

"Die with dignity?"

"As always."

"Salad, anyone?" said Evelyn. "This is low-calorie ranch, so you don't have to be afraid."

"Thanks, Mom." August let her scoop him a bowl. "How was Manda today?"

"To tell you the truth, I'm a bit worried," his father answered, accepting his own overflowing bowl of iceberg lettuce. "She just doesn't seem herself. With all the attention, I'm not surprised—Manda was always such a private girl. But this is different. She hasn't been to visit the babies yet. She hardly says a word to anyone."

"Maybe she's suffering a touch of postpartum?" August ventured, coloring slightly. "I've certainly seen the cows go through it."

"You know, they say she was getting a little hysterical, even before the babies," Mrs. Vaughn interjected. "Throwing things and raging around, just like Mary Todd Lincoln. I wouldn't be surprised if they diagnosed her with MS."

Both August and Pastor Vaughn stared at her quizzically. Mrs. Vaughn lightly tapped her forehead and laughed.

"No, not MS," she said. "Oh, Leland, what is it called? What is it we get?"

"PMS," her husband replied.

"Yes, PMS. They think now that Mary Todd Lincoln had it, and I'll wager Manda Frank does too."

"Could be." Both men nodded and returned to their low-calorie ranch.

"I just hope I did the right thing, counseling her to have all eleven," Leland said after a while. "Seems like everything she had went into making those babies and there is nothing left for her."

"How can you say that!" Mrs. Vaughn exclaimed, "It's been a miracle right here in Three Chimneys, and you're partly responsible for it. No one thought they could all be born alive, except you, and I know how hard you prayed. Now, they're not out of the woods yet, but they will be, and Manda, when she comes back to her senses, will bless you a hundred times over for the Christian guidance you gave her."

August could tell it was what his father wanted to hear, but it brought Leland no solace. The priest dug into his salmon unenthusiastically.

"You know, I had the baby blues with you, sweetheart." Mrs. Vaughn took away the dishes and reset the table with dessert plates and coffee cups. "That's what they used to call it in my day. Maybe they thought none of us would fess up if they called it something so scary as 'postpartum.' I know I wouldn't have. I would have just kept quiet."

August tried to remember if he had detected a change in Margaret after Polly was born. If anything, August had taken her postpartum upon himself, sighing to see the three so happy together—Francis at his kindest and most goofily adoring; Margaret glowing. And in the midst of their happiness, August prowled with anguished fear, for his model of maternity was his own miscarriage-plagued mother, and then there was Patty Jefferson, lost to her husband at the height of their love for one another. August hung back in the early days after Polly's birth, sitting alone for hours in the field, worried this birth would be the event that finally stole Margaret from him completely. But of course, Polly thrived and Margaret with her, and his bachelor worries soon grew awkward and ridiculous.

His parents had years ago stopped asking why he didn't get married, settle down, and start a family of his own. They would never be willingly rid of him, but the way they watched him every time he received a letter with an unfamiliar postmark or a phone call after eight o'clock at night reminded him of how happy they would be to have him in love as they were. He looked fondly at his parents, thoughtfully scraping up their cobblers and blowing in perfect synchronicity upon the headwaters of their coffee. Married for forty years, they were in perfect tandem, barely needing to speak to communicate, united in their unconditional love for their only son. August Vaughn was the luckiest of men. Jefferson lost his father when he was thirteen and his mother when he was thirty-three. He lost his best friend and his wife and four of his children. August still had everyone who mattered. And if he didn't have them in exactly the way he desired, well, at least God would not be jealous.

He helped his mother clear the table and made her sit down to her new Mary Todd Lincoln biography while he did the dishes. He found his father's reading glasses behind the electric can opener and placed them on his head when the priest wandered through the kitchen on his way out to the old chimney. It was little more than a kudzu bump in the landscape now, but long ago, it had served its patriotic duty by providing for the likes of Washington and Madison, Jefferson and Aaron Burr. The stewardship of the tavern had historically fallen to the elder branch of the Vaughn family, while the younger shoot entered the clergy at St. Barnabas Episcopal Church next door. Between the two branches, the Vaughn family covered the spiritual and corporeal needs of the antebellum community quite nicely: A Vaughn christened a man's son, and a Vaughn poured the spirits to toast his health. A Vaughn married a happy couple, and the Vaughn next door served the nuptial dinner. For over half a century these geographical first cousins—church and tavern—pursued a convivial dialogue. That is, until the day the tavern succumbed to a "conflagration of righteous retribution," which is one of the many nicer terms arson goes by.

August knew this chimney meant the world to his father. He was the sort of man who felt almost physical pain at the thought of losing anything, even if it was something he had never had. Love letters tossed in the fire, disintegrated baby blankets, books lost or casually loaned—*never to be returned*—these were the things of nightmare for Pastor Vaughn. A family had so little, inevitably lost so much along the way; who could conceive of destroying what remained? August often watched his father pat the old chimney's thick neck when he went to the mailbox in the morning for his paper, and he knew that in the evening, when putting together his sermons, his father loved to look out his study window and see the Old Man (as he called it) standing in the moonlight, steadfast as an Indian lookout. Through the window over the sink, August watched his father totter off to the Old Man now for inspiration on this Sunday's sermon, and thought, as he did almost every night at precisely 8:30, what a good thing it was to grow old in the company of these worthy old men.

CHAPTER FOUR

When the morphine first kicked in, Manda felt like she'd been turned off the leash. Here, finally, after months of being held back, straining to run, was a wide-open field: rocks to climb, stumps to leap. Space. Now Manda slipped her collar and raced through the morning meadow, hot on a scent, tonguing her excitement. In her life she'd raised hunters who tailed and watched the others, hunters that refused to hark and move up with their running mates. Some she'd been able to correct, others continued on their stubborn way and were of no use to anybody. She'd raised quitters and babblers, and potterers and ghost trailers, but never, until the morphine, had she run alongside them, stride for stride, understanding how easy it was to get lost in the rapture of pure forward motion. Could she blame those dogs for losing sight of why they ran, when the running alone was more than enough? Nearly seven months she'd been kenneled by what was growing inside her, but at last, inside the morphine, she was free. At least for as long as they continued the drip.

But Manda was young, and her body healed more quickly than she was ready for, and she nearly wept when the nurse turned the cock on the clear plastic bag and declared, *That should have seen her through the worst of it,* and instead of renewing her blessed drip, handed her a pleated cup in which two white pills rolled lonesomely. Manda's open field shrunk to the size of a common backyard, the pain returned, and she was tied to a clothesline, allowed just enough leash to choke herself.

"I understand you're going home today," Nurse Reynolds said, checking the dressing over her incision. "Are you excited?"

Manda nodded. She was sitting up now, and taking a few tottering steps. Her voice was the last thing that struggled to come back.

Manda noticed that the nurse didn't say she'd miss her, or that it would be sad to see her leave. All these months, Manda had just been the pen, looked through like a chain-link fence.

"Are we feeling up to going downstairs today?" asked Nurse Reynolds brightly, her eyes encouraging the correct answer. Manda struggled to think. What would Pastor Vaughn say? For days she'd been able to lie in bed without having to worry about them, and everyone said, *Just give her time. It takes some a while to adjust.* Jake went down and told her all about them, so it was like she had seen them. He memorized all the confusing incantations the doctors re-cited over their heads, words like craniosynostosis and asymmetrical with clonus, conditions that sounded like weed killers: RSV and NEC and Grade 4 IVH. How did all these abbreviations come out of her body? Manda wondered. How was she supposed to understand all this?

"I think you'd be happier if you saw them before you left the hospital," said Nurse Reynolds.

What would Pastor Vaughn say? He would say, Yes, go see them. They are your children. The pain would be as great here or there. Go see them.

It was her last day, so Manda let Nurse Reynolds help her into a wheelchair and roll her down to the Neonatal Intensive Care Unit. The halls outside were decorated with paper pinwheels and sick children's drawings: monkey faces, houses with yellow suns, blood red poster-paint handprints. Inside the double doors were a wraparound desk as one might find on a spaceship and, directly in front of her, a bulletin board of babies' faces. Healthy babies. Fat babies. Babies who made it and went home to those brightly painted houses with suns, and stupidly grinning parents, canary feathers peeking from the corners of their mouths. They had all gotten away with something, sneaking their tiny children past death. Now they sent pictures back of quadruplets dressed in matching kilts and first birthday faces smeared with cake.

It was very quiet in NICU and napping dark, disturbed only by the monitor lights and the whirring beeps of respirators. Capable women in pink scrubs, girls who had come from backgrounds similar

to Manda's but who had done something with themselves, they'd be
the first to tell you, padded silently, scribbling on clipboards. Nurse
Reynolds wheeled her around to the left, where her babies were arranged in four rows of what Manda thought were incubators, but which
she learned were now called isolettes. Babies A–K. Ranging in weight
from 2 pounds, 8 ounces, all the way down to the smallest at 16 ounces,
a size, Manda thought, more fitting for a Coke than a baby. Nurse
Reynolds passed her off to one of the pink nurses, a kindly-faced but
no-nonsense woman from the Islands. She removed a quilted blanket
from the bubble of the closest isolette to reveal the tiniest of liver-
colored babies, barely bigger than Manda's hand, but perfectly formed,
with matchstick fingers, a raisin nose, and eyelids so sheer, Manda
thought she could see the dreaming pupils underneath.

"It's good to finally see you," said the nurse. "Your babies were
wondering where you were."

The infant inside the bubble was hooked up to a circulatory
system of tubes and lines, held in place by white adhesive tape. A
red light flashed at her heel—the pulse oximeter, the nurse told
her—and a CPAP tube protruded from her nose. She was being fed
intralipids, fats injected straight into her veins. Any activity burned
off precious calories the baby needed to grow, so she was sedated,
against pain and to keep her from moving. Manda remembered a
conversation with one of the many doctors who saw her in the early
days of her pregnancy, who had gone to great lengths to explain
the heightened sensation receptors in fetuses. You know how you
should speak to your children in the womb and play soothing music for them, he said; well, if you believe they can feel the good
things, you must admit they feel the bad. He spoke in words she
barely understood. Of the developing thalamus, able to transmit
pain response by eight weeks. Sensory receptors appear on the face
and genitalia by the eleventh week, he said. They spread to the
palms of the hands and soles of the feet, and by the twentieth week,
the baby can feel everything. He spoke of heart rates going up and
oxygen saturation going down in response to pain stimuli. How some
babies flailed wildly and how others, overcome by the intensity,

went numb and shut down for days. Fetuses feel everything, he said; it's a medical fact. And they feel it far more intensely than even newborns do. Only after she'd thanked him and left the office did she realize that he told her all that in the hopes of dissuading her from having a selective reduction.

"Which one is this?" asked Manda, embarrassed that she didn't recognize her own child beneath all the tape and wires. She should know each one by instinct, shouldn't she? Hadn't she known Rose?

"Baby I," replied the nurse, double-checking the chart. "Infinity."

Manda winced at the name. Infinity was the name of a rich person's car. While Manda was in the recovery room, the news crew from CNN had begged Jake to let them be the first to break the babies' names, and eager to please, he went ahead and named them without her, pulling from the spiral notebook of names they'd been collecting, putting together first and middle names with no rhyme or reason— Brianna Arianna, like a cheap Italian countess, or worse, Kaylee Lea— names that obviously didn't flow, because inside his man's head he had no rhythm at all, just the jangle of his own nervousness. Manda woke to find the television broadcasting these names, she saw them printed in the newspapers and was embarrassed, because names were what you wore forever, and she felt she'd sent her daughters out in tacky rabbit fur coats when they should have been wrapped in mink.

"Would you like to hold her?" asked the nurse. "Just for a minute?"

Manda looked at the nurse in surprise. Why would they let her hold something so easy to break? The nurse took her silence as a yes, and gently untangled the tiny infant from her tubes and lines, lifted her from the bed, and placed her against Manda's chest.

In the rush of hormones returning to her body, Manda had grown a peach-fuzz beard that was now falling out. She watched a few blonde hairs sift upon the baby's forehead like the feathery clippings of her first haircut. Gently, she wiped the fuzz away, and her finger looked enormous against the tiny skull. Rose had been a big baby—nearly ten pounds—and energetic right from the very beginning. This baby moved like she was still underwater, slowly uncurling her fingers and turning her head. She opened her eyes and looked up at Manda. Glittering black fathomless eyes, full of seawater and accusation.

"She's in remarkable shape, considering," said the nurse. "Yesterday, we had to treat her for an intraventricular hemorrhage. The vessels to her brain weren't strong enough to carry the blood and it was leaking out. It happens in such small babies."

"She's all right now?" asked Manda in alarm.

"It was a level two. Not too serious."

This baby's brain is bleeding. What was she supposed to do? What would Pastor Vaughn do?

"It's going to be all right, Mrs. Frank," the nurse crooned with her comforting Island lilt. "These children have made it this far. They are born fighters."

The nurse's voice was so kind and hopeful, Manda didn't know why she started to cry. She just felt so ashamed. Ashamed she hadn't carried them better. Ashamed of all the times early on at home she'd snuck to the bathroom or the kitchen when they'd absolutely forbidden her to get out of bed. Ashamed of her children's littleness. Ashamed of their names. But most of all, she was ashamed of this numbness she felt. She felt like one of those teenage mothers who had given birth in the bathroom of her senior prom and then gone back to the business of slow dancing. She had carried eleven children seven months, even going without solid food herself so that they would have more room to grow; and yet all along, she'd felt like she was doing a very large favor for a friend. If she just got through it, she could give these children to their rightful mother and her life would finally get back to normal. In third grade, her math teacher had tried to teach them the concept of a million. They were to collect bottle caps and put them in a box. By the end of the year, they'd collected only eighty-five thousand. That's not even a tenth of a million, her teacher said, though it seemed so very many. Imagine this many bottle caps times ten. She only had eleven babies, Manda kept telling herself, but eleven might as well have been a million, for all that she could conceptualize it. And now they were out and everyone was looking at them and they were like the idea of a million and she was so ashamed.

Manda let out a single, hoarse sob and all the baby's monitors went off, the beeping pulse oximeter and the CPAPs and the temperature probe. Around her thick white respirator tube, Infinity tried to cry, but it came out just *whoosh-hiss, whooosh-hiss.*

"Take her, quick!" Manda wailed, feeling like she'd been caught trying to shoplift her own daughter. "Something's wrong."

"It's okay." The nurse swooped down and wrapped the child in a blanket to get her skin temperature back up. "She's just responding to you. You need to be strong for these little ones. They feel it when you start to give up."

Manda felt so ashamed.

She was supposed to go home in a few hours, leaving these babies behind, and the worst thing was, she was glad. She was glad to be putting thirty miles between herself and these suffering children, with their flayed maroon skin, and no-chins, and thin, splayed sea-monkey fingers, reaching up to something, reaching out to her. But how could they possibly have a concept of Mother? How, with their bleeding brains?

Manda wiped her nose on the sleeve of her gown and fell back against her wheelchair. Her milk had come in yesterday, and now it ran in two warm streams down the front of her gown and over her belly. She looked around for someone to bring her a diaper.

"Knock, knock." Pastor Vaughn was tapping on a pretend door.

"You can come over, Pastor," said the nurse, who seemed to know the minister well. Jake said Pastor Vaughn had been here every day.

"I brought the getaway car," Pastor Vaughn said, using the joke he'd tried out on his wife this morning. "I'm here to break you out of this joint."

Manda was happy to see him. Now that he was here she could let go and have him take over. He knew what she should be feeling. He would tell her what to do.

"What's wrong, Little Mother?" asked the pastor, seeing her swollen eyes.

"The baby's brain is bleeding," she said.

He peered into the child's isolette, where the baby now lay like a butterfly pinned in place.

"She's so small," Manda whispered.

"It's a shock, I know," said Pastor Vaughn. "But you'll get used to it. Why, Jake and I are old pros already. What's important is that you have come."

He stepped behind Manda's wheelchair and pushed her down the row of babies. "Look," he said, "look how beautiful. They have no idea how special they are, or how many people are praying for them. They are the most famous babies in the world, Manda, and you are their mother. You should be proud of them. And proud of yourself."

He did know what to feel. And she would do her best to feel it too.

"That one looks almost fat," said Manda hopefully.

Pastor Vaughn studied Baby C carefully before calling the head nurse. "Regina," he said, "Does Chase's stomach look normal to you?" He was sure, his smile said to Manda, that it was nothing to worry about.

The NICU nurse frowned over the obvious distention in the child's abdomen, and pulled an army green screen around his isolette. Manda heard her voice call out over the loudspeaker: "Doctor Khenesi to the NICU stat. Doctor Khenesi to the NICU stat."

"What's happening?" Manda asked, all her fears rushing back.

"The doctors are just coming to take a look at little Chase," answered the reverend, trying to keep his voice calm and even.

"What's wrong with him? Is his brain bleeding too?"

"I don't think so, dear. It's probably fine."

Dr. Khenesi, who had charge of neonatology, walked through the door and straight to the screen without even acknowledging Manda's presence. She felt like she should be doing something to help her own child, boiling water or fetching blankets, but she was just their kennel, she remembered, just a rusted old pen.

"Manda, you've trusted God this far," Pastor Vaughn said. "He won't desert you now."

"God doesn't care about these babies," Manda cried, surprising herself, for she had never spoken to her pastor like this. Everyone assumed she must be the most Christian of mothers, or why else put herself through this? But the joke was on them. She didn't always believe in God. Sometimes she thought she even hated God. She simply hadn't been able to decide what to do, and then it was too late. Everyone said it would be fine, but it was *not* fine.

Now Chase's monitors started beeping furiously, touching off the same response in Jake Jr.'s and Devon's and Ember's, and suddenly Manda felt as if every vessel in her own head was breaking. "If God had cared, He never would have given them to me. I never wanted them. Take them back."

Pastor Vaughn took a step away at her vehemence, and she was happy to see it. What could God possibly have been thinking? All she had ever wanted in life was to be left alone. When she was a girl she used to imagine herself a mushroom on the underside of a fallen tree. Away from all her brothers and sisters, she could grow, pale and hidden, shaded, unnoticed. Is she dangerous? Is she poison? people would wonder as they passed by, and because no one could be quite sure, they would leave her alone. Now God had seen fit that she should never be alone again. She would always have this menagerie of sick, helpless, beeping things, and with them the news crews back every birthday and graduation and speeding ticket until the day she died. The lights over Chase Andrew's crib was so bright, just like the camera lights, she thought her face would crack and spew spores all over Intensive Care.

"Manda." Pastor Vaughn spoke sternly to try to snap her out of her fugue. "Manda. What are we by nature?"

The girl stared at him blankly, awash in panic and sorrow.

"Manda," Pastor Vaughn repeated. "What are we by nature?"

"We are part of God's creation, made in the image of God," she mumbled.

"And what does it mean to be created in the image of God?"

Take pity on us, she begged with her eyes. "I feel like my brain is bleeding," she said.

"What does it mean to be created in the image of God?"

"It means that we are free to make choices: to love, to create, to reason, and to live in harmony with creation and with God." Once

memorized, the Episcopal catechism, like her multiplication tables,
had never deserted her. She repeated it by rote.

"Why then," asked Pastor Vaughn, "do we live apart from God
and out of harmony with creation?"

"From the beginning, human beings have misused their freedom
and made wrong choices."

"Why do we not use our freedom as we should?"

"Because we rebel against God, and we put ourselves in the place
of God." For the first time, Manda thought she saw what he was trying to teach her with this quiz. The monitors were slowly starting to
beep at their normal metronome pace, and her heart was calming
along with them.

"What help is there for us?" Pastor Vaughn urged, his voice warm
and insistent.

Manda looked her pastor in the eye and was very ashamed of all
she had said. She didn't want her babies to die. They didn't mean to
be unnatural. "Our help is in God," she answered, at last.

"God chose you for a reason, Manda," Pastor Vaughn said. "It is
not for us to put ourselves in His place."

The NICU nurse pulled the screen away and laid Chase An-
drew flat on a warming table that looked like an overhead projector.
Manda perked up when she saw him. "That's a good sign, isn't it?"
Manda said. "Having him in the open air like that."

Pastor Vaughn patted her hand. He hadn't the heart to tell her
that only those children who require constant critical attention are
ever placed on the warming table. Liberation was reserved for only
the sickest of the sick.

"Our help is in God," he said.

Manda was scheduled to be discharged at 5 P.M., in time for the live
feed of the nightly news. Her mother was working to get her present-
able, squeezing a blizzard of Johnson's baby powder onto her unwashed
long black hair to absorb the oil, and roughly brushing it through.
Manda had been in a hospital gown for so long, she didn't even own

maternity clothes the right size, and so she was wearing one of Jake's enormous T-shirts (just riding over her sagging whale's belly) that on the front showed a weight lifter Jesus pumping a cross, and on the back read: *This Blood's for You*. She stretched a pair of leggings over her swollen, varicosed calves and thighs, and slipped a pair of red plastic flip-flops on her feet. Her mother ordered her to sit still while she waved her mascara wand over Manda's stumpy lashes. Jake kissed his wife's cheek and told her she looked beautiful.

Everything seemed dreamlike to Manda in her wheelchair—the nurses lined up along the hallway to wave her good-bye, the bouquets of flowers thrust into her lap from the patients nonterminal enough to stumble out of their rooms, the flashbulb click and ratchet of disposable cameras. Forced roses and baby's breath slipped from her lap as the Chinesey-looking woman who pushed her wheelchair turned corner after corner in this forever hallway. Her mother ran back collecting the stray stems until she soon had a nosegay fit for a bridesmaid.

When at last they reached the main entrance, the wheelchair came to an abrupt stop. There it was, a wall of cameras, reporters and news vans, joyfully weeping women, and obvious Catholics. All the well-wishers of the world, like the faithful waiting Judgment Day in the valley of Jehoshaphat, but instead, here in the parking lot of this teaching hospital in this middle-sized town in Virginia, turning their faces to her, mother of the Frank Eleven. They did not look at Jake, grinning nervously beside her. No, he was like the groom in wedding photos, who fades behind the star in her big, white dress. All eyes were trained on her. All cameras on her. All the love and support and enthusiasm. On her.

"Mrs. Frank, how do you feel about leaving the children behind?"

"Mrs. Frank, how do you answer detractors who have called for your fertility specialist's suspension?"

"*Senora Frank, tu tienes niños favoritos?*"

Jake continued to grin, not knowing who to answer first, while her mother took this opportunity to disappear for a desperately needed Virginia Slim.

"I think I speak for the Franks when I thank each and every one of you for your support and prayers," said Pastor Vaughn. "There is nothing harder on a parent than leaving a child behind."

A thousand questions followed, but Pastor Vaughn sensed Manda's terror and steered her toward the car. With special dispensation, he'd been allowed to park his sherbet orange 1970 VW bus right outside the door for a quicker getaway (as he joked with the hospital officials, getting more of a chuckle from them than from Manda earlier). Kessler Chevrolet had donated a brand-new minivan, but it was still at the dealership, being fitted for eleven car seats.

"Don't you think we should have stayed to talk a while?" Jake asked. "I mean, all those people came just to see us."

"I think we should get your wife off her feet," answered Pastor Vaughn, strapping Manda into the front seat. The belt hit her exactly on her incision, but Pastor Vaughn had been thoughtful enough to pad the strap with an old towel. He looked over at the new mother, who was staring straight ahead, oblivious to the crowd swelling around her.

"Manda, let me tell you a little story," said Pastor Vaughn, backing out and trying not to run over Girl Scout Troop 419. Jake put his head out of the back window and told the girls please, if they wouldn't mind, he needed to get his wife off her feet.

"I once counseled a woman who had twins and decided to give them up for adoption."

"That's terrible," said Jake from the backseat. "I could never do that."

"Well, sometimes it's necessary," answered the pastor, "and in this case the boys found two fine, upstanding homes.

"One child was adopted by a family from Egypt and named Amal. The other one went to a good family from Spain and was named Juan. Many years later, Juan sent a picture to his birth mother, and she wept with joy. She came to see me in my office, and said, 'Pastor Vaughn, this photo of Juan has brought me such happiness! If only I had one of Amal!'

"'Well, ma'am, think of it this way,' I told her." And here he gave Manda, seated beside him, a little wink. "'They're twins. If you've seen Juan, you've seen Amal.'"

When that didn't bring even the weakest smile, Pastor Vaughn knew Manda must be mightily depressed.

The dogs behind the chain-link fence barked furiously when she stepped out of the bus, and for the first time that day, Manda felt a little like her old self. She used to roll cotton and Vaseline into her ears against their constant braying, but today she could have lain down among them and taken a dirt bath in their noise. The dogs climbed one another fighting to get to her face, trying to lick it through the wire. She touched their noses and hot, wet tongues with the flat palm of her hand.

"The house isn't quite ready yet," Jake explained, as if she couldn't tell by the half-hung clapboard and random rolls of roofing paper. Yet, it looked even bigger in person than it had on TV. A hedge of gifts had grown up around the house, presents from well-wishers as far away as Nigeria and Rio de Janeiro, along with cards and letters and bouquets of daisies and mums. Jake helped her up the steep-raked two-by-fours where the front steps would eventually be. "Just wait until you see inside," he said. "It's like a palace."

Rose and old faithful Turbo raced downstairs to meet them, followed by Jake's mother, who seemed chagrined to see no news vans (she'd spent twenty-five dollars that morning getting her hair done). Jake grabbed the dog's collar before she could leap on his wife, but he wasn't so quick with his little girl.

"Mama!" Rose grabbed Manda around the waist, just where the seat belt, though padded, had dug in, but Manda would not let her daughter see she'd hurt her. She bent down and showered her girl's dirty cheeks with kisses.

Oh Rose, Rose, what have we done to you? Manda thought.

Jake had brought the plans to the hospital, but Manda had never seen the inside of her new house. It was a half-finished masterpiece straight out of *Southern Living*. Inside, the kitchen floor waited for its no-wax linoleum, the blue slate counter spanned empty recesses where a paneled dishwasher and refrigerator would be fitted to umbilical pipes. Vast rooms of low-pile beige carpet stretched out before her, broken by archways and track lighting and unpainted French doors. There wasn't a normal light switch in the house; they all ran on dimmers.

"Mama, look!"

Rose ran to the top of the beige-carpeted staircase and slid down on her butt. *Bump. Bump. Bump.* Her grandmother put a swift end to it, for she was not about to put cream on anyone's rug-burnt behind.

"What are we going to do with all this room?" Manda asked, opening a door she thought was a closet, but which was another half-bath.

"Mama, look!"

Rose ran to the top of the stairs and slid down the banister on her stomach.

"Is this the way you behave when your sick mama comes home?" Jake's mother asked her sternly, pulling the little girl's arm. "Go out in the yard and play."

Manda didn't want Rose to go, but the little girl had already raced out into the backyard, which was still a churned swamp of mud and straw.

"There are nails outside," Manda said weakly.

"She's fine," replied Mrs. Frank, lighting a Merit Ultra. "I played with nails all the time when I was a girl."

"I'll watch her," Pastor Vaughn offered. "You look around."

Never in her wildest dreams had Manda imagined such a house for herself. Jake led her upstairs to the babies' rooms, hastily painted and filled with cribs. Four in one, four in another, three in the third. They passed Rose's room, where her single bed had been brought over from the old house along with her Winnie-the-Pooh lamp, whose cord trailed across the floor and found an unplated socket. Down the hall was Manda and Jake's master bedroom, with their old king-sized bed. It had the kind of shelf headboard you could store books in if you so desired, but at the old house it was always full of coffee cups and hunting magazines. With no other furniture around it, Manda noticed every scar and scrape. It looked cheap and forlorn in the new space, like someone's overweight alcoholic uncle who'd come to stay.

"Manda, look at this!" Jake steered her into their master bath, shimmering in inner-ear pink and tan. He hit the switch on the Plexiglas Jacuzzi, which because it had no water in it sounded like a garbage disposal eating a spoon. "Calgon, take me away!" he said.

His mother caught up with them in the bathroom. "I think y'all've done right well for yourselves. I don't guess you could've ever afforded a house like this on your own."

"It's too big," Manda said, backing out into the empty bedroom.

"Won't seem so big," Mrs. Frank said through a drag of her cigarette, "when you've got twelve kids running around in it."

"Mother Frank, you won't be able to smoke around the babies," Manda said. They'd taught her all about secondhand smoke in the hospital, and in her effort to do better, Manda was determined to follow orders.

Jake's mother shot her son a look that said, Hormones. She flicked the butt into the toilet.

"People've been donating clothes," Jake said, opening the walk-in closet to reveal three big moving boxes of shirts and pants. "Some are for the babies, some are for you. And here is the baby-sitting sign-up list the school sent over." Her husband handed over the multi-folded banner, purple with teenage girls names.

"I don't guess we'll need anybody for another few months, until they come home."

"Well, I hate to leave you so soon, baby, but I'd better get my route taken care of. I'll tuck you into bed when I get home."

Manda hadn't even thought that her husband might have to go to work. But of course they still needed to make a living—they had little to live on until the book deals and movie-of-the-week offers came through. She looked at the pair reflected in the mirror over the bathroom sink—her skinny husband, the man who had loved her without interruption since they were both fifteen, and herself, bloated and wide, with her unwashed hair and pregnancy acne, as miserable as she'd ever been in her life. And yet his arms snaked around her as if she were the sexiest bit of ass on the planet and he couldn't get enough of her. He still loved her. Despite everything.

"Are we staying here tonight?" she asked.

"We've got a bed and we've got electricity. I don't see what more we need."

"I can order us up a Domino's," his mother offered.

This is my new home, thought Manda, leaning back against her husband's strong arms. This is the huge place where I'll raise my huge family. We'll all eat huge pizzas and we'll all get huge.

In the backyard, Pastor Vaughn was telling Rose a joke.

"Do you know why monsters were big and hairy and ugly?" he asked. Rose's eyes were huge, and she squirmed as if she could barely wait for the punch line before exploding. "Because if they were small and round and smooth, they'd be M&M's!"

The little girl laughed and laughed and laughed, then she threw herself in his lap and laughed some more.

Manda sent them off one by one. They ate their pizza from greasy paper plates and drank soda out of sweating cans, then Pastor Vaughn took his leave, promising he'd be back tomorrow. Jake's mother stacked the stuffed animal gifts according to color and size, tied all the balloons into one smiling teddy bear zeppelin, which drifted aimlessly through the house on the central air currents; then she went home to wrap her hairdo in toilet paper and hope for better camera luck tomorrow. At ten o'clock, Manda finally convinced her own mother and sister, who had shown up just in time for the pizza, to go home, too. You'll have plenty to do when the babies come home; I can handle Rose for tonight, she said.

When they all left, Manda collected the limp plates and emptied the Coke cans, with their felty jingle of cigarette butts, into the sink. Under the table, Rose had fallen asleep on the soft pillow of

Turbo's stomach, her head rising and falling with every breath the old dog took. Jake wouldn't be back for another hour at least. No cameras peered through the window. Manda was finally alone.

It felt wrong somehow for them to have moved into this big empty house, just she and Jake and Rose, the same family she had before she went into the hospital. What entitled them to all this space? What were they without the babies? Just people who barely made their mortgage every month, who drove a bad truck, who enjoyed NASCAR and rabbit hunting. This was not her house, Manda thought. This house belonged to the babies, and she was a trespasser here. She lumbered slowly through the house again, turning up the lights, taking in all that was done and undone. It was as if Francis Marvel had taken inventory of all he would have liked in a house and tackled that first, so that there was a sound system but no dishwasher, track lighting but no bathroom door. In the unfinished dining room, she found the thermostat and cut off the frigid central air. Then she flung wide the front door to let in the late-summer night, now full of the sound of crickets and pond frogs. There was a swamp not far away where she used to go frog gigging as a girl, she and her brothers and the boys up the road, taking their burlap sacks and long poles with two nails duct-taped to the end, fixing their flashlight beams on sloe-eyed frogs in the muddy swamp grass, who knew, with the falling of the shadow, that their time was up. The great-great-great-grandchildren of those frogs called now, Welcome home. And the crickets called, and the ticks in their underbrush and the chiggers in her soil. Welcome home, Manda. Welcome home.

But she was a trespasser, and this was not her home. She turned back to make sure Rose still slept, and she let herself out through the garage, shuffling across the yard to her real home. The dogs in their cages whined as she passed by and she heard them stand and thump their tails against their plywood house. Beyond the dog pen, the old shack sat still and dark, only its Depression glass windows winking in the reflected moonlight. No one had bothered to lock the back door, even though most of their things were still inside. She turned the knob and let herself in, leaving off the lights, just feeling her way around like she had many a night when she snuck in drunk and didn't want to get it from her daddy. Manda took a deep, private, home-coming breath, letting the place settle into her and work on her confused sense of direction.

Now, this close, pungent place—this smelled like home to her. Generations of laborers and hired hands had rocked back in their dinner chairs, and passed out drunk on the rugs until their sweat just seeped into the wood walls and floors, leaving a cuss-masculine smell that all the Murphy's oil soap in the world wouldn't get out. Manda felt her way to the small kitchen and ran herself a mason jar of water, taking two of the Percocet they'd sent her home with. Her belly still screamed from the surgery and she still felt nearly as heavy as she had before she gave birth.

There was a time when six children, two parents, and a grand-mother lived in this shack. As the youngest, Manda slept wherever there was space—sometimes just on sofa cushions on the living room floor, if her sisters had friends over. Now her two oldest brothers were in jail and the youngest in the military. One sister lived nearby and the other had moved to Raleigh when her husband repeatedly violated his restraining order. Both had growing families of their own. That's what struck Manda as so odd about this whole thing. If she'd spaced her children out and had eleven babies in eleven years, she would have been no better than her own mother and sisters: irresponsible, a welfare cheat, another bit of Sawdust Lane white trash. But as luck would have it, she'd had them all at once, and now she was, overnight, middle-class. And respectable. She lived in a house built by a man from one of the town's oldest families. She was cared for by a respectable minister of a respectable church. The whole town, who before would reflexively lock their car doors at the sight of a member of her family, was treating her like a favorite niece. She didn't know whether to be grateful or to spit on them all.

The Percocet was beginning to steal away a bit of the pain, and Manda settled herself in her father's old recliner. She pulled the brown and blue pilly afghan over her legs and let her heavy head fall back. It wasn't morphine, but it would do. Instead of the field, she felt a clear-

ing open up, just a break in the woods, but someplace to run, like the
place she used to run as a girl, down by the rushing creek, with its diamond mica banks and six-pack plastic logjams. In this primeval opiate
forest, Manda was thin again, and racing across the red-barked pine
tree that had fallen over the creek—her dog Turbo running ahead,
impatient for her to cross. Manda stopped to taunt the churning, spit-
ting water below, lifting one foot and hopping, her balance perfect,
her body hawk-light. Here in the center of the log, she could say no to
both worlds: to Turbo urging her forward—quick—to the other side;
to her mother who from far, far away was ringing the bell she always
used to call the kids in to supper as if they were wayward cattle and not
her own flesh and blood. We're running away, Manda shouted to the
woods; I'm not coming home for supper. But even half a mile away,
she could still hear the dinner bell, which was never disobeyed without a whipping, and could picture her sharp, carcinogenic mother, the
white fat on her upper arm rippling with the rhythm of that bell. Here,
Bobby, Nina, Benny, Randy, Manda, Sue. Come home, I say.

Manda opened her eyes in her dark kitchen, and still the bell
was ringing. She pushed off the afghan and stumbled onto the front
porch, from which the sound seemed to originate, but when she got
there, all was quiet. Just crickets and frogs, and the almost subaudible
hum of her new house, with all its window lights blazing. Then, there
it was again. The bell. And then Rose tiny in the lighted maw of the
new house front door, crying, "Mama! Mama! The phone is ringing.
Where are you?"

Manda shook her head hard to try and clear the Percocet fuzz
and walked toward her daughter. Together it took them another
twenty rings to find where the phone was hidden (in the utility
room, behind the door) and answer it. It was the hospital, suggesting Mr. and Mrs. Frank come back right away. Things had not gone
well with little Chase Andrew, they were sorry to say, and despite
the best efforts of their seasoned professional staff, the weakest of
Manda's eleven children had died.

CHAPTER FIVE

Everyone suffers with the death of a child, and Three Chimneys went into deep mourning at the sad news from Charlottesville. Citizens wore their Frank Eleven T-shirts with a new solemnity, and some especially sensitive ladies of the town stitched halos of gold thread over the tenth line-drawn child's head. The death of young Chase Andrew was an occasion for tear-streaked faces and much coming together at Three Chimneys Junior High School, where many of the girls who had signed up for baby-sitting felt especially stricken. They exchanged stories of others they knew who had died young; some told of shivering at church cemeteries before tiny tombstones whose birth and death dates fell inside the same week, while others thought it a blessing if it meant the child would no longer be in pain.

While the girls absorbed the full impact of the town's tragedy, the boys of Three Chimneys Junior High were not so evolved. They had felt the whole eleven-children thing to be as repugnant as walking in on their mothers in the bathtub, and were looking for any excuse to ridicule the sentimentality of the young ladies of their acquaintance. They made jokes like "One down, ten to go," and "Litters are for dogs and cats, not people." The girls were disgusted with the boys and told them to grow up. The boys stuffed backpacks under their shirts and waddled down the hall in a cruel imitation of poor grieving Amanda Frank.

Polly Marvel was among the crowd of distraught young women who had collected in the main hall by the auditorium to plan a candlelight vigil down School Street that night. Polly was deeply occupied with thoughts on the precariousness of her own childhood, for Manda's son was the first person she knew who had died at a younger age than she was now. It was all so fleeting, wasn't it? Polly thought, feeling adult and resigned, even as she mourned the loss of her own innocence. Childhood was not a safe place.

"Babies die all the time in Africa," Drew Powell sniggered as he walked past. "I don't see any of you crying over them."

"You're such a prick, Drew," Polly called after him. "You wouldn't know an emotion if it bit you in the ass."

"Perhaps we should watch our language, Miss Marvel," said a familiar voice behind her. "We wouldn't want our principal getting his nuts in a knot."

Polly spun to see Mr. March coming out of the men's faculty bathroom they had been unintentionally blocking. His round communist glasses were still misted with water from where he'd held them under the sink, and the short hair around his ears was damp.

"Aren't you due in class?"

It was a minute to two, and Mr. March was right. The other girls drifted away to their own classes, and the boys raced off to gym or shop or whatever boy-thing was next. Polly found herself alone, with no other choice but to walk beside Mr. March all the way upstairs.

"Isn't it just devastating?" she asked, after self-consciously adjusting the distance between them. She didn't want to hug the wall, but neither could she imagine her bare arm brushing that of his blue cotton blazer.

"Isn't what devastating?" Mr. March asked.

"Poor Chase Andrew," Polly replied, shocked that he had not heard the news. "One of the Frank Eleven. He died last night."

"Oh," said Mr. March. "You knew him well?"

"Well, no," Polly answered reluctantly. "Not well. He was only eight days old."

"But you'd been to see him in the hospital?"

"We were planning to, before . . . ," she replied, feeling a little foolish. "The Franks are our neighbors."

"Oh. Neighbors," said Mr. March.

"I just can't think of a single thing more tragic than the death of a child," Polly said, and was pleasantly surprised to hear the quiver in her voice. She'd never thought much about it, but, indeed, what could be more disturbing than a young life over before it began?

"Miss Marvel, you seem like a remarkably intelligent young lady." They had stopped outside his classroom door, and Mr. March looked down at her softly. "But until you learn to think for yourself, I fear you will remain remarkably dull."

"I don't see what's so wrong about mourning the death of a child," she said, stung, yet determined to hold on to her new-found sorrow.

"There is nothing wrong with it," said Mr. March. "So long as one does not take too much enjoyment in one's own grief. Why should the death of a child be more tragic than the death of an adult? Babies have no personalities of their own. At that age, they can be nothing more than the sum of their parents' projections. Mourning that is quite narcissistic, don't you think?"

"But babies are so innocent," insisted Polly. "They have their whole lives ahead."

"Yet how much sadder to lose someone you've grown to care about. If death should take you, with all your life experiences and potential, we should all mourn greatly, but don't ask me to get worked up over a baby.

"The concept of childhood is a recent phenomenon, Miss Marvel," Mr. March explained, with his hand on the door. "Before the nineteenth century, children were treated with far less sentiment and indulgence than they are today. They were dressed as adults and spoken to as adults, and given adult responsibilities. This cocoon of childhood is your enslavement, Miss Marvel, imposed on you by society. It is a construct, nothing more. Now, if you'll excuse me, I have a pop quiz to administer." He smiled at her over his shoulder as he disappeared inside. "Next period, I'll expect you to act surprised."

Polly watched him through the glass pane beside the door, before slowly drifting down the hall to algebra. She slipped in under the glare of Mrs. Knowles, and immediately Bethany passed her a note. *I saw you talking. Way to go. Tell your mom you're coming over to do homework, and we'll go to the vigil together.* To which Polly wrote back. *Bethany, get a grip. A vigil is just so remarkably dull.*

After evening milking and dinner, Polly climbed upon her Schwinn three-speed and pedaled back toward town. It was her favorite time of day, when the sun was just another stratum in the purple and pink sedimentary sky. She stood up on her bike, pedaling against the last exhalations of honeysuckle folding up for the night and the sweet cucumber smell of neighbors' newly mown grass. Snakehill Road wove in and out of woods, tall overhanging spruce trees cano- pied the road to chill her until she burst back out into the warmth of the setting sun. She raced up the rolling hills and flew down again, her wheaten hair streaming behind her, her shadow, with its night- promise pumping angles, almost beautiful, she thought, keeping easy pace beside her.

Polly took the two miles into town easily, slowing only when she was just on the outskirts, when the hay fields gave way to a final stretch of evergreen and sapling oaks that marked the last bit of wil- derness before Snakehill straightened into School Street. At the white paper box and a red reflector on a stick marking a hidden drive- way, she squeezed her handle brakes and coasted to a halt. A packed- dirt driveway growing a spine of scrub grass led about an eighth of a mile to a small frame ranch house. This was where he lived, she knew, from the police incident a few years back involving some failing foot- ball players who had drunkenly vandalized his house in retaliation for their bad grades. They were punished with a summer of commu- nity service, while the PTA volunteered to paint over the word JEW- FAGGOT that dripped from his doorway like lamb's blood. Before she really knew who he was, she would sometimes see a thin, dark- haired man jogging this way, his washed-to-the-point-of-transparency Columbia University T-shirt clinging to his narrow chest, his lean, hairy legs disappearing into the scantiest of terry gym shorts. He would turn into this driveway like a rabbit dashing for cover and vanish into the woods, only the rough echo of flying gravel serving to prove his existence. Polly sat for a moment on her bike, listening for those short, compact strides coming toward her through the woods. It was about this time of day she used to see him, back when he barely registered as anything other than an "older person" and thus unworthy of further scrutiny. How many opportunities had she wasted as a stupid kid, she thought, riding past his house with nothing more on her mind than an ice cream at Snow White's or a slumber party at Bethany's? If she'd only known then what sort of man he was, she would have thrown over all those childish things and ridden beside him on his nightly jog, his personal timekeeper and cheerleader and helpmeet. If only she had known.

She waited by his tubular paper box a good ten minutes, as the shadows lengthened around her and made her wish for a sweater. She memorized every nick in the white plastic box, dirty with years of newsprint and purple with bird droppings. Mr. March didn't seem to have a mailbox, which struck her as odd, for only a few people in town took boxes at the post office, and they were the sorts that seemed always to be addicted to record clubs or involved in mail-me-a-dollar, I'll-tell-you-how-to-make-a-million scams. Polly waited and listened, shivering in the twilight, until she saw the accusatory headlights of an approaching car taking the curve of Snakehill Road. Polly swiftly pushed off on her bike, pedaling furiously, trying to put as much distance between herself and the driveway as she could. If only he would jog out of the woods right now, she thought, he would catch just the glimpse of her disappearing like a fleet young nymph—a rush of hair, a flurry of limbs. Would that not be more enchanting anyway? Was not glimpsed-in-flight more seductive than doggedly-waiting-by-paper-box?

But what if that was *his* car, she suddenly thought, whose distant high beams swept over her like a prison searchlight? What if he was about to turn into his house when he saw her riding ahead and, almost against his will, felt compelled to follow her, his machine put in service of pursuing a nymph, like Apollo the god chasing a virgin until she dropped of exhaustion and succumbed? The feeling that he

was there, behind the darkened windshield of his car, his eyes, like
his headlights, fixed on her with a mute intensity of desire, came so
strong upon Polly that when she was finally forced to stop at the
town's only traffic light, she was almost terrified to turn around. She
struggled to catch her breath, for she could never remember racing
so hard, and she did not want to appear ragged and overwhelmed
when he caught up to her. The headlights were hot upon her now,
but even as the car approached, Polly knew her hopes were dashed.
It was no whiny idle of a Karmann Ghia behind her, but the wide,
boxy backfire of Jake Frank's mother's ten-year-old banana yellow
Cadillac. No swarthy face and burning eyes behind the windshield,
only a dentured smile and a friendly wave, as the car pulled through
the light, leaving her behind. Polly waved a disappointed hello back
to the older woman.

Trembling with exhaustion and thwarted adrenaline, Polly
wearily pushed off once more, headed now toward her friend
Bethany's house on Polk Street, at the corner of School. She noticed that the twenty-two trees had gone into mourning for Chase
Andrew Frank—the pink and blue ribbons overfitted with deep
purple sashes—but she had completely forgotten about the candlelight vigil until she saw it advancing upon her down the street.
Young girls dressed in school colors, older women in comfortable
slacks. The news crews walked backward filming the procession,
capturing for the nation the beatific candlelit faces of the girls from
Three Chimneys Junior High in front, their large blue eyes glistening with tears, their hands gracefully cupped around the flames.
Someone behind them was playing a flute and someone else was
asking Chase Andrew in a warbling treble "Did you ever know that
you're my hero?"—while others hesitantly joined in. If she didn't
know what the procession was for, she might very well have been
moved by the sheer simple fairylike beauty of the yellow flames. All
this for a baby who weighed not even two pounds, who had barely
drawn a week's worth of breath. Everyone was made serious and important by candlelight; even the girls her age seemed to approach a
more adult understanding of sadness merely by being removed from

their native electric element. She picked Pastor Vaughn out of the crowd, touching his candle like a chaste kiss to a famous blonde reporter whom Polly recognized from when she used to watch television. She saw the weatherman from Channel 5 who had been at school the other day.

Mrs. Frank's Cadillac pulled off to the side of the road, and the grieving grandmother melted into the procession, a dozen arms reaching out to pull her in. Most of the town was here, and many strangers, all joined in one grief, solemnly advancing as one extended family down School Street. Yet as they approached, weeping, singing, holding laminated newspaper photos of little Chase Andrew, Polly couldn't shake the thought that they looked as much like a militia of colonial soldiers, evenly spaced ten across, their legions stretching back for miles. She half-expected the first row to drop to its knees, take aim, and fire, before being mowed down and replaced by the brave, fatalistic column behind it.

Bethany was standing outside on her front lawn watching the procession when Polly pulled up.

"Man, that's something, isn't it?" she asked.

"It's so predictable," answered Polly, brushing her sweaty bangs off her forehead. She leaned her bike against Bethany's front porch and waited impatiently to go inside. After another minute, Bethany tore herself away and closed the door, though the parade of candlelight went on outside the living room window. Polly reached over and drew the shade.

"Where are your parents?" Polly asked, drifting toward the huge, modern kitchen and the gleaming double-door refrigerator where the Frasers kept their three-liter sodas. Bethany rooted through the cupboards for glasses and a bag of Cheetos.

"Some reporters wanted to interview them. They're down at Snow White."

Polly rolled her eyes. Sure, Bethany's father was a doctor, but he was a hand surgeon and not at all involved in female matters. Her mom worked for the School Board, so Polly couldn't imagine what she might have to say about the Franks. The soda she was pouring foamed over the glass and onto the countertop. Don't worry, Bethany waved her off, her mom would clean it up later.

"They were saying at school that Manda and Jake had sex eleven times in one night and that's how they ended up with eleven babies," Bethany said. "My cousin was in the same grade as Manda. She said she was a slut."

"That's not how it works," Polly answered. "You don't need to have sex eleven separate times."

"I know who you'd like to have sex with eleven times. " Bethany laughed.

"Shut up."

"I saw you with him outside of class. What were you talking about?"

"Stuff," replied Polly evasively. "Slavery."

"Polly." Bethany sighed. "If you want him to take you seriously, you can't waste moments like that on slavery. You have to ask him questions. Find out what he's looking for in a woman."

"He said the concept of childhood is manufactured," she replied. "That we're enslaved by it."

"Tell me about it," answered Bethany. "They expect us to buy all these clothes and CDs, but they won't let us drive to the mall to get them. If I'm old enough to have a credit card, I'm old enough to drive."

The telephone rang. "Maybe that's him," Bethany teased, lifting the receiver. "He's tracked you down. Hey, get this . . ." Bethany held out the receiver and a tinny voice spoke into Polly's ear.

"This is Governor Adams Brooke," said the pretaped message. "In the words of the undying patriot Thomas Jefferson, 'Farmers are the true representatives of the great American interest and are alone to be relied on for expressing the proper American sentiments.' As you know, I was born and raised on a small family farm in rural—"

"Governor Brooke," yelled Polly into the receiver, "what's your position on politicians invading our privacy?"

Bethany grabbed the phone from her friend and spoke into it. "Governor Brooke, what is your position on students dating their teachers?" She laughed. Polly shrieked and quickly pulled the receiver back.

"Governor Brooke, if you're elected, will you let my mother come to the White House and have sex with you?"

"Governor Brooke," cried Bethany, "ditch the toupee, you're not fooling anybody!"

"Abolish childhood!" yelled Polly. "Let my people go!"

"Yeah!" yelled Bethany. "Let my people go! Let my people go!"

". . . *corporations and give America back to the people. And so on November 3, tell Washington that Family Matters.*"

"Come on, let's go upstairs," said Bethany, unceremoniously dropping the receiver on the floor. Polly wondered if the governor was on an endless loop and would go on throughout the night, patiently soliciting the votes of Bethany's microwave and garbage disposal.

The girls took their snacks upstairs to Bethany's rock-star-wallpapered bedroom. Since Polly was not allowed to have cable television, or a CD player, or a computer to download MP3s, she was utterly dependent on Bethany for her musical education, and knew all these bare-chested young men by reputation only. Today's *chico caliente* was a twenty-year-old Cuban pop singer Bethany had discovered on Internet Radio Havana. As with so many inseparable teenagers, Polly and Bethany's friendship was in part founded on a certain knowledge of superiority each had over the other, and a certain amount of charitable pity for the other's failings. Of the two, Bethany certainly knew herself to be the cuter. She had dark brown ringlets that she wore stylishly clipped around her head, and a T-zone full of winning freckles. She had not been without a boyfriend since sixth grade, the grade when precocious girls first got boyfriends, and if some of her earlier experiments had proven themselves remedial by middle school, Polly's virtue was that she did not throw them in her face.

If Bethany was the more experienced romantically, she couldn't deny that Polly's parents' divorce had given her friend a sophistication and disaffection that she, the unfortunate daughter of parents who liked each other, could never hope to achieve. She had to acknowledge that a new glamour had settled over Polly, despite the best efforts of her mother, who wouldn't even let her daughter wear Lycra, but cruelly sent her out into the world dressed like a Pilgrim, in horrible home-made clothes. Bethany knew how Polly suffered, and how she had grown up, seemingly overnight, when the news spread around town of her father's affair with his secretary. Polly had returned to school with a secret knowledge of what boys might grow up to become—not ro-mantic lovers, good husbands, and kind fathers, but cheaters and liars and infinite disappointment. Obviously, Mr. March had picked up on her new aura of adulthood. Bethany thought only a blind man couldn't see how hot he was for her, and how they were meant to be together.

Polly pulled her reading assignment from her backpack, but Bethany had other plans before getting down to work. She reached between her mattress and box spring, retrieved a brown paper bag, and set it on her quilted bedspread. Polly could tell from the size and shape that it was a magazine, but she gasped in horror when Bethany revealed which one.

"Oh my God! Where did you get that?" she squealed.

"I wouldn't be caught dead buying it around here, that's for sure," Bethany giggled, blushing. "I got it last time we went to Charlottesville."

On the cover was a petal-fresh girl frothed with tulle and raw silk, the blush high on her cheekbones, her face half-hidden behind a bouquet of fat pink peonies. They stared at the cover for a long time, neither daring to reach out to flip it open.

"Put it away," Polly said at last.

"No, we have to look at it," answered her friend. "It cost me four ninety-five."

Polly couldn't explain the feeling at the pit of her stomach as she turned the pink and pearl pages of *Bride* magazine. It was Sep-tember's issue and young women were shot romping through mown hay fields, summer's last rays igniting their windswept veils, rakish men in tuxedos chasing gamely after them. This is not for me, Polly thought queasily, I should not be looking at this, her fingers reach-

ing out involuntarily to reveal the next spread of carefree girls laughing into blue skies. She paused at a soft-focus picture of a young
woman in a claw-footed bathtub. Her head was thrown back and her
hands caressed her tanned, athletic calf, while a thousand candles
burned around her. It accompanied an article titled: "How to Make
Your First Night One to Remember."

"First night," Polly snorted. "No one is a virgin when they get
married anymore."

"Sex is different on your wedding night," Bethany explained.
"It's like starting all over again."

They devoutly flipped through every page of the thick magazine,
including the advertisements—especially the advertisements, because
that's where the prettiest dresses were. They were in absolute agreement about what sort of gowns they loathed (anything with puffed
sleeves, anything with long sleeves, anything with too much lace), but
they differed in their preferences. Bethany favored an elegant sheath
with spaghetti straps, whereas Polly secretly wanted the works: tight
bodice, huge skirt with train, a veil that hid her completely. If she were
ever dumb enough to do it, she wanted there to be no mistake or suspicion of halfheartedness on her part. No boring bridesmaid dress ordered in white to save money, or short skirt, or modern *hat* perched
ridiculously on her head. If she were ever dumb enough to get married,
she would make sure the whole world knew she meant it, knew there
was no turning back. But who cared what sort of dress she liked, Polly
thought, shaking herself out of the pink, perfumed spell cast by the
magazine. She intended to take many lovers, and who knew, perhaps
even have a child out of wedlock, but as for being saddled with a husband for the rest of her life . . . well, no dress was worth that.

"Do you think if Scott and I are still going together by senior
year, he'll ask me to marry him?" Bethany asked.

"Probably," Polly said, giving the answer she knew her friend
wanted. "Would you say yes?"

"Probably," Bethany replied. "But have a four-year engagement
through college. What would you say if Mr. March asked?"

"God! He would never ask."

"But what if he did?"

Polly was saved from answering by the sound of the door slamming downstairs. Bethany's parents were home, and the girls shoved the magazine deep under the mattress. As Bethany quickly scattered schoolbooks around the bed, Polly was left with the same guilty hangover she got whenever Bethany convinced her to try on clothes at the mall she knew her mother would never allow her to buy.

"Bethany Renee Fraser, march yourself downstairs and clean up that soda," Bethany's mother said, thrusting her head into the room, where the girls sat studiously bent over their books. "Hello, Polly."

"Hello, Mrs. Fraser," Polly answered politely.

"My daughter needs to learn I'm not running a maid service."

Bethany sighed dramatically and followed her mother downstairs, leaving Polly to wait in her room. As much as she would have liked to reach under the mattress for the magazine, she felt looking at it now would be tantamount to drinking alone. She turned instead to the limpid-eyed rock stars on the wall, their chests free of hair, their lips glistening as if just licked. She knew other girls found them handsome, but she never understood why. These boys had no character, no torment. She wanted a dark, sardonic sort of man, one who had been wounded deeply and needed someone to teach him to love again. She wanted a man whose problems made hers utterly insignificant. These boys were for children, and she wanted someone who refused to think of her as a child.

Oh, Mr. March, thought Polly woefully. What did she even know about him? Her eyes slid to Bethany's desktop computer, decorated with glitter stickers and a blue-haired pop-eyed troll. Before Bethany's parents bought a filtering package, the girls had once dared to type in the word "fuck," learning firsthand the terror of pornographic screens popping up like some perverse Whack-a-Mole. But now, logging onto Bethany's AOL account, Polly was interested in something else entirely. She glanced over her shoulder, and furtively typed in a darker secret.

Harvey March. She didn't know what she expected to find on him. He wasn't famous, after all, he'd never won anything so far as she knew, hadn't written anything or been elected to office, yet here she was tapping the floorboards of cyberspace, looking for a secret cache, some divot where a key might have casually fallen that would unlock the secret to his personality. She clicked hopefully as a handful of genealogy sites came up—some other Harvey March born in 1871 and married to some Ellen Brewster in 1903. She knew he'd taught at other schools and thought she might find his face in a group photograph as sponsor of a debate team or an old syllabus suspended like a fly in an abandoned web. He took up such a large part of her life, she was troubled to find nothing existed about him in the greater digital world. It made her feel small to care so deeply about a man no one else seemed to see.

The name Stanley March appeared over and over again in her search, however, and for lack of better results, Polly finally clicked on him. Stanley March, sixties radical (she discovered), had fled America and the draft under suspicion of planting a bomb at the uptown campus of the City College of New York. An adjunct professor, he had left behind a wife and ten-year-old son, Harvey Dylan March, then living in Montclair, New Jersey. When President Ford pardoned the draft dodgers in 1975, Stanley March elected to remain in Canada, where he had begun a new family, overlooking the small detail that he had never officially divorced his first wife. After challenging the bigamy statutes and serving three years in an Ontario minimum security prison, he went on to write many books about politics, the inequalities of the American legal system, and the impending death of capitalism, most published by Freak Tank Press (whose online catalog, Polly learned, contained such other titles as *Home Brew LSD, Grow Your Own Machine Gun,* and *The Cheney Diaries*). Other links gave variations on the story of this man whom she could only assume was her Mr. March's father, an assumption confirmed when she finally saw a picture of the radical Stanley, looking for all the world like her teacher, if Mr. March had lost all his hair and grown a wolfish beard.

Polly sat with this unexpected information for a long time. What she would have given to have a radical parent, one who believed in

something so completely he was willing to give up everything the
world thought important to follow his ideals. Mr. March was so lucky,
she thought, to have the spirit of resistance coursing through his veins,
to have rebellion genetically billeted in the double helix of his DNA.
Like most other kids her age, Polly had only a gauzy, pop-beaded
conception of the sixties as a paradise lost of teenage supremacy, one
long muddy Woodstock stretching from 1964 through 1972. To have
a freedom-fighting parent, one too busy burning the flag to police your
artificial preservative consumption, seemed the pinnacle of romantic freedom to her. No wonder Mr. March was so cool. She didn't
stand a chance.

"I hope you're going to make me your maid of honor," said
Bethany, suddenly appearing in the doorway with two fresh glasses
of soda. Polly swiftly closed the window on the computer screen.

"Just one word of advice," said her friend, smiling. "No matter
how great he is—don't let him do you eleven times."

CHAPTER SIX

The old glass thermometer on the side of St. Barnabas Church read 92 degrees the Saturday morning of Chase Andrew Frank's funeral. It was only ten o'clock, but it felt like deep-summer midday, and the paper funeral home fans cut the air inside the church like the lifting and settling of a swarm of locusts upon a field. If the fire marshal, who was in attendance, had been a man who followed the letter of the law, he would have escorted half of the exit-blocking congregation outside; but he himself was a father of four, and would not have dreamed of denying these fine grieving people the balm of a funeral service.

The camera crews had set up before anyone else arrived, and busied themselves in the recording of the town's grief. They panned the nearly three-hundred-year-old church, taking in the clear bubbled blown-glass windows, with their chipped, black windowsills; the mahogany pews, sticky with decades of tung oil; the brass plaques hung about the walls remembering departed benefactors of St. Barnabas—the inevitable Randolphs, and a Custis or two; many, many Colonel thises and Major thats, C.S.A. It was a typically spartan, postcolonial church, with little to catch a camera's eye, and the film crews from up North found themselves, by default, focusing in on the pastel paper funeral home fans—a doe-eyed Jesus gathering to himself all the little children—to provide the expected flavor of a Southern funeral.

On a pedestal, to the right of the altar, sat a small, shiny white coffin, like a cross section of a wedding limo, its lid propped open. The last of the congregation filed past to kiss the papery purple cheek of the tiny child, whose face had been unnaturally plumped with embalming fluid. The baby's parents and oldest sister, Rose, sat in the front row, the first time they'd ever earned the right to sit so close to the pulpit, a privilege usually reserved for the oldest and wealthiest families in town. The cameras caught Manda handing Rose a miniature golf–sized half-pencil and church bulletin with which to entertain herself throughout the service. They caught Jake red-eyed and haggard, as if he had not slept for days.

When the organ music paused and Pastor Vaughn walked in, the congregation rose to its feet. Pastor Vaughn made no opening remark, but began to read immediately from the Book of Common Prayer, 1928, the Liturgy for the Burial of a Child.

"I am the resurrection and the life, saith the Lord." Pastor Vaughn's voice boomed through the church. Not only was the sermon being recorded, it was being broadcast to well-wishers fifty deep in the churchyard outside. "He that believeth in me, though he were dead, yet shall he live: and whosoever believeth in me, shall never die."

The camera lights were an additional few suns on the already sweltering cleric, and he saw that their rays had caused a shrub of microphones to take root upon his pulpit. Pastor Vaughn had the strangest feeling of being disembodied before this enormous crowd, half of whom he did not recognize, another third of whom had not set foot in his church in decades. He had gotten used to crowds at the hospital, and crowds in town, but the crowd today inside his own sanctuary made him feel little better than a televangelist, conducting a funeral before the eyes of millions. He should never have allowed the cameras in here, he thought, even as he automatically recited the liturgy. "Jesus called them unto Him and said, Suffer the little children to come unto me, and forbid them not: for of such is the kingdom of God. He shall feed his flock like a shepherd: He shall gather the lambs with His arms, and carry them in His bosom. Let us pray."

The congregation bowed their heads and joined in. "The Lord is my shepherd . . ."

It was not often Leland Vaughn was expected to perform a burial for a child. In his thirty years, he remembered burying no more than five or six children, not counting the wayward teenagers who crashed their cars on prom night or drunkenly went swimming in swift currents. He had blessed many more silent blue stillbirths, but once a child took a breath in Three Chimneys, it seemed determined to stay here. Now, the familiarity of the psalm comforted him, and by the time he had moved on to "I will lift up mine eyes unto the hills," Leland had regained his composure. What harm did the cameras do, anyway? he thought. He could think of them as exploitative, or he could think of them as the means by which new neighbors joined the Three Chimneys community. The whole world had rallied around Manda and Jake when the babies were born, and the whole world might be expected to mourn the loss of their poor lamb.

"I know a good priest should never admit his own quaking terror," said Pastor Vaughn, carefully marking his place in the hymnal and looking out over his enormous congregation, "but I confess to you here today, that is all I felt that day back in January when our dear sister Amanda came to me for help. 'My doctor says there are eleven babies in my belly, Pastor Vaughn,' she'd said, sitting here beside me on a morning a good deal cooler than this one, I can tell you. Eleven babies." The priest shook his head in disbelief. "If she had said two or three, there would be no problem, right? But eleven? No one in the history of the world had ever given birth to eleven living infants.

"She said her doctors had advised a selective reduction, which is a medical term for aborting some children so that others might thrive. It is not uncommon in situations like this, and it seemed the best solution for poor Manda. I asked her to look into her heart and see if she could live with that decision, knowing it was best for her health, best for the surviving babies. 'But how do I choose among them, Pastor?' Manda asked me. 'How do I play God?'"

"I sent Manda home, and that night I walked down to my old chimney to pray. 'Lord,' I said, 'who is playing God in this case? The doctors for having coaxed eleven seeds to sprout? Or Manda for picking who shall live and who shall die? Do I even have the right to advise her? What is Your will, oh Lord?

"I sat for a long time down by my old chimney, where most of you know I do my best thinking. I thought of a thousand arguments for keeping the children and a thousand against. And then, after many hours of back-and-forth, a passage from the Book of Ecclesiastes came into my mind, laying a calming hand over what had become a tempest of indecision. It was from Chapter Eleven, verses five and six, and it goes: 'As thou knowest not what is the way of the spirit, nor how the bones do grow in the womb of her that is with child: even so thou knowest not the works of God who maketh all.

"'In the morning sow thy seed, and in the evening withhold not thine hand: for thou knowest not whether shall prosper, either this or that, or whether they both shall be alike good.'

Pastor Vaughn took off his glasses and wiped them carefully with a cloth. The crowded church was hot and heavy and he was tired just in remembering his struggle of that night. "My great-grandmother buried six children of her own," he said at last. "It was a time when parents tried not to get too attached to their young, for back in those days, children were sown back into the earth like fistfuls of corn. My great-grandmother lost two to influenza, one to diphtheria, two were born dead, and the last came, like our poor, dear Chase, too early; sent, so it seemed, by his lost brothers and sisters to fetch their mother home with him.

"Yet before she accompanied her final child to Paradise, my great-grandmother raised five other thriving, brawling, good-hearted children, one of whom grew up to be my grandfather and great inspiration, the former Pastor Vaughn. That made eleven children. Five on earth, six given back. My great-grandmother knew something that we seem to have forgotten: It is not up to us to decide who shall live and who shall die. That decision lies solely with God. It is up to God to play God.

"So then what does a parent owe a child?" asked Leland Vaughn. "I thought long and hard about that, down by the old chimney. Perhaps you'd say he owes his child a roof over his head. Food in his stomach. Some might say a good education. For those of you who grew up during the Depression, you might think you owe it to your child to teach thrift, so that she never struggles and suffers want as you did; those who became parents in the fifties and sixties might have thought all a child required was love and an allowance ample enough to afford a Beatles album. Perhaps a parent today decides he owes his daughter organic vegetables and SAT preparation courses and a well-maintained trust fund. Give and give and give unto your child until you can give no more, says our society. Give and you shall receive.

"But I tell you here today, friends and family, as it says in the Book of Ecclesiastes: All is vanity. The things I mentioned are what we do for our children out of affection, or guilt, or out of habit. As I stand here today, and at the risk of being politically unpopular, I declare there is only one thing we absolutely owe our children, only one debt we cannot dodge. My great-grandmother understood it. And Amanda Frank understood it. Both discharged their duty faithfully, and gave their children the one thing a child might honestly demand of its parent. Life.

"Life. That's all."

The room was silent except for the whir of cameras and a few sniffling congregants. The heat and the light had nearly transported Pastor Vaughn, and he felt as light-headed as he had that night back in January, when he had driven to Amanda's old sharecropping shack and promised his help and the help of the whole community if she decided to take a chance on life. He was unsure if his advice was right or wrong, but he knew one thing—he was in no better position to decide than she was.

"I know each and every one of you grieves for poor Chase Andrew, so briefly our neighbor here in Three Chimneys. Since his death, I have asked myself a hundred times, Should I have given his mother different advice, should we have done what the doctors thought best? But then I remember that only God knows who shall prosper, either this or that, and that all of our attempts to understand His will or anticipate it or explain it—all are vanity. We can but only love and accept, my friends, and your love and acceptance of Amanda and Jake in their hour of need has made me proud. As a priest. As a neighbor. And as a citizen of this generous country.

"Let us pray."

The congregation joined in with the Lord's Prayer, and after a few more readings from the Book of Common Prayer, rose and followed the tiny white coffin out of the church and into the well-tended graveyard behind. The baby's weeping father and bowlegged grandfather

were all the small vessel required to carry it, and Manda walked heavily
behind, her daughter Rose riding upon her hip. The massive crowd of
mourners trampled the plots of erstwhile Three Chimneyans, while
camera crews further disturbed their eternal rest by driving tripods into
their moldering rib cages. The baby was to be buried under a spreading
oak, beside a maternal great-great-granduncle who had ridden with
Mosby's Rangers and was thus awarded a hero's plot inside the wealthy
churchyard. Most of Manda's other relatives were buried out on their
land or in the poor cemetery six miles out of town. Jake's family were
all Baptists, and were thus buried amongst themselves.

"'In sure and certain hope of the Resurrection to eternal life
through our Lord Jesus Christ,'" Pastor Vaughn read as the coffin was
lowered, "'we commit the body of this child to the ground.'" Manda
put Rose down and told her to pick up a handful of dirt. It was to toss
into the baby's grave, she said. But when the time came, Rose had so
squeezed the clayey earth, it thudded on the clean white coffin.

"'For the Lamb which is in the midst of the throne shall feed
them, and shall lead them unto living fountains of waters: and God
shall wipe away all tears from their eyes,'" read Pastor Vaughn. "'The
Lord be with you . . .'"

"And with thy spirit," replied the congregation, drowning out the
small beeping in Jake's front right pocket. People surrounded the Franks
after the service and at the Vaughns' afterward, so it wasn't until he
checked his pager much later that afternoon that the grieving father
learned the hospital had been trying to reach them for hours.

"What the hell was I thinking? Eleven babies?" Francis Marvel mopped
his brow with a limp white handkerchief. Some vestige of familial grav-
ity took over at public functions, and Polly found herself standing with
Margaret and Francis at the end of the ceremony.

"We can build a smart bomb, but we can't keep one damn baby
alive?" he asked. "It's just my luck."

"Believe it or not, Francis, everything is not about you," said
Margaret.

"Well, it's going to be about *you* pretty soon if donations keep drying up," drawled Francis. "People don't give money to dead babies."

"Francis, you'd better not use that as an excuse," warned Margaret. "You're already five months behind . . ."

As she did whenever they argued over money, Polly tuned them out. In the year since her parents divorced, she had learned her exact worth: $490. She'd seen the complicated equation the court had used: her father's income minus any other alimony or children he was supporting, figured somehow against her mother's income plus any exceptional health care costs and day care, divided by her father's age, blah, blah, blah. The court had calculated her like a mortgage and come out with the sum of $490 a month. Not $500, a satisfying figure in her mind, the respectable burnt orange of Monopoly money, but $490, a savings to her father of ten dollars, snipped off each month like a lock of hair. She knew it was wrong, but she'd come to think of $490 as the sum she would fetch on the open market, or how much an insurance company would pay out at her death, or how much she was entitled to steal if she ran away from home. Every month when her father sent his check, *if* he sent his check, she hoped he would think to round up for her sake, just a little gesture, just ten dollars. It would have meant so much.

"It's not my fault," Francis was arguing. "Let one thing go wrong in a poor family and the whole town turns on you."

Margaret was about to answer when Pastor Vaughn appeared. "Well, this is a welcome sight," said the old priest, taking in the trio. "The death of a child makes us really appreciate our own families, doesn't it?"

"That it does, Leland," said Francis somberly. "If you'll excuse me, I want to go pay my condolences to the Franks." He kissed Polly and walked over to where Jake and Amanda stood surrounded by well-wishers. Polly watched as her father gave Jake a firm, manly hug and offered him his handkerchief to dry his eyes.

"I am so sorry my sessions with you and Francis didn't help," the priest said. "Evelyn and I have always been so happy, I think I am a poor excuse for a marriage counselor."

"Thank you, Leland," answered Margaret wryly. "Nothing could have helped by that point."

"Still," the priest said, taking her hand, "there is nothing worse than the dissolution of a family. I hope in times of trouble you will turn to your friends and neighbors for help."

"I appreciate it," said Margaret.

"We missed you at the candlelight vigil," said Leland, addressing Polly. "I thought for sure you'd be there."

"I had a lot of homework," answered Polly guiltily.

"I know you're a very busy young lady, but I'd appreciate it if you'd look in on Manda from time to time," said Pastor Vaughn. "It's hard to conceive at your age, but nothing destroys a parent like burying a child."

Pastor Vaughn was expressing the exact sentiments Mr. March had ridiculed her for yesterday, but somehow in the minister's mouth, the words sounded right and powerful. Polly found herself promising to look in on Manda and baby-sit whenever she was needed.

"I'll see you both at the rectory, I hope?" the old priest was saying. "Evelyn has baked a ham."

"Oh, Leland, I wish we could make it," Margaret answered, her voice full of regret. "But Polly and I have some pressing business down at Campaign Headquarters that simply can't wait."

Leland's face showed exactly how he ranked politics against neighborly solicitude, but he had been a priest long enough to know when to hold his tongue. "Well, I suppose we'll have crowd enough," he said, scanning the throng of well-wishers and reporters milling about the cemetery grounds. "It's incredible, isn't it, the outpouring of love in this community? Over the years we've had so many opportunities for division, but here we all are looking out for each other, sustaining each other. God has provided us a miracle, and I can't help but be proud of how our town has responded.

"Well, I should go get changed before the guests arrive. I'm about to roast in this wool jacket." Pastor Vaughn bid them good-bye, but then stopped and turned back. "Hey, that reminds me—did you ladies happen to hear the Mexican weather forecast?"

Pastor Vaughn's eyes lit up, and Polly braced herself to withstand this unbelievably stupid joke for the hundredth time in her young life.

"No, what did it say?" she asked politely.

"Chili today. Hot tamale!" He laughed with self-satisfied delight.

"Chili today. Hot tamale." Polly smiled weakly. "That's a good one. I'll remember that."

"And I won't even charge you for it." Pastor Vaughn smiled.

The deserted newspaper office, when Margaret let them in, was lit only by the red exit sign over the door, and Polly was once again struck by the smell that would forever be linked in her mind to journalism: the stale aroma of old food and old paper, heavy pork fat (from fifty years of sharing a wall with Snow White), decaying cloth from curtains imploded by mites, the parchmenty smell of bug husks in the light fixtures. Campaign Headquarters was a tiny room at the end of a musty, narrow hallway, cinched even tighter by stacks of Reagan-era yellowing back issues of the *Three Chimneys Register* and a slag of 386 IBM computers with 5¼-inch floppy drives that even the elementary school refused, but which the old editor in chief could not bear to throw out. Headquarters, which to the less politically savvy might be mistaken for a storage closet, was filled nearly to capacity with file cabinets and a newsprint-grimed water cooler, leaving only enough room for two chairs, a cigarette-scarred folding table, a typewriter, and two volunteers. Margaret had been in residence here for over a year, at the pleasure of Foster Lewis, a distant step-relation of the previous editor in chief who had bought the paper after the old man's last stroke. Foster Lewis was unmarried and unbecomingly fond of scandal—undoubtedly a muckraker, if ever the town had seen one. What had for decades been a sleepy, small-town newspaper, reporting the winners of 4-H scholarships and pound cake bake-offs, had seemingly overnight become a broadsheet of DUI convictions and marching band embezzlement exposés. Lewis was first to ferret the news of Amanda Frank's confinement—quite by accident, actually, for he had been having drinks with a Charlottesville General orderly in a location anonymously equidistant from both of their hometowns when the orderly, just to make conversation, mentioned that a woman from Three Chimneys had been admitted for a whole mess of babies. The "whole mess" turned out to be the unthinkable number of eleven, and despite a plea from Pastor Vaughn begging Lewis to preserve the Franks' privacy, the story became front-page news the following week. Foster immediately alerted his cousin, Patrick, the weather and features reporter for Fox News, Channel 5, and from there the *Richmond Times-Dispatch* picked it up, then the *Washington Post,* and then the world.

A four-line telephone with its chunky plastic HOLD button gave the appearance of serious matters going on inside, as did the grainy *Brooke for President* posters Margaret had photocopied from a circular. Because it went against her nature to join anything, Margaret worked unassisted by the Virginia Democratic Brooke for President organization. She had never understood the necessity of declaring a political party, or stumping for an entire ticket, when the only person she cared about, or believed in, was Adams Brooke himself. She preferred to do things her own way, outside of the machine, and though she cc'd them on all of her correspondence, she had never once asked for help or taken money from them. But her independence had come at a price; she bore the expense of her campaign efforts, including the rental of this room, and, as she learned when she missed Adams Brooke by minutes, she was woefully out of the loop concerning the governor's whereabouts.

Polly used to beg to come to Campaign Headquarters, back before the primaries, before her dad moved out. She had a kid's love of playing office, licking envelopes until her tongue went numb, staring into the corona of the brilliant Xerox as it generated galaxies of appeal letters and thank-you-for-your-contribution notes. She was sometimes allowed to answer the serious-matters telephone with the mantra "Adams Brooke for President, Three Chimneys Campaign Headquarters, How May I Direct Your Call?" before passing the receiver to her mother, the only direction in which it might go; and she was even written up as Three Chimneys' youngest little pollster.

But after her father left, everything changed. What had been a fun afternoon of make-believe once or twice a month became deadly serious business. The phone calls took on a harder, more desperate edge, the envelopes had to go out in such vast numbers, Polly's tongue was no longer an effective instrument, and was replaced by a bit of sponge on a blue plastic bottle. The past few months of her mother's election obsession had taken away any of the joy Polly used to feel, until she came to look upon Adams Brooke as a tyrannical step-father who, even in his absence, must be obeyed.

"What on earth?" said Margaret, playing back the phone messages. "Polly, listen to this."

Among the requests for bumper stickers from a local Brooke supporter, and another for fliers to pass out at next Sunday's Chicken Coop Gospel, there was a message on the machine from Sandy Jameson of the National Headquarters for Adams Brooke for President. *Your efforts on Governor Brooke's behalf have recently come to our attention,* said Mr. Jameson, *and we would love to talk to you. If you could return our call at your earliest convenience . . .*

"That's National Headquarters," said Margaret, dumbfounded. "I wonder what they want. Do you think it could be about the new slogan?"

Brooke No Opposition. It was her mother's latest, and Polly's reason for being pressed into service today. Polly had thought The Farmer's Friend was about as dumb as it got, but Brooke No Opposition, with its neofascist storm-trooper certitude, had pulled into first place.

"You know, Mr. March says opposition is absolutely necessary for our government to function," Polly said. "Thomas Jefferson founded the first opposition party. Are you against Thomas Jefferson?"

"Who is Mr. March?" asked Margaret, dialing the number left on the machine.

"My history teacher?" Polly answered. "Where have you been all year?"

"Obviously Mr. March doesn't have to run a farm," replied Margaret.

"I'm glad our Founding Fathers didn't think like you, or we'd all be eating fish and chips right now."

Margaret made the slicing "Be quiet" motion across her throat as the phone picked up on the other end. "Hello, this is Margaret Prickett from Three Chimneys Headquarters. To whom am I speaking?"

Polly couldn't have been more bored by the conversation, and turned away, idly opening a file drawer full of chronologically dated back issues of the *Register*. From what she could tell, there was a whole lot of nothing going on in this town before Manda's babies, just decades of bad hairstyles and embarrassing clothes, births, deaths, and 4-H prizes. It was the history of a town paying lip service to the passage of time, but fundamentally unchanged since its inception. Polly paused longest over the wedding photos, snickering at the seventies' limp cotton flounces and jute lace-up sandals, at the eighties' big sleeves and sequined headbands. She flipped forward through the file folders until she came to the week of October 20, 1990, seven months before her birth, and there she found a faded announcement for Francis Marvel and Margaret Prickett, two of the town's best kids, smiling formally for the photographer in a posed wedding photo. Her mother's gown was tasteful, being a modified version of her own mother's dress from the early sixties, and her father was in a traditional tux with a vest. Her parents had gotten married when they were both very young, and Polly squinted at the photo, looking for the telltale bulge of herself in her mother's waistline. But her mother was seated, snuggled up in her father's arms, and there was no trace of an unplanned child or a future divorce or a single day of trouble ahead. Polly looked over her shoulder at her mother on the phone, and contemplated waving the photo at her so that they might share a laugh. But then she remembered the day a year ago when she'd discovered some hidden love letters from her parents' first days of dating. She'd run downstairs to tease her mom and dad, and was dramatically disappointed when they did not find the letters charming at all. She learned later, that was the morning her father first admitted he was having an affair.

"I'd be happy to answer some questions, though I can't imagine what I could say that the governor doesn't already know," said Margaret, and from her exaggerated Southern drawl, Polly could tell her mother was speaking to someone more important than herself. Her accent only came out when she was trying to be accommodating. *Campaign speech!* she scribbled on the pad before her.

"What do they want?" asked Polly. Her mother snapped her fingers impatiently, pointed at Polly and then at the door. Polly closed the file cabinet and leaned against it impatiently. "Of course I understand all conversations are confidential," said Margaret with a nervous laugh. "I doubt I can give away any national cheesemaking secrets."

The conversation as Polly overheard it was full of pauses and nods as her mother answered a string of questions about the farm.

"We've been a dairy since just after the Civil War," Margaret told them. (Pause) "No, Jerseys exclusively. Holsteins are genetically engineered machines, and their introduction was the death of the family farm. My great-grandfather was a charter member of the Jersey Cattle Club, and we even have their slogan hanging in our cheese house, '*Omnis pecuniae pecus fundamentum.*' The herd is the foundation of all wealth. It's been our family motto ever since."

Margaret gave Polly a "Can you believe this?" smile as though she were talking to the governor himself. Polly couldn't imagine why his headquarters would want to speak to her mother.

"You know very well that ninety percent of all government subsidies go to five agribusiness crops," said Margaret. "We are an independent family farm. (Pause) Well, if I had to pick one thing, besides the subsidies, I'd guess it would be the estate taxes. You've just gotten out from one generation's debt when the next one dies, leaving the farm that much more burdened. You can't get out from under. The amnesty is the only thing that will save small farms like ours. (Pause) If I could speak directly to Governor Brooke? I'd tell him the individual is the only special interest any politician should answer to. Let him sell that to Monsanto. . . ."

Polly endured a few more minutes of one-sided conversation about poll numbers and good old-fashioned grassroots door-to-door before her mother finally hung up and she could satisfy her curiosity.

"What was that all about?" she asked. Margaret was staring absently into space, and Polly had to repeat her question.

"Governor Brooke's campaign headquarters has read all my letters and knows how hard it's been on our farm. They wanted permission to use us as an example in the speech he's giving."

"Us?" asked Polly.

"He knows who we are," said Margaret as if in a trance. "He knows who we are."

"I thought you didn't want to get involved with Campaign Headquarters," said Polly to snap her mother out of her reverie. "You said they were in the pocket of big business and did nothing but solicit soft money all day. You said you didn't want anything to do with them."

"I don't," answered Margaret. "I haven't. But I'm not going to ignore them if they call me."

"You're like one of those girls at school who pretends not to like a boy until he likes her, then suddenly she's in love."

"You know, you're getting a smart mouth," said Margaret crankily, turning back to her correspondence. "Why do you have to ruin everything?"

"I'm not ruining anything," said Polly archly, echoing her father. "I'm just telling it like it is."

"Polly, you are still a child. When you get older, you'll realize there are certain political realities that can't be denied."

"Like what?"

"Things you wouldn't understand."

"You know, I only act like a child because you treat me like a child," said Polly. "Back in the old days, parents considered their children smaller adults. They didn't try to protect them from everything like you do now. They entrusted them with important responsibilities."

"I let you milk the cows, and all you do is complain," Margaret answered.

"That's different," retorted Polly. "Those are chores, not responsibilities. Responsibilities require trust."

"I trust you to get working on the campaign posters," said Margaret sharply, ending their conversation. Everything was a battle these days.

The two worked in silence. Polly booted up the old computer Foster Lewis allowed for their use. It was so like her mother, she thought, to preach consistency and independence, then cave at the first nod from someone important. When she had children, she would never be like that. She would have a little integrity and set a good example. How was she supposed to respect a woman who constantly changed her mind?

Polly opened up Photoshop to the picture of Adams Brooke's fat, smiling head. The only reason her mother brought her along, she knew, was because Polly understood how to work the computer; if she didn't she would be utterly useless. She took out the text reading "The Farmer's Friend" and replaced it with "Brooke No Opposition" in blocky, black letters. When she reached for some paper to feed into the printer, she accidentally knocked a stack of mail from the table.

"What's this?" asked Polly, picking up the green-tagged certified letter from First Virginia Savings and Loan. Margaret had brought it to the office so that it wouldn't constantly reproach her at home, but she still had not been able to bring herself to open it.

"Put that down," said she. "It's nothing."

"Mom, it's dated. It says 'Open Immediately.'"

"I know what it is, it doesn't concern you."

"God, do you hear yourself?" asked Polly hotly. "'*You wouldn't understand. It doesn't concern you.*' You're always harping on Dad for not facing up to his responsibilities, and you're too afraid to even open a letter."

"Do you want to know what's in that letter, Miss Smart Aleck?" Margaret stood up and smacked her hands so angrily against the card table, the telephone fell with a Lucite thud upon the floor. "Your house. And your clothes. And your college education. That's what's inside that letter. And they are all about to disappear." Margaret hadn't meant to share any of her money troubles with her daughter, but the girl was so sanctimonious sometimes. "I have liquidated my pension. I have sold every stock and bond we own. I've taken out as many mortgages on the farm as they've been dumb enough to give me. But we are broke. Do you understand? We're going to be on the street and you are going to be sold into white slavery because your drunk, irresponsible father certainly can't afford to take you in, and the only person who stands between us and ruin is Adams Brooke, and if his campaign needs our help, then I am damn well going to give it."

"All you care about is money," yelled Polly. "I'm sorry Dad doesn't pay you, but it's not my fault."

"You know, I'd like to have fun sometimes too. I'd like to go out for a beer or take a vacation or do something other than worry about money, but how can I?" Margaret's voice cracked, and the tears that she was always fighting for Polly's sake threatened to overwhelm her. "Who is going to take care of you? Who is going to take care of the farm? All I want is for someone in this world to keep his promise. Is that so much to ask?"

"I'm sorry I'm such a burden," cried Polly. "I know you wish I were dead like Chase Andrew."

"Polly, that is a horrible thing to say," exclaimed Margaret. "How can you possibly believe that? That is a horrible, horrible thing to say."

To Polly's great satisfaction, her mother broke down in tears. The room was silent except for Margaret's soft weeping and the telephone, splayed across the floor like a murder victim. *"If you would like to make a call, please hang up and try again. If you need help, hang up and then dial your operator."* This message cycled through three times before the maniacal dial tone, scientifically engineered, in Polly's opinion, to manufacture as much anxiety as the human body could withstand, took over. This *was* what she wanted, wasn't it? To reduce Margaret to tears and make her hurt as she hurt? But even as she dispassionately watched her mother, an insidious, creeping fear stole over her. If her mother was afraid, perhaps she should be too. Polly remembered the night her father moved out, the evening she sat in her bedroom window, watching Francis load cardboard boxes and bulging green trash bags into a rented U-Haul, taking with him objects that had seemed, like herself, native to the house—the leather recliner, a framed print, the grandfather clock from the hall—but that she now learned had a specific owner, that had in fact come with, and would now leave with, her father. When at last he was gone, blowing her a kiss from the front yard, she had walked downstairs and through the eerily silent house to find her mother screwing a sliding chain lock onto the front door, a door that like every other door and window on the farm had been perpetually left unlocked the entirety of Polly's life. Until that moment, she had never once considered there was anything outside that might be in need of locking out. But that night in bed, she began listening for sounds—a creaking floorboard, the unexpected rustle in a bush—suddenly aware they were two women alone and unprotected. Polly was a clever girl, and she thought she knew all that could go wrong in this wide world, but her mother's tears today, like a locked door, said she didn't know the half of it. Slowly, she retrieved the phone and placed if back on the card table.

"I'm sorry, Mom," she said, through the rising lump in her own throat. "What can I do to help?"

Margaret cried all the harder and held out her arms for her daughter. Damn Francis who never has to go through this, she thought. What got into her to terrify Polly like that? She murmured a hundred apologies into her daughter's hair, hugging her as fiercely as if her epithets had in fact summoned a white slave trader, who was even now waiting in the hallway.

"I'm so sorry, Peanut," she said, using Polly's father's name for her, and Polly knew then that her mother must be very sorry. "It's the stress of the election. Things aren't as bad as all that."

Polly gently dried her mother's eyes and poured her a glass of water. "Leave it to me," she said, "Adams Brooke will win this election. I know he will. I'll do anything it takes."

"Don't worry, Mom," said Polly, gathering her mother into her arms, as she herself had so often been gathered. "Leave it to me."

CHAPTER SEVEN

  . Balanced budget, six years standing. ·
Ran clean campaign.
Ordered drug dealers out of town.
Opened his arms to the poor.
Kept at it, even when all seemed lost.
Embarrassed by wife's shoplifting? Not at all!

Near-death survivor.
Organ donor, and regular giver of blood.

Organized youth center for troubled teens.
Pardoned Jimmy Sands, an innocent man.
Put ducks in a row.
Orchestrated amnesty for
Small-time farmers and vowed to abolish excessive
Income tax for those who took the Family Matters Pledge.
Tough on crime.
Is one of us.
Oh haven't you guessed? The
Next President of the United States is Adams Brooke! Vote the
    Farmer's Friend!

She had no one to blame but herself. She had come up with the acrostic. She had carefully handwritten it in tall red block letters down two sides of a sandwich board sign. She had fashioned the straps and lifted the thing over her head. She had, of her own free will, offered to parade it down School Street, beneath the shade of the overhanging oak trees, from eleven on Sunday through three o'clock, when her mother would come pick her up and kiss her gratefully, and that kiss would make up for the utter humiliation of it all—all her own fault, she knew—but the kiss of pride and gratitude would make it all worthwhile.

"Brooke No Opposition. Adams Brooke for President."

Last night, it had been like old times between Margaret and Polly. She slept in her mother's room, curled inside her mother's arms, pulling Margaret's freshly washed, long wet hair over her own like a wig. She lay quietly on Margaret's stomach, letting her breath find the rhythm of her mother's, just drifting, as close to climbing back inside as a long, lean girl of thirteen could get.

"Vote the Farmer's Friend this November."

I would never want you dead, Margaret had whispered to her in the darkened bedroom. *I never want you to say a thing like that again. I would die a thousand deaths before I would ever let anything happen to you, Polly. I love you more than life itself.*

If her mother had been here, the two might have made a game of it: imagining Polly as a pair of dancing legs beneath a box of Lucky Strikes, hoofing it on *Ed Sullivan,* or pretending to be a singing telegram for social change. Last night, they'd been a team, coloring in the block letters and stapling buckram straps to the poster board, but today, her mother was entrenched in the cheese house and Polly was on her own, with only the heat of her own self-consciousness to keep her company. Did she think that up? asked Mrs. Vaughn on her way to Sunday school and taking an eternity to read each line. My, how clever. The priest's wife popped open her purse and handed Polly a wintergreen Life Saver to suck. You must be awfully hot in that thing, dear, she said. What a good girl you are.

With most of Three Chimneys sitting in the pews of St. Barnabas at one end of School Street or First Baptist at the other, the sidewalks were mercifully deserted. Polly handed flyers to a few aimless newsmen, who were so very bored with this nowhere town that a girl in a sandwich sign actually pricked their consciences. Most of them would much rather have been part of the election coverage than stuck on a dumbed-down human interest story anyway, and if even a kid, for Chrissakes, could care so much about politics, could they con-

tinue to believe they were anything other than infotainment sellouts?
The thought drove several of them into Drafty's for a round or two,
despite its being not quite noon.

She walked past Tinton's Grocery, closed on Sunday, in accor-
dance with blue laws that had long ago been repealed. She walked
past the feed store and the Community Center, with its white obelisk War Memorial. She paused and read the neatly chiseled names
of the Confederate dead, boys who fought with the 13th Infantry,
others who died with the Gordonsville Greys. Her mother told her
that every Memorial Day in her girlhood, the older ladies of town
would lay a grand rose wreath, larger even than what they awarded
the winning horse on Derby Day, at the foot of this obelisk, a practice that had been discontinued at about the time of Polly's birth.
Even the dead had a place to be on a Sunday afternoon, thought Polly
fleetingly.

A little after noon, the red doors to St. Barnabas swung wide,
discharging the overheated congregation. Polly was just past Snow
White when she saw Pastor Vaughn in his black cassock step outside to shake hands with everyone who left. Her father was not a
churchgoing man, and so her family, more often than not, had
stayed home on Sunday—there was plenty of work to do, and church
seemed just another chore—but secretly, she'd always envied the
girls whose parents got them up and then turned them out ironed,
combed, and polished. It was another form of solidarity, she thought,
seeing, even now, some of the girls from school descending the
church steps in their lilac and navy sweater sets, wearing panty hose,
even though it was about a hundred and fifty degrees outside. The
girls looked dewy and respectable, with their parents walking behind them, far enough behind to give them freedom, but there,
nonetheless, watching over them, keeping them within sight. They
cared that their children got into Heaven. But where was her
mother? Fighting on another front, Polly thought loyally, working
to better society instead of mouthing platitudes about it. But still,
she had to admit, those families looked so untroubled and certain

about themselves. These were girls who lacked nothing, who shared among themselves, like a sugary soda, the knowledge that all would go well in their lives, moving effortlessly from Homecoming Court, to an all-girls college, to the crisp, understated pages of *Bride* magazine. There was nothing messy in their lives, no registered letters or unpaid child support, and when the time came, they would produce tidy, happy, equally entitled smaller versions of themselves who would begin the whole cycle over again. Polly was only thirteen, but she understood, as surely as she wore this sign, that she was marked down as different from everyone else in this town. As she watched, her friend Bethany bounded down the stairs with her parents in tow, saw the other girls from school, and ran to join them. These were the people she went to when Polly wasn't around. Even between herself and Bethany, there would always be this great divide.

Polly suddenly felt like a homeless drifter in her jeans and cardboard, as though she might be advertising a strip bar instead of a political candidate. She remembered her defiant words to Adams Brooke's recorded voice, and didn't want Bethany to see her in this thing. Not knowing where else to go, she quickly ducked inside Snow White.

The restaurant felt cool and dark inside as the screen door swung shut on the stiff heel of her sandwich board. She took a seat at the counter next to a state trooper and settled the stiff slices of her sign over the stool. When after a few minutes Lucille took her order, Polly brazenly asked for a contraband Coke and chocolate cream pie with Cool Whip. The waitress clucked over so much sugar so early in the day, but if young ladies wanted to rot their teeth, that was their own business.

Snow White had not changed so much as a napkin dispenser in the thirteen years Polly had been alive, and if she'd ever bothered to ask her parents, she would have learned that the same greasy clock had hung upon the wall in their youths, that the same blocky hot sauce and vinegar cruets graced the same twelve Formica tables that had been placed there opening day 1947. This restaurant had

befuddled the out-of-town newspaper reporters, who found it perpetually closed whenever they sought to eat here, but the locals
knew the schedule, and kept the place as full as it could handle.
Everyone understood that Mrs. Hawks, the owner and sole cook, was
staunchly loyal to her stories, despite how smutty they'd become over
the decades, and opened her restaurant according to the ABC daily
lineup. Monday through Friday, she served food from 11 till 2 in the
afternoon, closed during *One Life to Live* and *General Hospital,* then
opened again from 4 until 6:30. Saturdays she was closed altogether
because she usually visited her out-of-town children, but Sunday she
opened for lunch after church, serving from 12 until 3. The hours were
posted nowhere, nor was there a menu to be found in the establish-
ment. Everyone knew what she had. Barbecue with or without slaw.
Navy bean soup. Egg salad sandwich. Fried chicken on Sunday with
pressure-cooker green beans and potato salad. Pies of three varieties.
Coke but not Pepsi, in glass bottles, for which she charged only 65 cents,
and which you had better not try to take out of the restaurant or she
would lose her deposit. No matter how cantankerous Mrs. Hawks had
grown over the years, no matter how tyrannically she set her hours,
Snow White was never without customers during its brief, gaudy hours
of operation. And everyone was perfectly content to wait.

At noon, the restaurant was full of churchgoers from the morning sermons, Baptists and Episcopalians alike, all gnawing legs and
thighs and center breasts. Polly was grateful not to know anybody too
well—there was no one under retirement age eating lunch so early,
unless you counted the toddlers with their grandparents, perched like
little despots upon their red plastic molded thrones.

"That'll be three dollars, sugar," Mrs. Hawks's Lucille said, and
Polly awkwardly pulled her arm inside the sign to get to her pocket.
It would be so easy to shrug off this sign, she thought, and leave it
like a shed skin here in the restaurant. Maybe she could tell her
mother she had been mugged, or was a victim of political sabotage.
But she knew that too many people had seen her come in with the
sign, and that someone would helpfully run after her if she left it. She
dug into her pie glumly.

Because my mother
Really
Ought to see a psychiatrist
Or other mental health professional, I am stuck in this hell.
Kill me, somebody.
Enough already!

Nobody cares about stupid
Old Adams Brooke,
Or his stupid campaign.
Please kill me now.
Please, somebody,
Or else I'll have to commit
Suicide.
I mean it!
Torture, is what this is.
I know a secret about Adams Brooke:
Old cow shit turns him on. Vote for cow shit lover!
Nature Calls!

Polly shoveled the last forkful into her mouth and left 50 cents by her plate. But there was to be no escape for her today. Just as she was rising to leave, the Frasers stepped in and waited to be seated. She could not avoid passing them; with no back exit through which she might vanish, there was nothing to do but awkwardly maneuver between the crowded tables and try not to embarrass herself further by toppling any unwary water glasses.

"Why, hello, Polly," said Mrs. Fraser.

"Hello, Mrs. Fraser," the girl replied. She glanced at Bethany, but her friend was staring at the floor, in deference to Polly's obvious discomfort.

"Having a relaxing Sunday?"

"Yes, ma'am. And you?"

"Just came from church," said Mrs. Fraser, making no reference to Polly's signage. "It was about a million degrees in there."

"I'm sorry to hear that," said Polly. "It seems summer just won't end."

"Seems so."

"Well," Polly said after a long, uncomfortable pause. "I'd better get going."

"Give our best to your mother," said Mrs. Fraser. "Tell her we're dying to have her over for margaritas sometime soon, if she can find the time."

"I will, thank you, Mrs. Fraser." Polly wiggled through the door, ignoring Bethany's wan smile of encouragement. Back on the street, the hot sun was high overhead, but Polly still had nearly three hours before she could go home. Try as she might, she couldn't summon last night's magical camaraderie. *I would never want you dead. I would die a thousand deaths . . .* , she heard her mother say, but the words now seemed to lack conviction, sounded cynical to her ear, as if this had all been an elaborate trick, one big joke on Polly. Why else would she be out here alone, while her mother hid at home behind her cheeses? What sort of mother sent her daughter out to be publicly humiliated?

"Hey, Francis, isn't that your girl?"

Polly was just passing the hot beery doorway of Drafty's when she heard a voice call out from inside. She squinted in to see who had recognized her, before realizing that she should have immediately run and precious seconds had been wasted. But it was too late. Her father was weaving his way to the screen door, a pint of Bud Light in his hand, though the glass said *Guinness*. Unlike the fathers in church, hers was unshaven and dressed in shorts and a University of Richmond sweatshirt.

"What in the hell are you wearing?"

"Adams Brooke for President." She smiled weakly, handing him a flyer. She could see behind him into the twilight of Drafty's, a beer joint she'd never dared enter. A television hung over the bar like the one in Manda's hospital room, tuned to the Redskins preshow, while the purple and red jukebox beneath twanged "Ghost Riders in the Sky." Several of the news reporters were eating popcorn from a plastic wood-grain salad bowl. Her father balled up the flyer and tossed it over his shoulder.

"Shrinky, will you come here," he called. "Have you ever seen anything so goddamn stupid?"

Andrew Friedman, the psychiatrist who shared office space with her dad, joined him in the doorway. He was a thickly bearded man with glasses, and as unlikely a friend as her father could have found. Like many Northerners who had moved south to stay, in a desire to assimilate he had enthusiastically taken up Southern ways, like frequenting beer joints on Sunday and eating grits. Her father used to say he would have hung a goddamned Confederate flag in his office, if he hadn't been told that no one clearing over $18,000 a year did that sort of thing anymore. Neither man was on his first beer, Polly could tell.

"What the hell has your mother put you up to this time?"

"For your information," Polly said, "I'm proud to represent Adams Brooke. He's committed to saving the small farmer."

"The only thing he's committed to is his own damn career," scoffed her father, "and if your mother can't see that, she's got her head even farther up her ass than I imagined."

Here, Andrew Friedman, psychiatrist, intervened. "It's important for teenagers to have role models, Francis. It's productive for her at her age to be interested in the world at large."

"Is it productive for her to be parading around town like a goddamn monkey?" Francis asked, and his face was a deeper shade of purple than normal. When he lived at home, he wouldn't have been able to make it to the bar this early, Polly thought. He would still be hosing down the milking equipment or spreading manure. How nice that he'd been able to more conveniently arrange his schedule.

"Dad, this is a free country. I am under no obligation to discuss my political convictions," Polly said primly, and turned to go.

"Don't you walk away from me, young lady. I am under no obligation not to whip your butt." He lurched a step toward her before Andrew Friedman stopped him.

"You can't take that beer outside," the psychiatrist reminded.

Francis stopped, his body outside, but his beer hand just inside the door of Drafty's. "Business is bad enough without you two making idiots of yourselves all over town," he said.

"You're working real hard right now, I see," Polly said with as much sarcasm as she could muster.

"For your information," said Francis, "I am meeting with a client. Shrink Wrap here is thinking of building a house."

Andrew Friedman chuckled at Francis's nickname for him. All her father's friends had nicknames for each other. Bethany's dad, the hand surgeon, was called Quack; Coach Emery, who graduated the same year as her dad, was Jock Itch; and Mr. Crenshaw, from First Virginia Savings and Loan, was known simply as The Jew, though his family had been Presbyterian for generations.

Her father stuck his head inside the bar to take a swig off his beer, and Polly used the distraction to walk away.

"Where the hell are you going? I'm still talking to you," he shouted.

He wanted to come after her, Polly could tell, but that would mean setting down his beer, and he and she both knew it wasn't worth it to him to take a step farther. He quickly shifted tactics.

"Come on, Peanut," he called, wheedling this time, "take that damn thing off. You look like a moron."

Polly stiffened her back and kept walking. Everyone on the street was watching her, having overheard the exchange. Beer, she thought. And friends. She moved them into the column of things that mattered more than her, along with ten dollars extra a month. Cheese. And Adams Brooke. When she was little she had foolishly believed herself to be the center of her parents' lives; nothing was her rival, nothing better loved or preeminent. But the older she became, the more surely she was learning her worth, and it was less than an amber glass of beer, and it was less than having her father's friends think him funny. It was less than a campaign slogan.

Polly had been brave all day, but now she felt self-pity threatening to overwhelm her. She walked to the War Memorial, where she figured she might as well sink down among the other casualties of war, for despite her mother's words of last night, Polly knew if she disappeared into the ground and never rose again neither of her parents would miss her.

"What sort of opposition is this?" a familiar voice called out from across the street. She looked up, and to her dismay saw Mr. March rolling down the passenger window of his green Karmann Ghia. His words were sarcastic, but his voice was more tender than she'd ever heard it. How long had he been there? she wondered. Polly swiftly wiped her hot, red face.

"You look like you could use a ride home," he offered, reaching across and opening the passenger door from the inside. "Come on, get in. I'll give you a lift. . . . though I'm not sure that sign will fit."

It was all the permission she needed. With a vengeance, Polly ripped the sign from her body and tore it in half. She left the letters scattered all over the sidewalk and defiantly slid into the passenger seat of Mr. March's cramped car.

"Polly Marvel, you've littered!" he exclaimed. "It feels good to be a lawbreaker, doesn't it?"

Mr. March pulled back onto School Street and headed out of town. For the first time in their acquaintance, Polly didn't even try to speak. She stared straight ahead through the bug-bespeckled windshield and simply breathed in the smell of him, of his stale navy polo shirt, slightly citrusy with Old Spice.

"It's been a rough year, hasn't it?" Mr. March filled the silence, and Polly merely nodded. "A divorce forces you to grow up fast. It exposes all the flaws of the two-party system, if you know what I mean. My parents split when I was ten. I acted out. Ran away from home. Stole a car."

"I think about that sometimes," she said. "Acting out."

"I can tell you're the rebellious kind."

Now he was making fun of her again, and Polly turned her face back to the windshield. What did he know about her? They drove past his driveway, and Polly involuntarily glanced over.

"That's my house," Mr. March said, noticing.

"Is it?" she asked disingenuously.

She felt his eyes on her then, though she kept hers fixed straight ahead. She had given herself away, and now he must know, without a doubt, that she was a pathetic, twisted stalker. Polly shrunk back against her seat miserably.

"You know, you're welcome to stop by anytime," he said, "if you ever need to talk."

Polly nodded, for her tears were too close to the surface to trust her voice. He was so good and generous and she was so unworthy. She couldn't believe how everything had turned against her. Finally, to be alone in the car with him, to have him speaking so gently, and for her to be swollen and red-faced, as humiliated an insect as ever crawled on the planet.

"I don't know why you agreed to wear that sign in the first place," he said.

"My mother was upset and I wanted her to feel better," she said. "It was my idea."

"One thing I learned from my own parents' divorce: Adults have their own agenda. You need to look out for yourself."

"She's my mom," said Polly. "I owe her."

"You don't owe her anything. Just because someone feeds and clothes you does not mean they own you. That is the very definition of slavery," he said earnestly. "You were born into a tradition of rebellion, Miss Marvel. When your forefathers saw oppression, they rose up against it. They threw off the shackles of tyranny and created a new nation. You are not an extension of your parents. You are not their instrument. You are you. In all of your Polly Marvelousness."

He was coming out of the canopy of trees on Snakehill Road and fast approaching the turnoff to her house. Polly Marvelousness. If she didn't tell him which driveway was hers, maybe he would just keep driving and they could go on like this forever. But he was already putting on his blinker and taking the left-hand turn.

They pulled into her driveway and rode the last quarter mile in silence. The cows were sleeping out by the old chimney and the fields were Sunday afternoon–still. The sunbaked smell of manure rose up to meet them, and Polly hung her head at the rusted farm equipment out front, like some redneck's old Camaro raised up on cinder blocks. When they reached the front of the house, Mr. March stopped the car, and once more reached across the seat to open the passenger door. As he leaned over, his face was nearly in her lap, and she could count the thin strands of dark brown hair arcing from his scalp. His arm casually brushed her shoulder as he sat back up. She felt the entire day's humiliation worth this unintentional caress.

"There is no better time than *childhood* to learn these lessons, Polly." Mr. March smiled kindly at her. "Jefferson said, '*The time to guard against corruption and tyranny is before they have gotten hold of us. It is better to keep the wolf out of the fold than to trust him drawing his teeth and talons after he shall have entered.*' Keep the talons out of your flesh. I don't think it's too late for you."

Her mother's truck was not out front. Nor was August's. Polly stood in the empty driveway as Mr. March pulled his car forward and peeled around. It didn't occur to her until much later that she hadn't had to tell him where she lived.

Harvey March did not drive straight home after dropping Polly off, but aimlessly turned down a succession of country roads in an effort to clear his mind. He didn't get out this way often, and was surprised to see the same trapping of grief echoed in the country homes as in those he was more familiar with in town. Nearly every mailbox was tied with a dark purple ribbon to honor Chase Andrew Frank, the fallen of the Frank Eleven. Every picture window sported a single Christmas candle screwed with a blue bulb, that like an eternal flame burned even in the daytime. How did these people instinctively know what to do? he wondered. Was there a guidebook to grief and grieving, some *Public Mourning for Dummies*?

The roads turned from unlined pavement to gravel to dirt the farther out he drove and the more spontaneous turns he took, until at last he considered himself officially lost. It was not such a bad feeling, and not one he was unused to. When he was a student at Co-

lumbia, he would sometimes take different subway lines to their ter-
mini just to wander an unfamiliar neighborhood, the more deserted
or dangerous the better. He liked being a stranger in a place no one
else would think to go.

Though Harvey March had lived in Three Chimneys for ten
years, he still felt himself as much an alien here as he had wandering
Canarsie or Van Cortlandt Park. Three Chimneys was, in fact, a sort
of self-imposed end of the line for him. While certainly no native
questioned as to why a young man of twenty-four with a master's from
Columbia University would have chosen to make a home in their
lovely town, his friends back home were mystified. Harvey's future
had seemed so bright. He had studied political science and interned
with a senator. He was peripatetic and urbane, able to order cock-
tails in five languages. But he was also a little unstable, and apt to get
into trouble. He sometimes spoke his mind to the senator, when even
the dullest clerk would have recognized the need for silence. He had
a bit of a reputation for creating his own bad luck, so when he was
dismissed from his internship, though everyone was sympathetic, no
one was truly surprised. Harvey had taken a midyear replacement job
teaching government at a private school in New Rochelle, and when
he was dismissed from that, people assumed it was more of the same.
Overqualified and too big a mouth.

And then he shocked his whole circle of friends, by abruptly
leaving town. No one even knew where he went, until he dropped
his mother a birthday card, postmarked from some nowhere town in
Virginia, of all places. No explanation, no promises of return. Just
the news that he'd taken a job teaching U.S. history to eighth-graders
and was renting a house. There was some speculation he'd met a
woman down there, but nothing more was heard about it, and after
a few years Harvey March was forgotten, so much so that even the
alumni fund-raisers no longer bothered to call.

He drove too fast for the narrow dirt roads, raising mushrooms
of dust and sharp chips of gravel that snapped at his windshield. The
woods around the road thickened as he slalomed downhill, the
bramble of kudzu and thorns tangling into a narrow green tunnel

around his car. He took a swift hairpin turn on the dirt road and pulled up sharp at the bottom of the hill. The road, without any warning, had whittled to a single lane that splintered into a wooden bridge over the lazy, orange Rapidan River. Shit, thought Harvey March, wishing he had turned around at the last fork in the road. His perverse desire to get lost had disappeared almost the moment it was achieved, and he was bored and ready to go home. Now he had no choice but to continue straight over this rickety bridge until he came to the next road or driveway or thickening wide enough for a three-point turn. The bridge was low and the water not even high enough to cover the sticks and discarded beer cans of its muddy bottom, but neither fact mattered to him. He was raised in the city and moreover had seen too many Amazon jungle movies to trust any crossing made of plank. He inched his car onto the bridge as gingerly as he would have led a spooked thoroughbred, and didn't realize he had shut his eyes until he looked up to find himself squared off against a large white minivan, its massive black bumper self-congratulatorily stickered with "My Child Is a Three Chimneys Elementary School Honor Student" and the ubiquitous, but now outdated, "We ♥ the Frank Eleven."

The huge vehicle bore down on the bridge, and for a second they were at an impasse. Neither car could move forward on the single lane, and neither was so discernibly past the middle as to claim precedence. Harvey looked into the windshield of the other car and saw a large smiling woman with four soccer-jerseyed kids—three husky boys in the back, watching cartoons from a television suspended in the backseat, and up front a girl rhythmically bobbing her head to the headphones covering her ears. Their mother shrugged at Harvey as if to say, What can you do? You're outnumbered, and waited patiently for him to back up.

For a moment, the history teacher considered resistance. Why should he make way for this minivan full of soccer hooligans? Because it was larger? Because such was expected of him as a gentleman, no matter how vertiginous it made him? Because he mustn't dare delay the soccer practice of a Three Chimneys Elementary School honor student, whichever of the four it might be? But then he realized why he would inevitably be the one to back up—because this woman, with her four kids and 2.9 percent–financed van with removable cargo seat, would never dream that he wouldn't. She perfectly understood that the past must give way before the future—her shiny van trumped his rusty Karmann Ghia, his sad bachelor existence was dust before the warm flesh of her progeny, and thus by divine right, she was entitled to put him in reverse, then back him off the bridge, onto the shoulder, and nearly into the ditch. His foot hovered over the gas pedal, ready to slam down and send her smiling face into the windshield, her kids flying over the seat like the Wile E. Coyote cartoon they were watching. It would be worth his own death, wouldn't it, to spare the future this bunch. But of course, when he did finally step on the gas, he was in reverse, and the woman in the van tooted her thanks and bowled on her thoughtless way.

Harvey sat for a long while, shaking in his car. Thank God for girls like Polly Marvel, he thought; they were the only reason to stay in such a godforsaken place.

Though the road was too narrow, he backed his Karmann Ghia into the ditch, whipped the steering wheel around, and floored it.

Then, as if it were a trail of crumbs left in the woods, he followed the minivan back to civilization, breathing its dust the whole ride home.

Sometimes Polly wished for the kind of house where a radio was left running. Or where a television blared the day's headlines in an endless loop of overwrought music and droning voices—anything to break the eternal quiet of her house when no one was home. After Mr. March left her, she walked inside to the still, hot kitchen. A trio of flies rose and circled and settled back on the wooden countertop, where they had been feasting on a puddle of tomato juice spilled when Margaret canned some of the season's last Better Boys. The jars still sat in their water bath on the stove, slowly cooling for storage in the pantry. Through the open window, she heard Sultana's pregnant lowing complaint. When her dad still lived here, he played bluegrass records on her grandfather's old stereo console. But after he moved out, her mother had given the stereo away. And she now kept the television in the closet, wheeled out for the late news and special occasions only. Her mother might find the silence peaceful, but it left Polly feeling marooned, afraid to make noise and disturb the heavy somnambulance of the quilts and hanging baskets and cluttered artifacts of Prickett relatives, buckets of their stripped hardware and toe-stubbing antique irons used for doorstops.

She would be in trouble when her mother got home, she knew, but she didn't care. Her parents had no problem being unreliable, why should she hold herself to a higher standard? She stood in front of the old Hotpoint refrigerator, staring vacantly at what there was to eat. Margaret had baked a gooseberry pie and left her homemade ice cream in the freezer, but Polly reached for the rasher of bacon and wound a raw piece around her index finger. She gnawed it while she poured herself a glass of vinegar and sprinkled in a little salt. It was her secret snack when her mother was not around to police her. She glanced at the kitchen table, where Margaret had left a to-do list.

> Shipment to Philadelphia
> Order cheesecloth
> Copy more flyers for Polly
> Note to S. Jameson
> Buy yarn, winter hat Polly
> Remind Polly Farmer's Market Saturday
> Election Day—sample ballots. Polly?

While she was making an idiot of herself on School Street, Margaret was planning her life through the autumn. Mr. March was right. Her mother saw her as nothing but a way of being in two places at once.

Upstairs, something thumped like a tennis ball thrown against the window. Polly stood motionless in the kitchen, waiting to hear the sound again. *Thump.* She heard it. Then again, a panicked patter. She set down her glass and climbed the narrow servants' staircase that connected the kitchen to the upper floors. The noise came from one of the unused bedrooms at the other end of the long hall, on the east side of the house. Last winter, the wooden eaves had rotted, and unable to afford to replace the roof, Margaret had simply shut the doors and avoided those rooms altogether. They were too expensive to heat, she said, and anyway, there was more than enough space for the two of them on the sunnier side of the house. With its bulbless light fixtures and sour carpet runner, that wing had become like the dark side of the moon, and Polly now found herself treading nervously. The thump came again from the white paneled door at the end of the hall, where her great-aunt Louisa had slept when she was alive. Polly knew her only from a few faded Christmas photos, for she had died long before Polly was born. But she had left behind a wonderland of fancy gloves, feathered hats, and costume jewelry that Polly used for dress-up, back when she played at that sort of thing.

Polly immediately felt a draft when she turned the white porcelain knob. Unattended, the leak in the roof had only gotten worse, and a deep brown water stain ran from the ceiling to the warped pine plank floor. She could see blue sky through the rotten section of roof, and beneath it, the feathers and twigs of a mourning dove's nest. One of the pale gray birds had become trapped inside, and fluttered madly around the room, knocking into her great-aunt's vanity mirror, the heavily carved rosewood chifforobe, the shut and locked uncurtained windows. Polly ducked as the bird skimmed her head, banking sharply to avoid the door and crashing dully once more into the mirror. Polly raced across the room and threw open the window, prying up the screen and pushing it out into the yard below. The dazed bird lifted up but seemed unable to find its escape, for all Polly's shooing. It flew drunkenly around the small bedroom until finally it hit the window ledge and bounced outside. Polly watched it fly to the corner of the east chimney, where it hunkered in the shadows, puffing itself to twice its size.

What a mess, she thought, surveying the water damage and dropping-streaked furniture. The pale pink and green wallpaper hung in strips, and the old iron Franklin stove that once heated the room had scaled with rust. It looked like no one had set foot in here for decades, rather than months. When she was little, she used to play inside this chifforobe, opening its many miniature drawers and rooting through its artifacts—cut-glass drops from an extinct chandelier, rolls of gauze bandage, red Lucite and rhinestone buttons snipped from a threadbare coat. She would drag blankets from the hall closet and read for hours, curled inside the armoire, falling asleep and alarming her mother, who searched the farm for her in vain. Now Polly instinctively opened the door and saw the goose-down comforter she had brought here well over a year ago, exactly where she left it; only it had been gnawed by something, for a cloud of feathers rose up to greet her. There was a family myth of silver hidden from the Yankees that, once the war was lost, never reappeared. Polly used to tap the walls for it and paw behind the canned goods in the cellar, until her mother told her that if such silver had ever existed, it had certainly been sold long ago to pay off debts. Still, she could barely stop herself from opening drawers and burrowing into pockets, and over the years, she'd mined the house of thirty-five dollars in loose change and stray bills.

The drawers of the chifforobe she knew well. One held nothing but linen napkins and browning lace tablecloths that Polly recognized from Christmas photos. In another were a few grimy toys, including a sky blue windup toy telephone that played haunting, off-key music in a minor chord that for some reason had terrified her as a child. She was tall enough now to reach the top drawer, and was rewarded with a cracked leather snap purse, hung by a thin gold chain. Inside was a plastic rain bonnet given out by the local funeral parlor, a few sticky bobby pins, and a small pink bud-shaped cup of something called Rose Milk. But Polly felt something inside the torn silk lining, and fishing around, came out with a folded blue airmail envelope bearing the postmark "Mecklenburg Prison, Mecklenburg, Virginia." From inside, she drew out a letter, typed double-spaced on an old-fashioned manual typewriter.

Though her great-aunt was long dead, Polly paused and looked behind her. Money was one thing, but the plunder of private corre-

spondence made her hesitate, as if discovering an old letter or even
a discarded grocery list might lay bare some dark family secret, like
an illegitimacy or the fact that she was adopted. She had especially
avoided love letters since the fiasco with her parents', but in the end,
her curiosity got the better of her, and she began to read.

Dearest Rudy, it said, *How I miss you. It is hell in this house with
Momma and Daddy and Abingdon and now Martha, for she has moved
in and acts like she owns the place, lording it over me who has lived here all
her life. I can't wait until you are home and we have a house of our own,
for being here is killing me, Rudy, and I count the days until I see you again.
Do they treat you well? Do you want for anything? Daddy sold off some
acres to those Franks to pay for what you and Winston have done and he
never lets me forget it. Day and night. I count the days, dearest Rudy,
until I see you again and we are out of here, for it is killing me . . .*

The letter went on in this vein, but in the blank space between
the lines, her aunt had received a reply in masculine cursive. *Dearest Lou, You know paper is hard to come by here, so I am sending
this back to you with these lines. How are you, honey? I am hurting for
cigarettes here and $20 would sure go far. Yes, $20 would sure help a
man out . . .*

Polly folded the letter and shoved it back in the purse. She knew
her great-aunt Louisa had never gotten a house of her own, but spent
the rest of her life here with Polly's grandparents and Margaret, and
had died in this room, which was now white with bird droppings and
ruined by water. The smell of dry rotted wood and wet plaster was
giving her a violent headache, and Polly suddenly found it difficult
to breathe. She thought of this house sucking in anyone who came
too close. Her grandmother Martha. Her great-aunt Louisa. Her own
father. She tried to imagine herself married to Mr. March and inviting him to come live here with her mother and the cows and all these
ruined rooms, but the thought was too ludicrous. Yet taking over the
farm was exactly the life her mother planned for her, as surely as if
she had scribbled it on her to-do list. Polly started at the sound of
footsteps in the hall. When she spun around, her mother, like a prison
guard, loomed in the doorway.

"Where have you been?" Margaret asked in annoyance. "I've driven all over town looking for you. I saw your sign on the ground, and I thought something had happened."

"*Keep your talons out of my flesh,*" Polly yelled, pushing past her mother to her bedroom, then slamming the door angrily.

Dumbfounded, Margaret stood beside the old carved chifforobe, while from somewhere uncomfortably close came the panicked flapping of doves.

CHAPTER EIGHT

After Polly's mutiny, Margaret abandoned Brooke No Opposition. She tried to keep her enthusiasm for the slogan, going so far as to take out a full-page ad in the *Three Chimneys Register*, fifty dollars she could ill afford to spend, before admitting that she, too, found the phrase a little awkward and somewhat musty. The Farmer's Friend had a lilting bounce, and she retreated to it, but when she was being honest with herself, she had to admit Polly's defection had swayed her. She couldn't look at the words without remembering the acrostic and the fun they'd had making the sign. Whatever the reason she'd turned against it—and her daughter steadfastly refused to talk about the day she ripped up her sign and abandoned her post—the slogan simply didn't work without Polly.

The last honorable man in America. On Channel 5, the mid-afternoon anchor was interviewing a former schoolmate of the governor's, asking if there was anything the American people should know about the man behind the candidate. *He's the last honorable man in America,* repeated George Shearling of Pittsboro, North Carolina. *I've known him all my life and I trust him like my own brother.* In the background, a clip played of Adams Brooke's high school graduation. In it, a tall, gawky teenager was reaching for his diploma and flashing the peace sign to the camera. Two years later he would enlist for Vietnam and be nearly fatally shot. *It changed his life,* said classmate George. *Before he'd been a regular farm boy, but after that he became a crusader. I've never known anyone like him.*

It was the third week in October, and Margaret had all but given up on hearing any mention of herself. It had been three weeks since National Headquarters called, and yet there had been no reference to Prickett Farm and its struggles in any campaign speech; in fact, she'd heard nothing of the amnesty at all, but instead a good deal of talk about health care and oil prices and our enemies abroad. No one had promised her she'd be mentioned, she had to remind herself, and for all she knew, she could have been one of a hundred farmers interviewed. But still, the phone call had felt like a promise, and now she was left with the hollow, queasy hangover that comes from hoping for too long. With her constant checking of the newspaper and television news, she felt like a moonstruck teenage girl obsessively calling home for her messages. She didn't want to believe, as Polly had taunted, that she played hard-to-get only when nobody wanted her. Margaret watched for several more minutes, until she was sure the election coverage was over, then unplugged the television and put it back in the closet.

She had no choice now but to make her reluctant daily trek to the mailbox, a walk she'd come to dread even before the last registered letter from First Virginia Savings and Loan. She'd identified a pattern to her collection notices—a review of the delinquent account on the 15th and a subsequent threatening missive fired off. By the 20th or so, the letter would arrive: *Attention Margaret Prickett: Because you have failed to act on our earlier notices, we have been forced to turn your account over to our collection agency for immediate action . . .* Each new letter took a line from the one that went before, building on its threats like a harmless bit of string evolving into a rattlesnake, until the final strike: stationery from a lawyer, the threat of repossession, the certified letter. After a while, she simply left the letters unopened, telling herself that the clock began ticking not when she received the letter, but when she read and could no longer deny its contents. Today, when she reached in she found the usual, and something else: a handwritten, plain white envelope with a crooked stamp. Inside was a piece of spiral notebook paper and the tortured block printing of Conrad Marcus, the man who picked up her cheese for delivery. His truck was so old and rusted, its tailpipe was held on by duct tape, and he himself was even older and more broken-down than his truck. *I am sorry, Miss Prickett,* he wrote, *because I have worked for your daddy and your granddaddy, but I really need you to pay what you owe because gas has gotten so dear of late and its hard for a man to make ends meet.* Margaret's face burned. She took a certain defiant pride in holding off the credit card companies, but to have overlooked a bill from Conrad Marcus made her sick with shame.

"August, I need to drive a check over to Conrad's place," she called into the barn when she got back. "Can you watch things for a minute?"

She looked down the long row of empty stalls, the floor still holding puddles from its recent hosing, giving off that clean, riverbank smell of wet concrete. Only heavy-bellied, swaybacked Sultana moved inside her pen, brought inside for the last few weeks of her pregnancy to rest and store up her reserves for the delivery. *August?* she was about to call again, when she heard someone speaking overhead in the hayloft. It was August's voice but not August's voice—a mellower, sadder baritone, different from his reedy Jefferson, the one that conjured ripping tinfoil no matter how accurate he told her it was. She followed the voice up the ladder to the wide-planked loft, where August was getting the place ready for a winter that seemed determined not to come. He had spent the morning restacking bales to make room for what was drying in the field, and had moved on to tarring the many hairline cracks in the ceiling. There was still so much seed and pollen swirling in the air, he was painting on a field every time he lifted his brush, and there some future archeologist might be able to determine what Virginia dairy cattle ate, circa the beginning of the twenty-first century, by bits of haylage, trapped like bugs in amber.

"And after she was gone," said August, ministering to the cracks in the ceiling, "His Heart cried out: 'Deeply practised in the school of affliction, the human heart knows no joy which I have not lost, no sorrow of which I have not drunk! Fortune can present no grief of unknown form to me! Who then can so softly bind up the wound of another as he who has felt the same wound himself? But Heaven forbid they should ever know a sorrow!'"

He was unaware of her presence, she knew, for he rarely spoke at length when they were alone together during the day, unless it was to pass on information about one of the girls. She stood for a moment at the top of the ladder, watching him work. He had tied a red cotton bandanna over his nose and mouth to filter the pollen, but a less-threatening bandit she couldn't imagine. He was simply too tall and gangly to take seriously, with hay poking like Indian feathers from his wavy red hair. His ears were red too, from the exertion of reaching for the rafters, and she could see where his loose white shirt drooped from his shoulders, from his ruddy farmer's tanned neck. He spoke again, this time changing the clip of his voice to one more impatient and didactic.

"And the Head replied: 'I often told you during its course that you were imprudently engaging your affections under circumstances that must have cost you a great deal of pain: that the persons indeed were of the greatest merit, possessing good sense, good humour, honest hearts, honest manners, & eminence in a lovely art; that the lady had moreover qualities & accomplishments, belonging to her sex, which might form a chapter apart for her: such as music, modesty, beauty, & that softness of disposition which is the ornament of her sex & charm of ours; but that all these considerations would increase the pang of separation . . .'"

August dipped his paintbrush in character and splashed tar passionately against the roof.

"'. . . In time, my friend,'" he continued in the same exasperated voice, "'you must mend your manners. This is not a world to live at random in as you do. . . . The art of life is the art of avoiding pain: & he is the best pilot who steers clearest of the rocks & shoals with which he is beset. Pleasure is always before us; but misfortune is at our side: while running after that, this arrests us. The most effectual means of being secure against pain is to retire within ourselves, & to suffice for our own happiness. Those, which depend on ourselves, are the only pleasures a wise man will count on: for nothing is ours which another may deprive us of. Hence the inestimable value of intellectual pleasures. . . .'"

He turned to dip his brush again, and in doing so caught sight of Margaret's wondering face. He immediately dropped his brush and retreated into mortified silence.

"That was quite a conversation you were having," said Margaret, climbing the rest of the way up the ladder. She was enjoying his embarrassment.

"That was Thomas Jefferson," August rushed to explain. "In Paris, he fell in love with a married woman, a painter, and to get over her, he wrote a dialogue between his Head and his Heart. I was just practicing parts of it."

"Oh," said Margaret.

"I'm giving a program for the Richmond chapter of the DAR next week. I thought a little romance might please the ladies."

"I guess election year is an especially busy time for Founding Fathers."

"I'd better go down and check on Sultana," August mumbled, unable to meet her eyes. "Let me get out of your way."

Margaret regretted mocking him and put out her hand as he walked past. "Is that what you do, August? Do you live your life avoiding pain? Do you only value intellectual pleasures?"

He dared a glance at her, unsure if she was being kind or still teasing. "I'm definitely more of a Head," he replied slowly.

"A head *case* is more like it." Margaret laughed. "Why do you spend so much time being someone else?"

He struggled for an answer. "Who else should I be?"

"August," she said, and this time there was no trace of teasing. "That heart of yours is wilting away here on this farm with us. I'm sorry that I've been monopolizing you so much since Francis left."

"I don't mind," said August, hesitating at the ladder. "I like it here."

"Still," she replied. "I'm going to start giving you more time off. But only if you promise to go out on a date every now and then and tell me what it's like."

She had meant it to sound lighthearted, but a bit of the hollowness she had been feeling all afternoon crept into her voice. August looked at her sharply.

"You know I could never do that," he said in a rush. "You know—"

"Margaret! Are you in here?"

Neither of them had heard a car pull up, but when Margaret went to the loft window she recognized the leased gold Lexus in the driveway. "It's Crenshaw from the bank," she whispered, sitting heavily upon a bale of hay. "Oh God, what am I going to do?"

"What's he come about?" asked August, immediately remembering her unopened letter.

"I have no idea," Margaret lied. "Listen, will you go downstairs and tell him I'm not here?"

"Your truck is right out front."

"Tell him it broke down and I'm out with a friend. Or that I was kidnapped by aliens. August, please, tell him anything," Margaret hoarsely pleaded. "Just don't make me talk to him. I can't face him today."

For all his Jeffersonian affinity, August had far more in common with George Washington where veracity was concerned. He could conceal, but he could not confabulate, and the idea of lying to a man from a bank especially filled him with horror. But then he looked into Margaret's frightened eyes, and knew it was in his power to take a little bit of that terror away. His Head told him it might very well be a crime to lie to an officer of a federally regulated institution, but his Heart led him to the ladder, where he descended like a martyr to the lion's den. He gave Margaret a brave smile and called out with forced cheerfulness, "Hey there, Bob, that you?"

The bald little man below threw up his hands in mock terror when August leapt down. "Don't shoot! I'd give you all my money but I left it at the bank."

August realized he hadn't untied the bandanna over his nose and mouth, did so, and hastily shoved it in his pocket. "Aw, come on," he joked to cover his nervousness. "A powerful man like you must carry a spare thousand or two."

"Wish I did, my friend," said Bob Crenshaw, laughing uncomfortably along with him. "Times are hard for everyone."

Like August, Robert Crenshaw had been born and raised in Three Chimneys, and like August, he himself had been more than a little in love with Margaret growing up. But his family had moved here within the last century, and moreover, had always been tied up in money, so they had neither Vaughn nor Prickett standing in the community. Still, despite their social inequality, young Bob Crenshaw had often fantasized about stealing off with the dreamy Miss Prickett and showering her with love sonnets, for like T. S. Eliot, he considered himself a banker-poet, and saw no incompatibility between love and lucre. He was here today on an unpleasant mission, though, and wanted to get it over with as quickly as possible.

"Where's Margaret?" he asked, peering behind the taller man. "I need to talk to her."

The lie came far more easily to August than he had imagined it would. "She's giving my mother a driving lesson."

"Your mother's learning to drive at her age?"

"The hospital's idea. They're running short of patients."

"Margaret's truck's in the driveway," Crenshaw said, skeptically. Margaret had received the bank's letter nearly a month ago and had never responded. He knew she had good reason to avoid him.

"They took our car. Margaret's is a stick shift. We want to teach the old lady, not kill her."

"Know when they'll be back?"

"They just left." August began to warm to his deceit. "I'm surprised you didn't pass them on the road."

Crenshaw nodded, and August could see the tiny furrows of hair transplants budding on his shiny scalp. He looked so utterly out of place in this filthy barn—scrubbed and plump and pinstriped, his polished wing-tip shoes sinking in the manure. Though the man made a pretense of believing August's story, he showed no inclination to leave. Instead, he walked away from his leather briefcase and peered into the cow stalls.

"This one pregnant is she?" Crenshaw asked, nodding at the lowing Sultana.

"Should lay down any day." August followed him nervously. "Good thing, too. Margaret can hardly keep up with orders from New York. Business is really turning around."

"Too little too late, I'm afraid."

"Don't say that, Bob." August wanted to uproot every blade of hair on the barren pink pate. How dare he stroll around this barn as if already taking stock for the foreclosure sale?

"She'd be better off filing Chapter 11 bankruptcy. At least then she could keep possession."

"Come on, it can't be as bad as that."

"August, you don't know the half of it." Crenshaw gingerly patted Sultana's fawn-colored head, and the cow lowed all the louder. "Her agent and I told her after the old man died, she'd better mechanize and join the co-op, but she wouldn't hear it. None of us blame her, mind you. Old man left her with a heavy load, but she won't do what it takes, and now she's going to lose it all."

Margaret file for Chapter 11? Admit to the world she was a bankrupt? August knew she would sooner sink into her grave than dishonor her family like that.

"How are your programs going?" Crenshaw asked to take the scowl off of August's face. "Will we see you on Election Day?"

"What's Election Day without Thomas Jefferson?" he asked.

"I sure do love your programs," said Crenshaw. "Though I must say, I'm a Civil War man myself. You know, my great-great-grandfather was wounded at Chancellorsville. It's important to keep the past alive. So long as you don't get stuck living in it."

Crenshaw looked once more around the barn, and his eyes rested briefly on the hayloft. "When she gets back from her driving lesson tell her to give me a call. She can't avoid me forever." At times like this, the banker wished he wore a hat, for he felt the end of their conversation demanded a polite tipping of one on his part. "Tell her what I said about Chapter 11," he said over his shoulder as he picked his way out of the barn. "I'm happy to help her with the paperwork if she can't afford a lawyer."

"Will do," said August, telling his last lie of the day. He watched the banker slip into his leased Lexus, with its white leather upholstery and its global navigation system, as if Crenshaw were likely to drive anywhere he might get lost. His briefcase was expensive, and his suit was expensive, and his car, which he didn't even own, but would upgrade every other year, was expensive, and August felt such a rage against money it nearly choked him. He stood up beside Margaret every day, saw how hard she worked, and how little it rewarded her. He knew she didn't sleep most nights from gnawing anxiety, and yet she was never too exhausted to make her daughter's breakfast, or say a kind word to a frightened cow, or pay her help, a personal check every other week, written in her fine, no-nonsense hand, in home-made black ink that faded to purple if not cashed promptly. He had never known a richer woman with less money in his life.

"Well, I have to get that check to Conrad," she said, climbing down the ladder.

"Did you hear any of that?" asked August, surprised by her non-chalance; he'd expected a tirade or defiance. Margaret looked at him sharply.

"We still have two weeks," she said. "He's out of his mind if he thinks I am going to do anything before Adams Brooke wins this election."

My Dear Madam—Having performed the last sad office of handing you into your pickup, and seen the wheels set to motion, I turned on my heel & walked, more dead than alive, to my own carriage, where I drove in suffering silence, home.

My father was not at the table at the usual appointed dinner hour, and my mother had not heard from him since he had received a summons to University of Virginia Hospital earlier in the day. She was in a most melancholy mood, much given over to talk about the "old days" and how complicated things had become in the intervening years. "Take me, for example," she said. "I tried for years to have more children after you, dear, but the good Lord did not will it so. And did I rush out and buy some eggs or have your father do his thing into a cup? Heavens no! We might all be a good deal happier if we were more content with our fate."

I thought long and hard about what she said—what it meant to be content, and how tricky that one word: fate. I thought of you, dearest madam, fated to carry the load of many spendthrift generations and perhaps, I feared, to sink under it. Then I thought of myself, destined to stand eternally at the leeway of your life, to watch impotently and offer undesired help. I wondered if contentment must forever pass us by, when with only a few words, all might possibly be different. Thus engrossed in thought, I sank into my father's living room chair. As luck would have it, PBS was running a Founding Fathers marathon, and so seated by my television, solitary & sad, the following dialogue took place between my Head & my Heart:

Head: Well, friend, you seem to be once again in a fine state.

Heart: I am indeed the most wretched of beings. One who touches me deeply is in the gravest of trouble and I am forced to sit helplessly by.

Head: And yet that trouble is not your trouble, so why do you disturb our equilibrium with it? Has your friend in question given you any cause to think she would desire your help?

Heart: She has in fact done just the opposite, and bid me not concern myself.

Head: Then as the voice of reason, I would advise you to obey her.

Heart: Oh, that is easy for you to say! You who live cloistered like a monk, never having felt the pang of admiration for another.

Head: If I do prefer the pleasures of solitary scholarship over crass carnality, is it really so surprising? Have I not been taught by a thousand different lessons that longing brings only pain? Have you already forgotten that day in our youth when you won me over to your side, when we called a truce to our perdurable war, and united in our devotion to the woman in question? She was not even a woman then, but a mere girl of sixteen, thin and ripened by the sun. We had spent a summer working for her father just to be near her, while she, lazy nymph, read novels in

the hayloft and sunbathed on the new-tarred roof of her porch.
She had no thoughts of responsibility back then, her narrow
shoulders were unbowed by debt or disappointment, and we
loved her in her indolence. How often did we pause in our
journey from stable to cheese house, sweating can upon bony
hip, just to adore her gorgeous inactivity? Then how often shy
away, when her eyelids fluttered in our direction? On the day in
question, just as summer was setting and the chill wind of a
school year gathering, we screwed up our courage and invited
her to climb the hill behind her house, where the old chimney
flared. This had always been our favorite spot on the farm, and
we learned it was hers, too, as we hiked up, our bare paired feet
sweaty in our sneakers, the rhythm of our walking in perfect
partnership. You and I spread a blanket we had found, full of
fleas it turned out, but they were a cause for much merriment
and slapping, and it didn't matter that she had come along out
of boredom more than anything else, because all of her real
friends were off at the beach or touring in Europe. She was
speaking to us as if we were one of those friends, as if we had
shared secrets and might do so again. It was a magical afternoon, if you recall, as we bit into acid-sweet tomatoes like
apples and wiped the juices from our chins. We passed a ther-
mos of iced tea back and forth like a jug of whiskey and pretended to be drunk. Then you, my friend, emboldened me to
slice a wedge of her mother's sharpest cheddar and hold it to
the daughter's lips. Our eyes met as she slowly bit it from the
knife, and it seemed in that suspended moment that all we had
so desired might very well come true. . . . .

Heart: Ah, what joy your words give me! How blissfully I remember that day.

Head: Shall I remind what grew out of that cherished moment on
the hill? Nothing! You had not the courage to kiss her then,
and I argued it was premature. And then the school year
started, and then she met that boy, and Polly sprang a few years
later, and she never glanced again.

Heart: Why must you torment me so?

Head: To show that you have barely changed! You still yearn like a lovesick boy and yet are not man enough to act.

Heart: But now I would declare my love, yet you hold me back!

Head: If I gag you, it is to spare you, friend.

Heart: But we must help her! You have been hoarding money in that trust account of yours for years.

Head: She will never accept a loan from me. Not even to save her farm.

Heart: Not from a friend . . . but perhaps from a closer relation . . . ?

Head: Surely you cannot flatter yourself that she will marry you?

Heart: Why should she not? Could she find a more devoted servant than I? Could she find a more adoring father to her daughter or more tender minister to her fields?

Head: You read too many novels, my friend. True love often goes down in defeat when not protectively pressed between the pages of a book.

Heart: We hesitated once before and lost our opportunity. You cannot stop me now. Not when we must lose her for good if she herself loses the farm. I will speak to her, and when I am ready, you, sir, must open your mouth to let my words pass through. There will be no barring of the gate this time.

Head: You are a fool! There is nothing but heartache ahead—!

"Dear, do you mind if I flip over to Channel 12? I was hoping to catch the eleven o'clock headlines."

August started from his reverie at the sound of his mother's voice. How long had he been sitting in this recliner, fighting his internecine battle? The credits were cycling past and that aching Appalachian fiddle that had come to stand for all American music pre-1920, melancholically filled the room. His mother was in the doorway, backlit by the kitchen lamp, wiping her hands upon a shadowy dish towel. August flipped over in time to catch the top story: The presidential race was too close to call, with a few key states hanging in the balance.

"I do wish your father would phone," Evelyn Vaughn said, not staying to watch the headlines, for she had suddenly remembered some cherries that needed pitting if there was to be a pie tomorrow. "I worry about his driving at night. Especially in that beat-up old van."

"I'm sure he's fine," said August, still caught in the undertow between Head and Heart.

"It's only held together by rust and the Lord's Prayer," she called from the kitchen.

August kept up an abstracted conversation with his mother, grunting and "hmmming" enough to be polite. But his thoughts were all given over to Margaret and his bold new plan to speak his mind. If only he could woo as Jefferson had—courting his beloved with the strings of a violin instead of his own weak, tuneless words. When they'd overheard the two lovers in perfect accompaniment on fiddle and piano, suitors to the young Martha Wayles Skelton had thrown up their hands and walked away, knowing their cause was lost.

"In local news," the television anchorwoman was saying, "two more of the eleven children born to Amanda and James Frank of Three Chimneys, Orange County, are dead tonight. Doctors at University of Virginia Hospital state that Baby B and Baby F succumbed to complications following surgery. They were among the largest of the children at birth and had received a better-than-average prognosis. The other eight children remain in critical condition. As you recall, Amanda Frank made history last month with the first-ever recorded live birth of eleven infants. She was being treated with the fertility drug Pergonal."

The rectory door opened just as a grim-looking hospital spokesperson appeared on the television to give a statement.

"Leland!" Evelyn cried, racing to take her husband's jacket and briefcase while August vacated his father's recliner. Leland Vaughn leaned in the doorway like a man just returned from war, grateful to be out of the trenches, but still wearing the sad dust of all he had seen. He let himself be led to his favorite chair and deposited into it heavily.

"Oh, dear," Evelyn fussed. "We had no idea. We just heard on the news."

"Can I get you anything, Dad?" asked August.

"A cold beer if we have it, son, would be great," the priest answered.

"How is poor Manda?" asked Evelyn.

"She is holding up about as well as can be expected," the priest said, allowing his wife to remove his clerical collar and loosen his top button. "She has to be strong for the other children. Jake is taking it mighty hard, though."

"I should make them something," Evelyn said, thinking of the cherry pie that moments before she had been planning for her own enjoyment. It would go straight to Manda and Jake's in the morning, along with a second of blueberry.

August returned with a Heineken that had spent the past two years sandwiched between Worcestershire sauce and sweet relish in the refrigerator door. It foamed up Pastor Vaughn's nose as he tried to drink it, but the priest barely noticed. He downed it in four long swallows.

"I've never seen anything so sad," he said at last, wiping the corners of his eyes. "They had to fit both children with shunts to draw away the spinal fluid leaking into their skulls. There was no way they were going to escape severe brain damage, but the doctors thought they might still live . . ."

"You don't have to tell us about it, Leland," said Evelyn, patting his shoulder. "You should rest."

"I gave them Holy Unction this morning, and then we spent the rest of the day waiting. Watching the doctors treat their seizures, watching them go cyanotic. They had to sedate Jake—he was raging around like a wounded bull—but Manda just sat there, holding their tiny blue hands and waiting for the inevitable. I tried to comfort her, but she seemed beyond reach, like she'd put away some part of herself or, I hoped, given it over to a higher power—I couldn't tell which. The worst thing is, Evelyn," he said, reaching up for his wife's hand, "I don't know if it's strength or despair that's driving her. She's so stoic, and she won't talk. I'm beginning to think we should get Dr. Friedman in to see her."

"Oh, Leland! A psychiatrist?"

"Mom," piped in August, "if she is depressed she could harm herself or the children."

"Manda would never do that," Evelyn replied, scandalized that her own son could think so ill of a neighbor. "Shame on you."

With a deep sigh, Pastor Vaughn hefted himself out of his chair and took his beer bottle to the kitchen, where the fluorescent strip under the cabinet gave off a thin blue light. In the deep porcelain sink, a paring knife lay bleeding beneath a colander of stemmed black cherries; on the counter, carefully filmed in saran wrap, a dinner plate of roast chicken and mashed potatoes awaited him. Everything seemed so normal and familiar compared with the beeping, whirring chaos of today. Leland rinsed his bottle and dropped it in the recycling bin. From the kitchen window, he could see the old kudzu-covered chimney shining in the moonlight, its brick bench beckoning him to sit a while. Evelyn was calling him to come along to bed and August was bidding him good night, but he felt if he just had a moment or two alone, he might be able to make sense of this awful day.

"You all go on, I'll be up in a minute," he told his family, unlocking the back door and stepping out into the overripe night. It shouldn't be this hot so late in October, he thought, and maybe that was part of what had him so unsettled.

Sometime early in life, so long ago he couldn't even remember when he'd heard the tale, a cousin had told him that this plot of land had once been an old Indian burial ground. He didn't doubt his cousin's story, though the boy was an inveterate liar, because over the years he'd found gnawed obsidian arrowheads alongside the broken crockery and melted nails from the tavern fire. Leland had cut his teeth on the history of his family's tavern, yet in his imagination, its chimney had been standing just as it was long before any white man had ever set foot here. He even imagined a legend for it, like the legend of Virginia Dare turned into a white doe, but in his tale, an old Indian chief refused to abandon his post during an attack from an enemy tribe. He guarded his camp faithfully, allowing many women and children to escape, and did not budge even when about to be hacked to death by naked young warriors. Then, in good

Ovidian fashion, just as the enemy hatchet was about to cleave his head in two, the Indian gods took pity on the old chief and turned him into a funnel of stones, a ghostly sentinel to forever watch this plot of land. When the boy Leland shared his hopes and fears with that ancient pile of bricks, he more than half-felt he was whispering them in the wise Indian's ear, and that no matter what, the chief would watch out for him.

He brought a heavy heart out to the Old Man tonight. Ever since he could remember, he had been imagining his home the site of great events and adventures. It seemed so long since anything of note had happened here. His great-grandfather could remember bloody Confederate engagements fought nearby, and *his* great-grandfather lived among older relatives with recollections of James Madison and Thomas Jefferson. Leland knew from the crop in his backyard that history had passed by his very house, for splinters had broken off in proof. And yet all day, ever since he had oiled crosses onto those two small swollen foreheads, he had been fighting the fear that he had pushed too hard for history to once again pay a visit to Three Chimneys. What if it was his desire to see his town once more at the center of things that had pushed his parishioner Manda Frank to have all eleven babies, when every doctor she consulted was against it?

Had he not for years now felt a spiritual drift in his community—felt the modern world, with all its allurements and inevitable tensions, pulling at his congregation, leaving more pews empty every Sunday, putting up walls between neighbor and neighbor? Had he not prayed for some cataclysmic event to unite them all in a common cause, as once a war or a flood might have done? Manda had been the answer to his prayers: a modern miracle to reclaim those adrift, a natural disaster in which no one would be hurt, but instead, lives saved, and even better, before the eyes of the whole country. Looking back on it now, after the deaths of three of those innocent, unsuspecting children, Pastor Vaughn couldn't believe he had thought his advice victimless. Yes, he'd convinced himself he was saving those babies from the abortionist's needle, but had he not become a more vicious murderer? He had thought he was leaving it up to God

to play God, but now he felt Satan had come to his church that day
in the guise of a confused young mother, and Leland had counseled
her out of his own ennui and desire to bring glory to a forgotten town.
Manda and her children had been his means to his selfish end.

It was in this position of despair that August found him, leaning his cheek against the Old Man and staring at the moon. August
had scared up another beer from the refrigerator, thinking his father
might be in need of it.

"The Old Man giving you any inspiration?" August asked by way
of letting his father hear his approach. The pastor seemed so lost in
thought, his son didn't want to startle him.

"He seems pretty silent tonight," replied the priest.

"Dad, you know it's not your fault."

"I wish I did know that, son."

The two men were quiet for a time while Leland drank his beer
and offered the occasional sip to August. For all Leland's skill in counseling parishioners, there had always been an uneasy silence between
him and his only child, and Leland often felt, without his wife to act
as mediator, a shyness around his son. He was grateful the young man
had come out to console him, but he didn't exactly know how to
say so.

"I have to write a sermon for those two poor children," the priest
said at last. "What can I possibly say about them that I didn't already
say about their brother?"

August shook his head. For that, he had no answer.

From the one lit window on the back of the house, a lone figure was
watching the men below. Evelyn had wiped the cold cream from her
face and neck, then slipped her recently salon-styled hair into its protective net and pinned it at her temples. She had brushed her teeth
and thought guiltily about flossing as she did every night before de-
ciding she was too tired and would most definitely get around to it
tomorrow. She had exchanged her poplin shirtwaist dress for a thin,
faded flannel nightgown, and now she sat in the window seat of the

bedroom she had shared with her husband for the past thirty years, listening to the metal box fan rattle against the wooden sill. Around the corner of the fan, she could see the two of them out there by the chimney, passing a beer back and forth. (*Two* for Leland? He only drank at Chinese restaurants, and then only a small glass of plum wine to keep her company.) Not until she saw her husband rise to leave would she abandon her post and slip under the cool sheets of their pencil-post bed, pretending to have been reading the whole time. Until then, she would sit and watch, and if they needed her, she could be outside in a second.

Evelyn put her mouth close to the fan blades and spoke slowly, "Aaaaaaaay. Eeeeeee. Iiiiiiiii. Ooooooh. Youuuuuu. And sometiiiiiiiiimes Whyyyyyyyyy?" She repeated her drawn-out vowels, savoring their robotic choppiness inside the fan. "Aaaaaaaay. Eeeeeee. Iiiiiiiii. Ooooooh. Youuuuuuuuu. And sometiiiiiiiimes Whyyyyyyyyy." Ever since she was a girl and had discovered the joys of reverberation, she could barely pass a fan without whispering something into it. She used to croon Bobby Darin off-key when she was alone, or recite the Preamble to the Constitution, or like tonight, simply say her vowels and listen to them come back to her in a stranger's voice.

She wished her men wouldn't take things so hard, sitting out there alone in the dark as if their worlds were coming to an end. August had seemed preoccupied all night, and she wondered if he wasn't nursing some heartache that he was reluctant to share. She tried not to put pressure on her son, but the one thing she desired more than any other in the world was a grandchild to spoil before she claimed her small plot of God's green acre. She had wondered off and on if her son might be gay, and had tried to discuss it with him, noting, for instance, just how charming those Village People were or pretending to seek his opinion on a new sofa fabric. But he had never taken the opening, and Evelyn had never had the courage to ask outright. She'd noticed that his moods had been more erratic over the past year, since Francis Marvel and Margaret Prickett had separated, but she hoped his heart did not lie in that direction. Margaret was a hard woman, for all of her good qualities, and one who had never shown the slightest interest in her son. It would be a shame for him to break his heart against those particular rocks.

And as for her husband, downstairs suffering for his part in poor Manda's tragedy, Evelyn felt the fiercest loyalty. He had done absolutely nothing wrong, she believed, in counseling Manda to have all eleven children. As a man of the cloth, was he to encourage her to murder half of them in the womb? Where should he have drawn the line? At four? At three? At two? Any self-recrimination, she felt, should be saved for the doctor who got her into this mess in the first place. Evelyn was a firm believer in "What is done is done," in its being best not to dwell on what might have been. Everything had its own inevitable rise and fall. Over the years, she had developed a personal cosmology to suit her way of looking at the world, one that she was convinced Science would eventually prove correct. Like the seasons, everything in life followed in cycles. She believed not in reincarnation per se (that would be un-Christian), but in the endless rise and fall of life and life energies. She believed that one day they would find proof that other advanced civilizations had existed long before this one, that they had flourished, become proud, and annihilated themselves, as this one was bound to do. The Earth's molten core was made up of the souls of all these men—well, not so much their souls (those were in Heaven), but their life energies—like one giant nuclear explosion, or electrical coal pressed into fiery diamond. She had once broached this view with Leland, who hadn't taken her seriously at all and had tried to argue her into line with periodic tables and Scripture. But though Evelyn was as God-fearing a woman as the next, she knew, as Leland obviously pretended not to, that there was much in this world unaccounted for by the Bible. And if he wanted to argue science, she might say that life was like Newton's third law of thermodynamics, which she had learned all the way back in high school: Matter is neither gained nor lost, it is only transformed. Leland might feel the lives of those poor young children were wasted, but Evelyn knew they were ultimately part of God's grand recycling. They would pass through the crucible at the center of the Earth and eventually, along with Atlantis, and Ancient Egypt, and Medieval Rome, give their energies back to the world.

"Aaaaaaaay. Eeeeeeee. Iiiiiiii. Oooooooh. Youuuuuuuu. And sometiiiiiiimes Whyyyyyyyy," she repeated, letting the blades chop her words and fling them across the humid night. Out by the chim-ney, Leland and August had ceased talking, and each now stared off into his own corner of night. Evelyn would have laid down her life to make these two men happy, and yet looking upon them from her vantage, her heart ached with something akin to the pain of unre-quited love. After only a minute more, she pushed herself up from the window seat and crawled slowly into bed. What was done was done, and no amount of watching was going to transform those dreamy, anguished faces. She knew, with a wife and mother's intu-ition, that a woman occupied the thoughts of both her husband and son. And yet she also knew, with a wife and mother's infinite, re-cycled sadness, that in neither case was that woman her.

CHAPTER NINE

Block by block, and tree by tree, the banners came down along School Street. One child dead was an honest tragedy, but three children dead had become, by unspoken agreement, a source of public embarrassment. No candlelight vigil celebrated the short lives of Baby F and Baby B as they were eased into the ground by their brother's side. As Leland presided over the funeral, the family was in attendance, a few curiosity-seekers, and no one else.

With the Frank story taking such a mournful turn, the television crews, too, were gone, having packed up their cameras and headed off in search of other news. A pretty blonde five-year-old had disappeared in California, and a prominent senator was a close, some say too close, friend of the family's. A heretofore-unknown mosquito had materialized in Mississippi, bringing in its whiny wake an outbreak of suspiciously malarial symptoms. And of course there was the election. All the reporters not assigned to missing children and tropical outbreaks went into the scandal-digging business with the gusto of resurrection men.

A thick warm drizzle was falling on School Street a few days before Halloween as Leland squinted through the ineffective windshield wipers of his old VW bus. It hadn't rained for weeks and he drove especially carefully, minding Evelyn's warning that the lightest rain was always the most treacherous, and out of deference to the blinding headache he'd had since this morning. It was the barometric pressure, most likely, or the fact that he needed new glasses, but he had been so distracted of late, he'd missed his last two eye exams. Slowly he crept past the fog-shrouded War Memorial, the empty Drafty's, the empty grocery, the empty hardware store. The spreading oaks, out of decorum, had renounced their brilliant fall foliage, which with-ered yellow on the branch and fell in diffident soggy barrows along the storm gutters. Leland supposed downtown had always been this quiet and lonely during the day, but he had grown so used to seeing people on the street and cars parked tightly together like happy sunning flocks that normalcy now seemed meager and undernourished by comparison. Neighbors had begun to avoid one another, crossing the street so as not to have to say hello, giving each other wide berth. They were behaving like the sheepish victims of a pyramid scheme or survivors of ergot poisoning, rubbing their eyes as if waking from a collective bad dream. He'd noticed the change today in Snow White when he'd had his morning cup of coffee; faces had darkened at the mention of irresponsible Amanda Frank, giving birth to eleven children she couldn't possibly afford, and hints had been dropped about her extended family's dependence on the State. And then there were the mercenary regrets of the town's businessmen, who'd sat sullenly eating their breakfast. For all the disruption the news crews had caused, profits had risen 40 percent while they were here, and local merchants had begun to look forward to an elevenfold life span of remunerative notoriety. Notorious was how Three Chimneys felt now—famous not as the birthplace of the Frank Eleven, but, instead, as their ill-omened grave site.

Pastor Vaughn was on his way to the Franks this afternoon because of a phone call he had received from Jake last night. Every day since Manda's discharge, the parents had driven the thirty miles into Charlottesville to sit with the babies. There they stayed until lunchtime, after which Jake would make his rounds collecting tin and paper while Manda worked with her hunting dogs until Rose came home from kindergarten. But for the past few days, Jake told him on the phone, Manda had refused to go to the hospital. She wouldn't say why, she simply wouldn't get in the car, and Jake had been forced to go alone. Not that he minded, he explained, but the nurses were telling him that with any luck the strongest babies would be able to go home soon—that is, if the family seemed emotionally ready. Would Pastor Vaughn, if he had a minute, if it wasn't too much trouble, mind coming out to have a few words with his wife?

The dogs in their wet skins set up a furious racket when the minister pulled into the driveway. In the beginning of her pregnancy, Manda, not yet enormous, had tried to keep working. She bred her best hunter and intended to get one last litter in before the babies came; but the dog delivered while Manda was on bedrest, and with Jake too busy to do much more than feed them, they had grown like wild animals—black and tan missiles that launched themselves upon the unwary visitor, too steeped in their dog chaos to take and follow a command. From what Jake told Pastor Vaughn, Manda had been out in the pen working with them every day since she got home from the hospital, hoping to undo the damage, and that was where the minister found her, ankle-deep in mud, scrubbing down the kennel's rusting corrugated tin roof.

"Shut up, you," shouted Manda over the yelps and howling. "*Shut up*, I mean it."

Manda fixed the twelve compact beagles with her stare. The dogs squirmed to an uneasy silence, whining and pawing at the ground, but even sitting still, their skins jumped and their ears vibrated; they were barely domesticated, Leland saw, holding themselves together out of desperation only.

"Hello, Manda," said Pastor Vaughn, and she clapped her hands to release them. The dogs rushed the fence as she closed the gate behind her.

"Hey, Pastor Vaughn," said she, walking to the shed behind the pen. She was wearing nothing against the rain, just an old flannel shirt, gray sweatpants, and a pair of plastic boots. Her lank black hair hung about her pale face, still swollen from all the extra weight she'd put on. Before the pregnancy, any two of the dogs could have knocked her over, but now she seemed like an unassailable stone wall.

"Where's Jake this nasty afternoon?"

"On his rounds, I expect," she answered, still not looking up. She was emptying a thirty-pound bag of Buckeye Hi-Performance into a trash bag–lined steel bin. Pastor Vaughn rushed to help her.

"Shouldn't you be laying off the heavy lifting?" he asked. She shrugged.

"And where's Rose today?"

"In school. Mother picks her up."

"So you're here all by yourself?" he asked. "I guess you should enjoy it while you can."

"I guess," answered Manda, measuring out each dog's ration. She planned to run them on some swamp rabbits in a few weeks and had put them on their conditioning feed.

"So Jake told me the good news that some of the children might be coming home soon," said Pastor Vaughn, a bit too brightly. He found himself unexpectedly nervous around the silent mother, who robotically measured two cups of food into each of the twelve stainless steel bowls. "Will you be happy to have them home?"

Manda looked grimly over the pen, lost in thought. "I think these dogs are ruined," she said at last.

"Manda, could I trouble you for some Tylenol? I have a vicious headache," said the preacher, wanting to break the depressing spell cast by the wet dogs and the musty food, the unmucked pen and the relentless drizzle. He was getting soaked, and a dull pain was blooming behind his left eye.

"I've got Percocet if you want it," she said.

"No thanks, Tylenol will do."

He followed her through the garage, where she stepped around a large pile of donated toys, many still in their original packaging, many more obviously used: a chipped train set; a doll bruised with dirty fingerprints, her joints arthritic with Cheerio dust. She didn't bother to take off her muddy boots, but tracked brown sludge across the new white carpet on her way into the kitchen. She ran a glass under the tap and placed two round, red pills on the counter.

"Thank you," said Leland.

Manda's old dog Turbo lumbered in from the family room. Her thick nails clicked across the plywood floor as she made her slow, stiff way over to Manda and sat down just where Manda was standing at the sink. Pastor Vaughn's eyes strayed to the unwashed dishes stacked in the sink and the dried cereal stuck to the countertop.

"Why are some dogs house dogs and others outdoor dogs?"

Manda asked, reaching down to rub Turbo's wiry gray muzzle. The dog's formerly brown eyes were now blue with cataracts. "Why do I let this one come inside while I make the others stay out in the rain?"

It was the most Manda had said since he'd arrived, and it gave Leland hope. He took a seat on one of the torn vinyl kitchen chairs and beckoned for her to do the same.

"She could track a swamper four or five hours without ever giving up. With the pack. On her own. She always got her rabbit. If I could have bred her, we'd have had state champions," said Manda, rubbing the old dog, who had flopped heavily onto her side. "But she just wouldn't take. She's one of a kind."

"Manda," said Pastor Vaughn, willing her to look at him. "These have been rough days, I know. No woman should have to go through what you've been through. But you can't lock away your feelings like this and expect to get by alone. You need to reach out. To your husband, your doctors, your church, your neighbors. We are all here for you."

Manda nodded, then took the minister's empty water glass to the sink. She set it in the pile of dirty dishes.

"Jake says you've stopped going to the hospital," he continued. "Do you want to talk about it?"

"I have a lot of work to do, Pastor," said Manda, looking out the window toward the pen. "You see what shape they're in."

"But your children need you most of all," said Leland gently. "They need their mother."

Manda looked at him quizzically. "They've got all those doctors and nurses. These dogs've got nobody."

"But these dogs are just dogs. Your children are your children."

Manda nodded.

"So you'll go back to the hospital?" asked Leland. "You'll be strong for your children?"

"Yes, Pastor Vaughn," said Manda.

"Manda, everyone is praying for you. Everyone wants to help you and Jake through this." Leland tried to make the lie sound convincing, wanting to believe it as much for his own sake as Manda's.

"Once the children are home, you'll see. You'll have more help than you know what to do with."

Manda nodded.

"Three Chimneys is a family," said Leland with finality. "We won't let you down."

Manda rubbed Turbo's belly as if to raise a genie from a lamp.

"Is there anything I can get for you?" asked the priest. "Anything you need?"

"I don't think so," said she. "I think we're good."

"All right then," he said, not wanting to go, but having no real pretext for staying. Despite what Evelyn said, he thought it best to give Dr. Friedman a call. "I'll check in on you later this week."

Manda led him back through the utility room, where piles of Jake's work shirts and pants were heaped atop the washer. If she was this overwhelmed now, he feared the worst for when the babies came home. Manda noticed his frown and automatically stuffed the clothes inside the machine, but didn't bother to turn it on. As she led him to the garage, the phone in the utility room rang.

"Aren't you going to get that?" asked Leland when she kept walking. He imagined the hospital calling or Jake anxiously trying to get through. Manda stopped at the door, but made no move to answer the phone.

"It's just going to be another one of those," said she, without elaborating.

Pastor Vaughn lifted the receiver. "Frank residence," he said.

"*God has cursed you!*" screamed the shrill voice on the other end. "*It's unnatural what you did and now you're being punished. I hope they all die, I hope—*" Leland slammed the receiver down in horror.

The sound of barking dogs, high-pitched and insistent, followed him down the road, so far that he knew he must be imagining it, but then again, maybe it was a trick of the fog, which like a feathery set of gills exhaled every sound and smell in this stretch of woods. His heavy breath obscured the windshield, but when he turned on the defroster, it made the bus so hot, he had to switch it off again. This would be the weather in Hell, Pastor Vaughn thought dully. Not an infinite inferno, but one long unsettled day in between seasons, too hot to wear a sweater, too rainy to go without one, a muggy, clammy, oppressive sort of day, when all the world's sins would stick to a man like dust from the road.

The world was full of hatred, he knew, but out there, not inside his house. His community was a helpful community, not without its foibles, but generous and kind and open-minded. The call obviously came from that vast wilderness beyond, where the Devil had wedged himself between men and their better natures. That world was full of inconstant people, he knew, ones who promised warmth and support but who, when things became difficult, had their own hearths to tend.

When he returned to the parish house, Leland determined, he would get back on the phone himself and make yet another round of calls to all the book agents and movie scouts, the PR firms and Website designers who had contacted him in the early days of the Frank Eleven. His attempts so far had been greeted with embarrassed silence from the assistants on the other end, or, worse, with blithe good cheer. "*Certainly, Mr. *** will get in touch with you right away. He has the number, right?*" Leland would dutifully leave it again, and stress how deeply the Franks needed support in light of their recent tragedy. He understood the story would be a more difficult sell, but all of those people couldn't possibly turn their backs, could they? He thought about the signed contract he had FedExed for that movie-of-the-week, though now he realized gloomily that he'd never received the countersignature.

Fog wrapped the road in a sticky, white cocoon, and Leland was forced to pilot Snakehill Road by instinct alone. Only once before had he ever seen fog so thick, rushing down from the mountains like soup overboiling a pot. It was the night he drove Evelyn home from the hospital in Charlottesville, the long terrible night she miscarried their first child, a girl, not quite five months. The doctors had performed a D & C, and Leland wanted to rent a hotel room rather than face the long drive home. But no, Evelyn had insisted quietly, she wanted to sleep in her own bed; and so he had driven in the worst fog of his life, weather that caused a kind of hysteria, with elderly women stopping their cars in the middle of the road, too afraid to drive on, and young men speeding around them to their near-deaths in oncoming traffic. His wife had fallen asleep in the overheated car, the chocolate brown Plymouth they had back then, her pale cheek resting against the cold window, her young face slack and tired. Now, driving home from Manda's, Pastor Vaughn could barely tell if it was day or night, for it seemed the fog had stolen into the bus and behind his eyes, filling his brain with cobwebs. His headache had assumed the form of a deep red pitcher plant, luring whatever random thoughts crawled near. It was so hard to concentrate. Mary Todd Lincoln suffered from migraines, he thought incongruously. Maybe I have MS.

Leland blinked, and a figure separated itself from the fog directly in front of him. A dog, of all things, dead center in the middle of the road, just inches from his bumper. The black and tan beagle sat unconcerned and serene, like a grinning canine incarnation of the Buddha. Leland slammed on the brakes and turned the wheel sharply to the left, but felt the sickening lurch of his tire going over something brittle and softly resistant. And then he was woefully off balance, the nose of his bus angled into the ditch, where it hit with the wicked retort of a discharged rifle, sending him sharply into the steering wheel. With a gulp, the pitcher plant swallowed his eye and vomited it out again.

From somewhere far off in the woods, Leland heard a mournful howl; it took him a long minute to realize it was not animal, but the echo of the VW's horn, depressed by his bleeding cheek. I hit that dog, thought Leland weakly. I hit that dog. But even as his eyes were shutting and his fingers losing their grip on the steering wheel, he thought he saw, from the corner of his throbbing eye, something black and tan wriggle out from beneath his bus and bound joyfully off into the mist.

For the final presidential debate, Margaret broke her rule about watching television during dinner. She wheeled the small set out of the closet and into the kitchen, where she and Polly watched the proceedings in black and white, through static not quite controlled by the coat hanger over the antenna. Night had gathered, but the two sat cozily at the long kitchen table, safe inside a yellow circle of lamplight. The room smelled like a Norman Rockwell painting of dinner: Margaret's home-made meat loaf, mellow orange winter squash baked with butter and cinnamon, an apple crumb. Polly ate hers over her history homework, her textbook opened to the Election of 1800—one of the most bitterly contested in American history, Mr. March said. Jefferson created the first opposition party, and factionalism was born.

Margaret thought that so far, Adams Brooke was clearly win-ning the day. Though he was dressed identically to the president—in a dark suit, white shirt, and yellow tie—he came across as someone who had pulled on his clothes in a hurry and couldn't wait to get out of them again. His tie was infinitesimally askew, loosened moments before he went on the air; his hair, too, was not worn laquered to his head, as per Beltway fashion, but rumpled rakishly, as if he'd just re-moved a John Deere cap after a hard day's work. His lack of pretense was what she admired most about him. When Adams Brooke rolled up his shirtsleeves you saw, rather than the pale extremities of a leg-islator, the tan, muscular, pre-melanoma arms of a man who'd spent his life outdoors, on the farm, on the battlefield, in the service of others. The current president played golf. Adams Brooke built houses for the homeless. Maybe no one else noticed these things, but Mar-garet did, and it sometimes seemed to her that this close race could come down to something as subtle as that—were you the sort of voter who wanted your president comfortable in a suit?

"Mom, do you think August is in love with you?" asked Polly, looking up from her textbook.

"What?" exclaimed Margaret, taken completely by surprise by the question.

"He spends an awful lot of time here," said Polly, helping herself to more acorn squash. Her mother now only allowed them to eat what was grown locally and in season, so there would be no more juicy to-matoes or sweet corn until next year, unless she ate what they'd canned. The pollution created from trucking vegetables, even organic vegetables, all the way across the country was simply not worth it, her mother said.

"August is an old friend," replied her mother. "I've known him longer than I have your father."

"I can't imagine August in high school." Polly laughed. "Did he wear his Jefferson costume back then?"

"I don't remember much about August in high school. He worked for Grandpa. He seemed completely normal."

"Well, I think he's in love with you."

Margaret frowned at her daughter. "Pay attention to the debate," she said. "This is history happening."

The two turned back to the television, eating in silence. Adams Brooke was explaining his Family Matters Pledge. *We are all a family,* he was saying. *Those within our own houses and those outside our borders. We must discipline fairly and we must forgive and embrace, even the prodigal son. As a superpower, we should be a benevolent father, but as a member of the global family, we must also be a respectful brother, listening to the voices of others. First and foremost, both at home and abroad, we must understand that Family Matters—*

"Mom," asked Polly, interrupting. "How can you tell?"

"How can you tell what?" asked Margaret, with one eye still on the television.

"If a man is in love with you?"

Margaret turned to face her daughter. So this was what all her erratic behavior had been about. Polly was in love. Of course, she should have seen it months ago, but it had never occurred to her that the moodiness and rebellion might be the by-product of her first crush. She had much to say to Polly on the subject, and much to warn her against, but she really wanted to hear the debate.

"There are a lot of ways to tell," said Margaret, waiting until the governor finished speaking and the president began. "He pays attention to you. He makes you feel important. When others are talking, he listens out for you, and answers as if you were the only one in the room. But Polly, you are too young to be thinking of love. You have your whole life ahead of you."

"I'm not thinking about it," said Polly defensively. "I was talking about you."

"Don't worry about me."

"It's just that you haven't been on a date since Dad left," Polly
said, then added under her breath, "and Adams Brooke is already
married."

"Why is it," asked Margaret, "that everyone thinks if you admire
and believe in someone, you must be in love with them? Adams Brooke
is an honest and morally upright politician, and one who stands to help
us. I'm no more in love with him than August is with me."

"If you say so," replied Polly skeptically. "But don't you think
it's funny that you and I will start dating at the same time?"

"You're not dating for several more years," said Margaret, "and
I'm never dating again. I'm done with men. Now, be quiet. I want to
hear this part."

Adams Brooke was talking again, answering the president's
challenge about his stance on homeland security.

With terrorist threats against our water and food supply, Adams
Brooke was saying, *now, more than ever, we need to turn our attention
to the predicament of the American farmer. In these troubled times, it
is irresponsible to have our nation's agriculture concentrated in a few
megafarms owned by centralized agribusiness. If for no other reason than
our own safety, we need to return to the ways that made our country
great—by growing and eating locally. And that can only be achieved by
supporting America's small farmers.*

"Hear! Hear!" said Margaret, pounding the table in approval.

Let me give you an example, said the governor, lowering his voice
and speaking into the camera. *There is a family farm in Three Chimneys, Virginia, owned by a struggling young mother named Margaret
Prickett—*

"Mom!" cried Polly. "Oh my God! That's you!"

Margaret paused with her fork halfway to her mouth. He said her
name. On national television. Not in a stump speech in a cornfield
somewhere, but during a national debate, watched by millions of people
across America. Campaign Headquarters hadn't lied to her—he really

did know who she was. Margaret felt her cheeks burn as if the entire country had suddenly swung around to look at her.

Margaret is struggling to keep her dairy farm afloat in the face of mounting debt and government indifference, continued Adams Brooke. *Her family has worked the same piece of land for two hundred years, since the founding of this great country, but she is about to lose it all. It's for small, hardworking farmers like Margaret Prickett of Three Chimneys, Virginia, that I am proposing my onetime amnesty under the Family Matters Act—*

"Mom! Oh my God! He's talking about you!"

Margaret barely heard her daughter through the roar in her head, the thunderous applause of the House and the Senate and all their invited guests as she stood up to be recognized during President Brooke's first State of the Union address. *"It was for people like Margaret that I worked so hard to see this amnesty through, and now that you have passed it in a tremendous show of bipartisan support, her farm, like that of so many other brave Americans, is safe at last."*

I understand the pain of farmers like Margaret, because my grandparents owned a small dairy farm in North Carolina, Adams Brooke continued on the TV, telling the story Margaret cherished above all others. It was how she knew he would follow through on this promise, even if he broke all others. *I worked there every summer of my boyhood and let me tell you, it's hard work. It's backbreaking work. But it's also rewarding work, and it should be lucrative work. My grandfather had a saying, one he repeated so often he put it over the door to his milk house. He used to say to me, "Adams, Omnis pecuniae pecus fundamentum." And I'd say, "Papaw, in English, please." And he'd translate, "The herd is the foundation of all wealth." Small farmers in this great country should be able to earn a living wage, and if I am elected in November, I will see to it they do!*

"Mom?" Polly said, aghast. "Did you hear that? Did you hear what he said?"

But Margaret wasn't listening. She could not take her eyes off Adams Brooke's kindly face and easy, gap-toothed smile, his eyes crinkling at the corners as he joked about his grandfather's gift for Latin.

She was suddenly seized with the same pit-of-the-stomach feeling she'd had the day she glimpsed Francis in his pickup, a woman's head, so very obviously not her own, nestled on her husband's shoulder.

"Mom," cried Polly. "He stole our saying."

"Be quiet," Margaret snapped, needing desperately to think. "We don't own that saying. It's from the Jersey Club. Maybe his grandfather was a member too."

"They called you a few weeks ago," Polly said. "I was right there. You told them all about it."

"Everything you heard in that room is confidential," said Margaret swiftly. "It's like a doctor's office or a confessional. You swore."

"I didn't swear."

"It's got to be a coincidence," said Margaret, trying to calm her pounding heart. "Adams Brooke has his own family history. Why would he need ours?"

"If he'd lie about his own grandfather, what else is he lying about? Mom, you've got to tell somebody."

This brought Margaret up short. A few reporters still lingered from the Frank Eleven story; the last thing she needed was for one of them to overhear Polly talking to one of her school friends. "Polly, don't tell anyone about this," she said.

"You can't censor me," retorted Polly. "I have rights under the First Amendment."

"You have no rights in this house," said Margaret hotly. "Too much is riding on this election for you to be childish right now. I need you to give me your word."

The two stood locked in mutual defiance, neither willing to back down, neither willing to call the other's bluff. On the television, the president was saying that our enemies were developing weapons of mass destruction and it was only a matter of time before they used them.

"Hello," a muffled voice called from the back door, causing mother and daughter to flinch at the same time. "Is anybody home?"

Reluctantly taking her eyes off Polly, Margaret strode across the kitchen. The fog was so thick outside, she couldn't make out who was standing there, until she opened the door and Leland Vaughn all but fell inside. His face was pale and a thin line of dried blood ran from a cut on his forehead down to the corner of his mouth.

"Oh, my God, Leland!" cried Margaret, helping him into the room. "What happened to you?"

"Just a little run-in with the ditch," he said, joking weakly. "Long time since I've seen fog like that."

"Where is your bus?"

"About a mile up the road toward town," he answered.

"Let me call you an ambulance."

"No," said Leland swiftly. "August will be home soon. He had a program tonight. I'll phone him to come get me."

"For goodness' sakes, Leland," said Margaret, thinking swiftly, *August had a program. He won't have seen the debate.* "I'll drive you home. But I think you should see a doctor first."

"It's nothing, really," said Leland. "Just a little bump."

Over his protests, Margaret led the priest to the sink, where she found a clean cloth and ran it under warm water. All the wrinkles invisible from the pulpit revealed themselves under her kitchen light, a busy network of laugh lines and crow's-feet, the decoration of a life well lived. Leland was getting old. She held his familiar face in her hands, gently washing the blood from its folds and creases—the cut was only a superficial head wound, but everyone knew how badly those bled—and he shut his eyes, drifting almost to sleep, letting Margaret take care of him as he never would have allowed an emergency technician. It's all about trust, she thought. Just as Polly said. Gingerly, she painted his cut with the dropper from her tiny vial of iodine, and brushed his silvery bangs forward. If he didn't tell, no one would even suspect he'd been in an accident. Still, when she was done, Leland's eyes remained closed, and his head rested heavy in her hands.

"Leland," asked Margaret gently. "Are you sure you're all right?"

The priest opened his eyes and looked around the kitchen slowly, unsure, she could tell, as to where he was. What was this wet, warm cloth? This kerosene lamp? This counter with its butter churn and coffee grinder? Then his eyes lit on Polly, watching worriedly over her mother's shoulder, and he seemed to come back to himself.

"Just let me catch my breath," said Leland with a reassuring smile. He walked unsteadily to the kitchen table, and with a sigh lowered himself into the chair Polly had vacated. The priest stared apprecia- tively at the leftover food steadily cooling on the young girl's plate.

"That looks like some mighty delicious. . . . some mighty deli- cious . . ." They waited for him to continue, but instead his tired eyes went to the old black-and-white set, where the debate, completely forgotten by the two women, was wrapping up. In one of those tricks of science whereby a person's own electricity clears the picture, as Leland leaned forward, Adams Brooke's face emerged from the static, as wholesome and inviting as a fresh-baked pie. Leland smiled at the screen.

"I sure do hope he wins," said the priest. "That Brooke seems like a boy to make his father proud." Polly shot a wry glance at Mar- garet, who did not respond. On the television, the moderator thanked the participants for a lively and informative debate.

"Meat loaf," said Leland, his eyes lighting up, as if the very syl- lables of the word he suddenly found in his mouth contained all the flavor of the thing itself. "That looks like some mighty delicious meat loaf."

CHAPTER TEN

"So he really mentioned you in the debate?" asked August over the scarred card table at Campaign Headquarters. "I can't believe I missed it."

"It was no big deal," said Margaret.

"How can you say that? He singled you out—you, out of all the people in America."

"They do that. It's politics."

"I meant to be home to watch it," August said. "My program ran late."

"Really, you didn't miss anything," Margaret said, dialing the heavy four-line telephone. "How is your father?"

"They towed the bus, which was mostly fine," he replied. "Only a crushed bumper. Dad said he hit a dog, but we looked and didn't find a dog. Thanks for driving him home."

Margaret nodded, but she was barely listening. She was extremely grateful August had showed up, but she was in no mood to talk. The polls had not agreed with her that Adams Brooke had trounced the president in last night's debate, and so the race, on this, the eve of the election, was still maddeningly deadlocked. Margaret's solution was to personally phone every name in the thin county phone book. She had made it up through the Ks and was about to start on the Ls, with only three hours left before people would be in bed, when August, her savior, had showed up and, on his private cell phone, begun working backward from the Zs.

"I finally convinced him to see the doctor—" August broke off as the answering machine at the number he was calling picked up. "This is a reminder from the Friends of Adams Brooke." He spoke slowly and deliberately, as to an especially dense child. "Tomorrow at the polling booth, show America that Family Matters, and check the box marked 'Governor Adams Brooke for President.'"

He pushed END on his phone and looked at his watch. "It's past dinnertime. I know a lot more people are home, but no one is an-swering the phone."

"If you can take some constructive criticism," said Margaret, "you're not putting a lot of heart into it. Listen to me . . ." Her line picked up, and she began enthusiastically: "Hello, this is a neighborly reminder from the Friends of Adams Brooke—No, wait, don't hang up, I just need a moment of your time—" Margaret found herself speaking to the dial tone. "Screw you, then."

"Yes, that's much better," August said, smiling.

But Margaret was in no joking mood. Since the debate, every-thing felt like it was unraveling. They needed a hook, something to convince people to listen past the first "Hello."

"August," she said with sudden inspiration. "Why don't you phone people as Thomas Jefferson. Adams Brooke is always quoting him, and what better endorsement could he get?"

August was silent as he dialed the next number. "Go ahead," Margaret urged. "Do your Jefferson."

"This is a neighborly reminder from the Friends of Adams Brooke . . . ," he began, speaking into yet another answering machine.

"No," whispered Margaret. "Your Jefferson. *Your Jefferson.*"

August tried to continue, but Margaret's frantic gesturing threw him into confusion. Without finishing his speech, he hung up the phone. "I can't 'do' Jefferson. It doesn't work that way."

"What do you mean?" asked Margaret in annoyance. "Don't tell me you need to get into character. You're not one of those method actors?"

"No, I mean I've never used Thomas Jefferson. When I became a living historian, I made a compact with myself—never to put him in the service of anything other than history. I don't want to turn him into just another pitchman."

Margaret sullenly watched him dial the next number, get a busy signal, and hang up. She continued to stare at him until he squirmed uncomfortably in his chair. "Why don't I go next door and get us some coffee," he said. "I think I can catch Mrs. Hawks before she closes."

"I'm sorry I snapped," Margaret said wearily. "With the race so close, I was willing to try anything."

"I know," he said, slipping around the card table and out the door. "It's just that some things are more important than politics."

For her part, Margaret couldn't think of any. Every night except last night when she stayed home to watch the debate, she'd been in this cramped, stale office until well after midnight, making phone calls and typing letters; or driving around in her car, nailing *Brooke for President* posters on people's trees. Some nights she didn't get to bed until well after 2 A.M., after she had finished baking cranberry muffins, or composting, or washing clothes. And then she had to be up by 5 A.M. to start the day all over again. Today, she'd been on the phone since milking this morning, with only the briefest interval for milking this afternoon. Chores around the farm had fallen far behind, and the girls were on a subsistence diet of whatever they could forage from the field, supplemented with a few hastily baled forkfuls of hay. Their milk production had dropped off with the disruption of their familiar daily routine. They were used to being coaxed and sung to, carefully curried and practically tucked into bed. For the first time in her life, Margaret regretted having so lavishly spoiled her cows. She was merely quick and efficient with them these days, yet they were punishing her as if she had suddenly started beating them and taken away their television privileges. It was like having a stableful of teenagers as ungrateful and difficult as the one who slept down the hall from her in her house.

". . . Hello, as you know, tomorrow is Election Day, and the race is neck and neck. Adams Brooke hopes every American will exercise his or her sacred right and come down to the polling booth to vote. And he hopes when faced with four more years of corporate greed, you'll say, 'No, *my Family Matters. I choose Adams Brooke, the Farmer's Friend.*'"

"Maggie? Is that you?"

What had she done? Margaret frantically ran her finger down the tight lines of the phone book until she hit the name Marvel. In her haste and fatigue, she had inadvertently dialed the seven poisoned digits belonging to her husband.

"Never mind, sir," she said coolly. "I know how you are going to vote."

"I'm voting for the man whose grandfather is a whiz at Latin."

"You saw the debate?" she asked queasily.

"Of course I did. Congratulations. You're a celebrity."

Margaret had forgotten about her ex-husband, who, of course, remembered the sign in the cheese house. "Listen, Francis," she said sternly, "his campaign headquarters called me and I gave them that motto. They had my permission to use it."

"Whatever gets you through the night, Maggie." Francis said, laughing. "He's just a lying scumbag like all the rest."

"What are you going to do?" she asked.

"Do?" he asked. "I'm not going to do anything. I just want you to remember my generosity next time I'm ten minutes late with a check."

Margaret slammed the receiver into its cradle, then lifted it and slammed it a few more times for good measure. August stepped into the room with a cup of steaming coffee, fixed just as she liked it, extra milk and no sugar. He stood still and watchful, waiting for her to calm down before he spoke.

"You need to go home," August said with quiet authority. "We don't have that many more people to call, and I'm happy to stay here and finish up."

Margaret looked at him through the sweaty tangle of her hair. She hadn't gotten more than three hours of sleep any night in nearly a month, and she was beginning to hallucinate. Was that a golden light around August's head or just a weird refraction of the compact fluorescent?

"You drive yourself home and go to bed," he said, daring to order her. "Tomorrow is going to be a busy day and you need to be rested."

She thought about fighting with him, but tears welled in her eyes at the idea of eight whole hours of sleep. "You really don't mind making the calls?" she said at last.

"Not a bit."

"And you'll make them all?" she couldn't help but add. That extra nudge would have sent Francis off the handle, but August merely smiled patiently and swore he would make every last call before he left the office.

"I don't know what I'd do without you," Margaret said, rising and giving his rough hand a squeeze. "I'll see you tomorrow?" she asked, gathering her pocketbook and sweater.

"What's an election without Thomas Jefferson?" He looked up briefly, for he was already dialing the next M in the phone book.

Margaret left her full cup of coffee cooling on the table and drove herself home.

She knew, when she nearly hit her daughter, who was running along the edge of the stubbled field like a panicked rabbit, that there would be no full night's sleep tonight. Before she could even roll down the window, Polly had ripped open the passenger door and breathlessly told her that something was wrong with Sultana. She'd tried to reach her at Election Headquarters, but August said she'd left already. Margaret fought the urge to back down the driveway and leave the old cow to deliver her calf all alone. She could get a hotel room somewhere on the Interstate, unplug the phone, drink a fifth of Jack Daniel's, and let nature take its course. Instead, she told Polly to get in, and together they drove up to the barn.

They found the expectant mother laying awkwardly on her left side with her thick gelatinous eyes rolled up toward the tarred barn roof, vainly seeking heavenly intervention. Her other stock waited dully through labor, panting and grunting and each delivery seemed to take less time than the last. But Sultana, her prized milker, was as dumb and nervous as a new heifer. She had been bred six times already, yet each birth presented a new horror and opportunity for bovine melodrama. Sultana had been lowing loudly ever since Margaret left, Polly told her, and had broken her water about an hour ago. Polly knew calves came relatively quickly if all was well. Most calves arrived unassisted in the middle of the night, and by the time she arrived for morning milking, the fresh-licked little one was lustily nursing or bucking about. She had never seen one of her mother's cows in such distress before. She feared that sweet, stupid Sultana was dying.

After just a brief glance at the downed cow, Margaret ordered Polly to fetch the iodine soap, then went to wash up in the barn's splash sink. She was so tired, she just stood there scrubbing her nails and forearms, chafing the skin all the way up to her already reddened elbows. The hard plash of the water, mixed with the cow's piteous bellowing, seemed to carry with it the pleas of her own epidural-free, torturous delivery of Polly and the cadence of her newborn daughter's first-breath wails. The sound of a female in agony had its own hypnotic power, Margaret thought, soaping and scrubbing with the mindless repetition of a hospital resident at the end of a thirty-six-hour shift. It was the first, most reliable sound any child born would ever hear.

"Mom, wake up."

Margaret shook herself. She had to deliver this calf. She dried her arms, stripped off her good shirt so that she was wearing nothing more than her white cotton bra, and fitted herself with a fresh pair of plastic OB sleeves. Polly placed a pair of Plexiglas welder's goggles on her mother's nose and, carrying the bucket of iodine and a Coleman lamp, followed Margaret to Sultana's stall.

"It's okay. It's okay," Polly whispered to the miserable cow, who scrambled to her feet at their approach. She followed her mother's orders to slip a halter over the animal's neck and tie her to the stanchion. "We're just here to help you."

The lights were low throughout the barn and the Coleman lamp threw a shadow herd against the wall. Sultana's restless sisters paced their pens, rattling their feed trays and craning their shaggy necks to see. They watched Margaret lubricate her arm up to her shoulder and approach their sister's washed backside. Tails switched and pink grapefruit uteruses clenched in sympathy.

With her arm deep inside the cow, Margaret felt for the calf's position. She should have been able to grasp two front fetlocks and make out the calf's cone-shaped head. To her dismay, however, instead of a muzzle Margaret felt a bony ridge of tail, and instead of the front knees, the hocks. It was as she feared—the calf was turned completely around and was coming out back legs first.

"We're going to have to pull her out," she announced wearily, resting for a minute on a bale of hay. "I'm going to need you to help me."

"Shouldn't we call August?" Polly asked. Margaret glanced at her watch and figured that he could only be up to the Ps in the local phone book. It was more important for him to remain where he was, she decided. They would have to do it without him.

She dispatched Polly for the calving chains, while she inserted both arms deep into the cow and worked to expand the birth canal. She had never delivered a posterior calf alone, though she had assisted her father twice, tugging her length of chain at his command, easing off when a contraction let up. They had saved one calf and lost one calf, when the umbilical cord kinked and the animal gasped too much fluid in utero. She and Polly would have to work fast once the legs presented, and pray they had the strength to tug a fifty-pound infant from its mother's flesh. It would be a bloody and dangerous business.

Why was this happening tonight? Margaret railed to herself, using twine to tie the animal's tail to her collar so that it did not lash the midwife blind. While other campaign workers were drinking coffee and laughing over doughnuts, locked in the punch-drunk confraternity of a college all-nighter, she was up to her armpits in gore and placenta, easing a life into being that might very well be snuffed if those same hypercaffeinated, sour-breathed soldiers in headquarters across America didn't take tomorrow's election. Somewhere in the sky above block-printed states, her Adams Brooke was napping on a plane, resting his voice for his final twenty-four-hour campaign blitz—a rally at midnight for night-shift workers at an Arkansas Toyota plant, a 3 A.M. call to arms in a Kansas cornfield, 5 A.M. pancake breakfast sermon with United Garment Workers Local 215 in Seattle. As she relubricated her arms and looped the birthing chains over the stuck calf's rear dewclaws, she pictured herself there beside him in the roomy airline cabin, watching him in the dim half-light, pinpricked with reading lamps others had forgotten to turn off. Instead of hooking easy-grip pull handles to a link of chain, she was leaning over her candidate with a blue plaid wool blanket; instead of calmly explaining to her daughter the necessity of working with each contraction until the legs emerged, she was easing his bifocals from his nose and folding them into his pocket. She might be pushing Sultana onto her side to give the calf a better angle, but in reality, she was easing herself into the seat beside her candidate and gently tugging a corner of his blanket for her own cold, weary body. "*I'm sorry I stole your family history,*" he whispered, just as she was falling asleep. "*As soon as I win, you can have it back.*"

"Mom, are you okay?"

Margaret focused on her anxious, excited daughter. She had never allowed Polly to help with a birth before, and now together they were going to tug another creature into being. She made Polly grasp the handle at one end of the chain and on Sultana's next contraction gave the order to pull—gently but forcefully, the bottom leg only. They felt the calf give internally an inch or two before the contraction eased and Sultana closed her eyes to rest. They didn't have long before the next pang, and this time it was Margaret's turn to pull upon the chain, coaxing the top rear leg as far along the birth canal as Polly's had come. They took turns this way for nearly an hour, not daring to pull too hard and risk tearing the mother or injuring the calf. They traded off, barely speaking, watching the cow for the first signs of tensing, then tugging up to follow the natural curve of her cervix, before they would tug down to arc the calf all the way out. After about half an hour, the sharp dark hooves presented. Another fifteen minutes and a set of flopping blue hind legs dangled from the mother's vulva like a second slimy tail.

Only then did Margaret order Polly to pull with all her might and not wait for the natural rhythm of the contractions to aid them. They dug in their heels and planted their rumps on the stale wet straw, arched their backs, and pulled like biblical oarsmen, tugging for the life of this calf, who would suffocate if they didn't get it out quickly once its cord was pinched. Margaret's arms trembled and screamed, and she couldn't imagine how her much younger daughter was bearing it, but when she glanced over, Polly's eyes were clenched in concentration and her knuckles were white around the grips. She was not going to let this calf die any more than Margaret was, and the older woman was overcome with a love so fierce and all-consuming, it took all her will not to drop the birthing chains and embrace her sweating, blood-smeared daughter. "*Pull,*" she heard herself grunt like a boatswain, "*Pull,*" and they gave one last final heave before the tension evaporated on the chains and a limp, helpless animal slithered out onto the straw. Margaret didn't know where she found the strength in her used-up arms, but she immediately hoisted the blue calf by its back legs so that the fluid might drain from its lungs, even as she yelled at Polly to dump a bucket of cold water over its head. She grasped its skull as if to kiss it, and ran her trembling thumbs from the bridge of its nose to its muzzle to expel any mucus in its sinuses. Polly followed her mother's instructions to tickle its nostrils with a piece of straw, and was rewarded with a bombastic sneeze and the new calf's first terrified bellow.

They'd done it. And it was a heifer. Margaret's first cautious thought concerned the profitability of the herd. But August's fear of twins was still with her and she knew she needed to examine Sultana again for signs of a second calf. She'd have to wash her arms and Sultana's rump before slathering herself with more lubricant and starting the process all over again. She looked over at Polly to tell her they were not done yet, and saw that her daughter had turned away.

Margaret crawled on her knees to where her daughter sat spilling hot tears over the sticky new calf. Sultana was too exhausted to clean her, and Polly was gently wiping the cheese-bloody afterbirth from the baby's soft hide. Laughing and crying at once, Polly looked up at her begrimed mother, much as Margaret herself had done when the doctor had placed the hard-won infant Polly on her naked chest.

"How can you stand to love something so instantly?" Polly asked.

Sultana was lowing again, and Margaret feared what she would find when she once more groped the recesses of the cow. She tried to prepare Polly for the possibility that another calf was still inside and that it might well be a male, and that if so, it would mean the heifer she now wept over, the one they had struggled so hard to deliver, was a freemartin, and thus sterile. She tried to explain the biology behind opposite-sexed twins in cattle, how their blood mingles as they float in their mother's womb, how the heifer drinks of her brother's testosterone and in so doing unsexes herself. She might look perfectly normal on the outside, Margaret went on, but inside she is blighted and undeveloped and unable to have offspring or give milk. She is an utterly useless creature.

Polly nodded her impatient comprehension, but Margaret could see the girl was unconvinced. There was no such thing as a useless creature to a thirteen-year-old. Polly could not accept, Margaret saw, that the life of one must sometimes be spared for the survival of the herd. Maybe she had been wrong to shield Polly from the realities of the farm for as long as she had, but she remembered her own attachments to certain of her father's stock and how heartbroken she had been to see them culled and shipped away. After what they had just been through together, Margaret didn't have the heart to deny her daughter's weeping request: If Sultana did have twins, they would keep them, wouldn't they, Mom? They would never kill something they had worked so hard to save, would they?

It was nearly midnight before she'd cleaned up and forked fresh bedding into Sultana's stall. She had waited to make sure the mother was letting the twins nurse their critical share of colostrum, and had only left when each infant was firmly fixed to an udder. She had sent

Polly in to wash up and go to bed over an hour ago, but as she herself
was scrubbing her chest and shoulders at the kitchen sink, she spied
a washtub of laundry she had forgotten before she left for Election
Headquarters however many hours ago it was now. A pile of whites
had been washed and blued and wrung and left to wait hanging on
the line when she got home. If she didn't put them out tonight, they
would mildew and she would have to laboriously wash them all over
again tomorrow. With her last bit of strength, Margaret tugged a thin
cotton house shirt over her stained white bra and dragged the metal
tub of laundry out into the yard.

The air had finally cooled some, though it was still twenty degrees too warm for the beginning of November. She shivered under
her open shirt and stopped to button it, but her fingers were too stiff
and she gave up. The porch light had burnt out a week ago, and so
she followed the moon to where it dusted the clothesline and felt in
the dark for the pins she left hanging there. Margaret shook out a
cold damp bedsheet and flung it into the dark, pinning instinctively
at precise lengths. Polly's simple cotton underwear and ribbed cotton tank tops. A slip that had belonged to Margaret's mother that
she herself now wore as a nightgown. She remembered, almost as if
it were a dream, a night just like this when she was a girl: the night
of the comet. The same anticipation hung in the air, the same thrilled
foreboding. The wind lifted her hair just as it was doing now, while
she and her cousins raced like blinded bats across the field between
her grandmother's house and the railroad tracks. There was supposed
to be a comet that night and they were going to stay up to see the
fiery red ball streak across the sky and set the world on fire.

They ran and shrieked and played until something moved in
the air, and the moon went dark, and collectively, like animals
huddling before a storm, they came together in a clump at the center of the field. A strange electricity tickled their skin and caught
in their lungs and they knew as sure as they lived, the comet must
be at hand. Far away, as far away as Richmond, thunder grumbled.
The cousins held hands and waited with an anticipation and desire so great it seemed to lift them off the ground and leave them

hovering over the mowed stalks of field corn. What would the comet look like when it came? Would they be instantly combusted and tossed as sparks through the black night sky? Would they ever be the same? Then suddenly, just as the anticipation threatened to explode them from within, there was a flash, and a streak of lightning, emerald green and thick as a girl's arm, hit down just in front of them. The cousins scattered. Margaret, cheated of her comet, opened her mouth to cry *What happened?* but all she tasted was metal on the railroad tracks.

A set of headlights swung up her driveway, and Margaret blinked in the glare. She paused with her mouthful of clothespins to see who could possibly be driving up at this hour and was greatly relieved to see August Vaughn step out of his truck and come toward her across the yard. He looked as tired as she felt, and she realized for the first time the sacrifice he had made in staying behind at headquarters, for talking on the telephone surely took as much out of a man like August as delivering a whole herd of breech calves. He didn't speak at first, simply took the wrinkled sheet from her arms and gently eased it over the clothesline.

"Sultana had her calves," Margaret said as he fished in the tub of women's underclothes for something less personal to hang.

"Polly called right after you left. I came as soon as I finished up. I thought that's what you'd want."

"Thank you," said Margaret. "It was a great comfort knowing you were there."

"So it was twins?" asked August.

"Male and female. We should sell them for veal, but I promised Polly."

"Promised her what?"

"They were the first calves she's ever delivered. She's in love, but she doesn't understand how hopeless it is."

August nodded, took a deep breath, and hung a lacy slip. Margaret laughed at his obvious discomfort.

"I thought you would be in bed by now," he said. "I was just going to see about Sultana."

"I needed to get this on the line."

"Why don't you go up and let me finish," he said, confronting the remaining pile of soft white underwear and bras. "I'll come up and check on you in a minute."

She had already asked so much of him today, and still he kept giving. But it was a blessing to be able to surrender the last task of the day and finally creep up to bed. She thanked him gratefully and limped inside, leaving him in the moonlight with her soft, ghostly laundry. It wasn't until she was upstairs that she realized her shirt had been unbuttoned the whole time.

Margaret took a scalding shower, brushed her teeth with baking soda, and crawled naked under the clean sheets. She heard August moving around downstairs in her kitchen and wondered briefly what he was doing. She didn't pay him nearly enough to deserve such loyalty, but she would remedy that the first chance she got. As soon as Adams Brooke was elected, she would find a way to give August a raise, and more time off, because he was such a nice man and such a good friend to her. She heard him coming up the stairs and saw him standing in her door, filling the frame with his own gangly frame and long, sweet head. In his hands he carried a mug of hot steamed milk, fresh from her cow's udder, just in case she needed help unwinding. He gently set it on the oak table beside the feather bed her grandfather had hewn for her grandmother as a wedding present, and tucked the sheets more snugly around her freckled shoulders. He looked so tenderly down upon her, looked, in fact, for all the world like he had something desperately important to say to her, that Margaret struggled to keep her heavy lids from closing. *What is it?* her eyes asked. *I'm about to tell you,* his replied. *Best be quick about it,* her eyes blinked once. *I'm trying,* he opened his mouth to say, but sadly, he simply didn't get it out fast enough.

Within a minute she had lost her battle, shut her eyes, and fallen deeply, soundly asleep.

CHAPTER ELEVEN

Margaret overslept on election morning and awoke hungover from a dream that had been playing all night, resetting itself every time she rolled over or opened her eyes to look at the clock. Adams Brooke had won the election and Margaret had been invited to his inaugural ball. She arrived, clutching her engraved invitation, but no matter how hard she tried, she couldn't get to him through the crowd of wealthy supporters. She spent the whole night shouldering through men in tuxedos and women in sequins, but never seemed to inch any closer to the stage, where he was dancing in endless two-step circles with his wife. Rough hands shoved her back, disgusted faces turned away, and when she looked down, she realized she had never changed out of her barn clothes, that she was still painted with blood.

Polly was not in her bedroom when Margaret peeked in. Nor was she downstairs at breakfast. Margaret poured herself a cup of strong coffee and took it to the barn, where she could hear strains of Sinatra already playing over the loudspeakers. In their stalls, the girls lowed miserably, but Polly was not at her stool, either, which explained the swollen-udder lamentations down the row. Margaret knew where she would find her daughter, and sure enough, she was there, in the calves' pen, sitting watch over the brother and sister, who were themselves curled in a warm, brown embrace. When Polly saw her mother she smiled conspiratorially, but Margaret had to shake her head and make her get up. It was the hardest lesson to learn about motherhood, and one Margaret was not always sure she had yet absorbed; it was too easy to become lost in the miracle of childbirth, while the rest of the world stood by waiting, forgotten and miserable.

August arrived a few minutes later, and the three of them went about their milking as if today were just any other day and not the one that would decide the balance of their lives. August tried to be cheerful, trotting out some of his father's less moth-eaten jokes, but Margaret's mind drifted southward to the governor's mansion, where Adams Brooke would be sitting down to breakfast, pushing his food around his plate, scanning the morning newspaper for the latest poll numbers. Still too close to call, he would be reading, feeling, like her, the hopeful dread of the day. Margaret finished milking her cows, and when she carried the heavy, sloshing buckets to the cheese house to cool, she averted her eyes from the sign above the door, the words that reproached her like a neglected grave site or a grandparent sitting alone in a nursing home. "Foundation." "Herd." "Wealth." They were only words, she told herself. Keeping silent was no desecration. But even as she ducked beneath them she asked herself, as she had so many times since that infamous debate, *Why?* Why make up a detail that didn't add a thing to his public persona, that could easily have been omitted, that if revealed as the plagiarism it was would only get him in trouble? It was almost pathological, Margaret thought, like a boy who couldn't stop himself from taking a cherry when he walked past a fruit stand. It wasn't his, but it was no big deal. And who, he'd probably figured, would turn him in for such a minor infraction? Margaret, the injured party? Margaret, his biggest supporter?

An hour later, Polly and Margaret were on their way to Three Chimneys Junior High, where the school cafeteria's yellow plastic bucket chairs had been stacked into corners and the long Formica tables folded away; where the red, white, and blue bunting left over from Fourth of July helped, but did not completely, distract from the faintly sickening milk-and-pizza-mildewed-mop smell of the echoing room. Two tables had been left out, and here the matronly volunteers sat, vainly searching for a name in the roll register until it was helpfully pointed out to them, brightly smiling as they eviscerated it with their mechanical pencils and straightedges. Polly insisted it was inhuman to drag her to school on a day it was officially closed, but it had long ago been decided she would accompany her mother to pass out sample ballots, and so she waited next to Margaret in the long, slow-moving line of prework voters.

All around them, people were talking and laughing. Election Day
in Three Chimneys was not some grim, gray affair with steely boxes
and sour-faced volunteers sitting under limp American flags; this was
no soup line of a day. No, the town believed a nation's patriotic privilege could only be celebrated rightly with brownies and Brunswick stew,
raffle tickets and free cholesterol screenings. In stalls set up outside, all
across the front lawn of Three Chimneys Junior High, the Fire Department and the Police Department and the Rescue Squad and the American Lung Association vied with representatives from the Republican
and Democratic parties to claim the attention of each registered voter.
Yes to the president. Yes to the governor. Yes to two quarts of the most
delicious Brunswick stew cooked this side of the Rappahannock; it was
a shame the Fire Department made it only once a year—judging by
the line at their stall, they could have bought six new ladder trucks if
they sold it every week. Yet for all the festivities, fewer people turned
out each year to vote, and the midterm elections found the polls nearly
deserted. When Margaret was a girl, voting had been as ingrained in
the populace as waving hello when you passed a car on the street, or
phoning the sheriff if a strange person walked through your neighbor's
backyard; and that little needling "Have you voted yet?" asked only to
shame coworkers on election morning in other cities, was invariably
answered, "Of course—you?" by anyone hailing from Three Chimneys.
But now, few in line beside her were under sixty, and no one, certainly,
appeared as haggard and nauseated as she, wearing the desperate face
of an all-night gambler, someone who had literally bet the farm on the
outcome of a single contest. She inched forward in line.

"Hello, Evelyn," said Margaret to August's mother, when at last
it was her turn.

"Hello, dear," Mrs. Vaughn replied. "Sign here, please."

And then it was time. Margaret stepped into the confessional
of the voting booth and drew the silky blue curtain behind her. Somewhere in his local precinct, in a public school or a library, a hundred
flashbulbs exploded as the governor disappeared into a booth just like
this one, where he would face a similar dizzying array of names and
parties, State Supreme Court justices and initiatives; and where, in

that brief moment of privacy, perhaps his only one of the day, his finger would come down on the little red flag (checked and rechecked, then checked again), and Adams Brooke would confidently choose himself. Since the debate, Margaret was no longer confident of anything, but she, too, would choose—her future, her farm, her family— in the person of Adams Brooke; and so, with a trembling hand, she pulled back the heavy red lever that looked like the brake on an amusement park roller coaster, and heard the satisfying, permanent *chunk* of her political will be done.

"I'll be back in a few minutes." Polly called to her mother the moment Margaret stepped into the polling booth. It was the one time all day Polly could be sure of making a getaway, and she used the opportunity to skip out of the bright cafeteria and through the doors that led to the darkened school beyond. Margaret hadn't heard her, and was mystified to find Polly gone when she stepped out. Under normal circumstances she would have looked for her, but today she couldn't waste a moment, and so stepped the required forty feet from the polling site to pass out her *Brooke for President* sample ballots.

A school was a public place, like a church or a restaurant, and Polly found it especially lonely now, emptied of its student body. The low sun slanted through the front door windows, piercing the upper half of the blue and gray metal lockers, highlighting dust motes as if they were swirling plankton. Polly was hyperconscious of her hard-soled shoes' echoing down the freshly buffed granite hall; she paused at the corner, where the hall doglegged off toward the English Department and the sign for play rehearsal might as well have been written in Arabic and pointing the way to Marrakesh, so exotic did it seem without four or five overly emotive students standing next to it for context. One of her earliest memories, from when she was no older than four or five, was of coming to this school to vote with her father, being taken in his arms inside the booth, where he pulled the curtain on a wonderland of buttons and levers and windows and knobs. *Hold tight,* he'd said as he reached for the

big red lever to record his ballot, *we're in a time machine*. He pulled
it and Polly screamed, surrendering to her child's sense of vertigo
and the sensation of hurtling backward through space to that place
where her mother and room and toys were not.

After a brief hesitation, she took the stairs leading up, and was
swallowed in shadow before coming out onto the sun-drenched,
overheated second floor. From the second-story window she could
look down on her school's front yard. *Rebels Homecoming 11/7*, read
the large white letter board, and below: *Pray for Peace*. Polly told
herself she would walk by his classroom without cutting her eyes to
see if he was there. If he called out to her, she would go in, and if
not, she would use the rest room upstairs and return to her mother.
It was a childish game, for she'd seen his car in the parking lot, and
knew, almost for certain, he would be sitting behind his desk grad-
ing papers. Still, she took a deep breath and pretended to be studying her nails as she walked past the illuminated door.

"Polly Marvel!" She felt the flush of triumph when she heard
the familiar voice. "Is that you lurking in the hallway?"

"Oh, hi, Mr. March. I didn't realize you were here."

"And yet you somehow found yourself outside my classroom."
He smiled. "Well, come in. Would you like to help me make up your
midterm exam?"

He was dressed more casually than he would be on a school day,
which made him look younger, but less comfortable somehow. He
wore a pair of faded jeans and a dark red V-neck sweater over a white
T-shirt, from which peeked a few strands of corkscrewed chest hair.
Still, he was freshly shaven and smelled like limes.

"I think you should make it really hard so that only I will pass,"
she joked.

"Polly, you will always deserve an A," he responded gamely, "so
long as you maintain your charming criminal activity. 'Trespassing
on school property,' added to 'littering' and 'breaking and entering.'
I'm eagerly awaiting what you'll do next."

"I'm too tired to get into trouble," she said, somewhat melodra-
matically. "I was up all night helping my mother."

"Not campaigning, I hope."

"Oh, no," she rushed to say, but then became suddenly embarrassed at offering up the story of Sultana and her calves. He had never expressed the least interest in the natural world, and suddenly the intimate details of the story felt bloody and forward.

"So what kept you up till all hours?" he asked, leaning his chin in his hand. "Dreaming of me?"

"Mr. March!" squealed Polly, blushing furiously. "Our cow Sultana had twins. And we had to help her."

"Oh, I'm so disappointed," he said with a sigh, returning to his paperwork. "Even an old man likes to be admired, you know."

He was teasing her again. Polly drifted over to the window, where below, her mother accosted her neighbors with ballots. She had been thinking of Mr. March a great deal since the night of the presidential debate. He would be deeply disappointed in her not having spoken up.

"Polly?" he asked, looking up at her long silence. "Is something wrong?"

"Our twins can't give milk. One is male and the female is sterile," she said at last. "Usually, Mom would ship them off for veal, but she promised me we could keep them. I love them so much, I can't imagine being without them."

She had said the word "love." Even though she was talking about her calves, she had used the word in the same room with him. He watched her closely, and covered in confusion, she turned back to the window.

"Did you come all this way to talk about your cattle?" he asked.

She shook her head in embarrassment. Down below, on the front lawn, she saw August pass her mother on his way to his makeshift stage. As on every other Election Day, he was dressed as Thomas Jefferson, and now he bowed ceremoniously to Margaret before turning to the small crowd gathered to hear him. Her mother might not see that he was in love with her, but it was obvious to Polly. Poor, pathetic August, she thought. Didn't he know her mother had no room in her heart for anyone other than Adams Brooke?

"What are your parents like, Mr. March?" she asked.

"My mother was small, Jewish, very quiet. She died five years ago," he answered. "My father disappeared when I was ten."

"I thought he was in Canada," she said, before remembering she'd learned that bit of information off the Internet. Mr. March looked at her sharply.

"Yes, Canada. I didn't realize it was such common knowledge."

"It's not," Polly stammered in an effort to recover. "I just thought your father might be Stanley March, the writer."

"You've heard of him?" asked Mr. March archly.

"I was doing research for a paper on conscientious objectors, and I came across his name," said Polly.

"How fortuitous."

"You must be very proud that your father followed his conscience and left the country," she said passionately, turning back to the window, where below, her mother was pushing another ballot on another neighbor, stumping for Brooke as if the lie of the debate had never been uttered.

"'Proud' is one word for it."

"At least he was brave enough to make a stand," Polly insisted. "That takes a great deal of courage."

Mr. March pushed aside his paperwork and gave her his full attention. "Miss Marvel, what is on that prying little mind of yours?" he asked.

"Do you remember once you told us even an eighth-grader could affect the outcome of a presidential election?" she asked.

"I remember."

"Adams Brooke is a liar and a thief and I can prove it," she confessed. "But I haven't told anyone because my mother asked me not to."

"She has asked you to go against your conscience?" he queried. Polly nodded. "She has asked you to lie for him?"

"Not so much lie, as keep quiet," said Polly.

"But you're telling me," he said.

"I shouldn't be."

"It's right that you do," he answered gravely. "This is how people in power remain in power. Through fear and intimidation. If you go along with your mother, you are a collaborator. Do you know what that means?"

"It's not that big a deal," said Polly swiftly, seeing how seriously Mr. March was taking her. "It's not a huge lie or anything."

"You know a secret about Adams Brooke, and suddenly she allows you to keep two calves she would normally sell for veal?" he asked. "Don't you find the timing interesting?"

Polly looked down onto the school's front yard as if seeing her mother for the first time. Who was that stern, grim woman handing out flyers with the funereal sobriety with which one might distribute rocks for a stoning? Would she let anything stand in the way of getting Adams Brooke elected? Polly looked over to where August stood on his stage. He was addressing the crowd, but his eyes were on Margaret, speaking to the only person out there he cared about. We are her slaves, Polly thought suddenly. August and I live to serve and protect her. And she counts on that.

"Eventually, you are going to have to develop a system of values separate from your parents," said Mr. March. "You are going to have to start making decisions for yourself."

Polly nodded miserably.

"The old cliché," said her teacher, "is that history is destined to repeat itself. Those with power have always sought to enslave those without. They frighten, they coerce, they bribe, all to retain that power. But once in a great while, someone special comes along, a person who rises up and says, *'Enough. I won't follow the herd. I will think for myself.'* It is lonely to be that person, but, in the end, it is she who makes the difference."

Mr. March studied her over the rim of his steel-framed glasses. She felt him drinking in every atom of her face and body: her gray wool jumper and black oxford shoes, her prim white blouse, smocked along the collar with needlepoint turtles, her red hairband, her bit-

ten nails. She felt him measuring her as if whether or not to find her
worthy of an appointment or grand commission, like Meriwether
Lewis being tapped to tackle the dark, vast American interior.

"The question for you, Polly Marvel," said Mr. March, after a
long and thoughtful pause, "is which do you choose to be? The cycle
or the precedent?"

As he did every election year, to crowds increasingly smaller, August stood up as Thomas Jefferson and delivered the third president's
first inaugural address. In 1800, Jefferson had won the most closely
contested election in American history. John Adams, his former
friend and ally, quit the White House bitterly, refusing to see his
successor sworn in. He left in his wake a series of midnight appointments, including John Marshall, Jefferson's cousin and bitter enemy,
as Chief Justice to the Supreme Court. The election had been dirty,
and cruel, and violent, yet Jefferson considered it a triumph of de-
mocracy, a second American Revolution, for power had changed
hands without bloodshed or rebellion, and the infant American ex-
periment, which he'd feared might be stillborn, seemed destined to
thrive.

Dressed in his powdered wig and deep-cuffed coat, August
mounted the hay trailer that served as his stage on these occasions,
and spoke passionately to the handful of his neighbors who had shown
up to vote.

"'It is proper you should understand what I deem the essential
principles of our Government, and consequently those which ought
to shape its Administration,'" he quoted, catching Margaret's eye.
She gave him a brief, distracted smile before handing a *Brooke for
President* flyer to Dr. Fraser, Bethany's father.

"'Equal and exact justice to all men, of whatever state or per-
suasion, religious or political; peace, commerce, and honest friendship with all nations, entangling alliances with none; the support of
the State governments in all their rights, as the most competent ad-
ministrations for our domestic concerns and the surest bulwarks

against antirepublican tendencies; the preservation of the General Government in its whole constitutional vigor. . . . a well-disciplined militia, our best reliance in peace and for the first moments of war till regulars may relieve them; the supremacy of the civil over the military authority; economy in the public expense, that labor may be lightly burdened; the honest payment of our debts and sacred preservation of the public faith; encouragement of agriculture, and of commerce as its handmaid. . . . ; freedom of religion; freedom of the press, and freedom of person under the protection of the habeas corpus, and trial by juries impartially selected. These principles form the bright constellation which has gone before us and guided our steps through an age of revolution and reformation. . . . Should we wander from them in moments of error or of alarm, let us hasten to retrace our steps and to regain the road which alone leads to peace, liberty, and safety.'"

Every difference of opinion is not a difference of principle, Jefferson had said upon his inauguration in 1801. *We are all Republicans, we are all Federalists*. August watched Margaret gravely distribute her flyers. He wondered what Jefferson would have said had he lost.

They came home briefly for afternoon milking, but Margaret was far too restless to remain at the farm, and so she left Polly with her calves and accompanied August back to the voting station, where they stayed until the polls closed at 7. At 7:30, with 70 percent of precincts reporting, the projected winner of Virginia was announced, and at 7:31, Margaret knew the worst. Afraid to leave her alone, August drove her to his house, where he said they would watch the results together. Virginia didn't mean a thing, he pointed out, not with all the states out west still to go.

The television was on in the darkened living room when the two arrived at the rectory. Leland was at the Franks, but Evelyn, taking one look at Margaret, immediately ceased cleaning out the refrigerator to brew a pot of crisis coffee. With twelve states reporting, only Vermont and New Hampshire had gone for Brooke, while the entire South, including the governor's home state, belonged to the president. The cheesemaker stared numbly at the red rash creeping across the U.S. map. She had felt him slipping away from her all day, from the moment they diverged at the polling booth, as if the very action of flipping the lever next to his name had let the air out of his campaign and begun its slow, inexorable deflation. As determined as she had been that he should win, she was now that fatalistic about his defeat. She should have known that someone as idealistic as Brooke could never win the country, that big business and special interests and corporate greed would take the day. And yet, whispered an insidious little voice in her head, wasn't it in some way fitting that he be punished? Could she not take comfort that lying and thievery went unrewarded, and the universe was just? As if to punctuate the sentiment, Georgia abruptly turned red.

"The chef of Montrachet in New York once offered me a job in his cheese cellar." Margaret turned to August. "Do you remember his name?"

"Don't talk like that," said August sternly. "It's only eight o'clock."

But they watched with mounting dismay as one state after another fell to the president. West Virginia. Kentucky. Tennessee. Rhode Island registered for the governor. With its two electoral votes.

Margaret had not been in Pastor Vaughn's living room since the death of her father two years previously. She had the same sense of unreality then as now, sitting on the Vaughns' pale blue chesterfield with a cup and saucer on her lap, nodding numbly as the minister told her what to expect at the funeral—a hymn, an anthem, a eulogy, a collect, a lesson, a psalm. During the whole time he spoke, her eyes had drifted to the daily artifacts of his life—the framed family photos on his mantel; Evelyn's green and red needlepoint cushions. Behind his head, inside his glass-front bookcase, she saw the family's heavy, embossed family Bible perched like a tombstone. So, when do we get to the grave? she wanted to stop and ask him. Everything else was preliminary, wasn't it, merely a way of easing the family toward the inevitable, like a long and pointless bedtime story for a child afraid of the dark. Now she watched

August's lips move as he reassured her about exit polls and closing times, but her mind had skipped ahead to the end, and she sighed with the sort of fatigue and loneliness that she had not felt so strongly since the last time she was here.

"Margaret?" asked August, when he noticed her staring into space.

Slowly, she reached into her front pocket and removed a folded envelope. It was warm from resting against her body all day, and its seal was slowly coming unglued. She had brought it with her to rip into pieces when Adams Brooke gave his acceptance speech, but now she finally slipped her finger inside and loosened it the rest of the way. "I guess I might as well open this," she said.

"Margaret, don't—," began August, but she cut him off.

"It doesn't matter, it will be public soon enough." She removed the letter from the envelope and smoothed it on her lap. "August, I'm afraid you are going to be out of a job."

They both stared at the paper, with its lurid red header. "Can't you restructure?" he asked, helplessly. "Consolidate bills?"

"I did that last year," she said. "It's over. Adams Brooke was our last hope."

"Children," called Evelyn from the next room. "I have some pot roast still warm in the oven. May I serve you some?"

"No thanks, Mom," answered August impatiently. He lowered his voice. "There must be something."

"I'm just so sorry to put you in this position," said Margaret. "I wish I had some sort of severance package to offer you. I don't know what we would have done without you over the years. Especially this last one."

"Margaret," called Evelyn. "Pot roast?"

"No thank you, Mrs. Vaughn. I've got to get home to Polly." Margaret stared at her foreclosure notice for a long minute, then rose and reached for her pocketbook.

After missing his chance last night, August was determined not to let her walk away tonight without declaring himself. He cast a quick look into the kitchen. If only he could go down on bended knee without his mother barging in with a tray of food.

"I know you don't want to take money from anyone—," he began.

"I would take money from an orphan right now"—she tried to laugh—"if I could just get Bob Crenshaw off my back."

"Then take it from me," August said, summoning his courage. "I've got plenty in the bank. I live at home, I never go anywhere. I don't have kids. I've got plenty saved, and it's yours if you need it."

But Margaret was waving him off even as his passion built. "I cannot take money from you, August," she said. "I *pay* you. Or at least I did. If I took money from you, you'd be working for free."

"Let me work for free," he offered.

"I won't hear of it. I'll file Chapter 11 first," she said.

How he wished he'd had the courage to ask her last night in the twilight of her bedroom, her body naked beneath the sheets, as vulnerable and approachable as he'd ever seen her. How much easier to ask her to marry him there than here in his parents' living room, sitting awkwardly in his mother's chintz chair, the singularly unromantic smell of pot roast wafting from the next room. "Would you take money from a relative?" he asked, as suggestively as he dared.

"A relative?" She laughed. "Who, Francis? Oh wait, I have a second cousin in Durham; I'll give her a call."

"No," said August quietly. "What if you remarried?"

"I'll never marry again," Margaret declared, patting his shoulder as she walked toward the kitchen. "It's not worth it. The smartest thing you ever did, August, was stay single."

He knew Thomas Jefferson would never give up so easily. He would find just the right elegant phrase to stop her from walking away; with truths self-evident, he would open his heart and declare his desire to form a most perfect union. He watched her kiss his mother's cheek and thank her for the coffee. He tried to picture his strong, capable Margaret bent over a cheese board at some fancy New York City restaurant, calmly explaining the subtle interplay of aromas to drunken bond traders, who snaked their arms around her waist and murmured endearments, and the idea filled him with despair. For all the years he'd played Jefferson, August had never

understood politics on a personal level. He had studied the philoso-
phies and embraced the theories, but until tonight, he had never
experienced the loss of a cherished dream. There must be something
he could do to save Margaret. He could not let her walk out of his
life.

"Hello, all," called Leland wearily, coming in the front door and
hanging up his coat. "Who's winning?"

As August turned to bid his father hello, he glanced over at the
television. For a moment he couldn't believe his eyes. Hope had come
from a most unexpected quarter.

"Margaret, put down that letter and come here," August said,
excitedly.

Margaret and his mother stepped into the living room, where a
flashing boot of blue filled the television set. In a shocking upset that
was taking even the veteran newscasters by surprise, Florida, with its
twenty-five blessed electoral votes, had gone for the governor.

"Florida," cried August. "He took Florida!" If he could take
Florida, thought August, Illinois was almost certain. New York and
California had been guaranteed from the start. If he could take Michi-
gan and the other farming states, the day would be his.

Margaret dropped her pocketbook on the floor and sank back
onto the couch. It was going to be a long night.

Just after one o'clock, Adams Brooke ascended the platform erected
on the front lawn of the governor's mansion to address the red, white,
and blue crowd of supporters and press who had been camped there
all night. He looked haggard and when he began to speak, his ragged
voice backfired like a rusted carburetor. He thanked his rival, the
president, speaking of their spirited battle and the will of the people
and the wonders of the democratic system. He thanked his supporters and his wife and two grown daughters. He thanked God for allowing him to be born into this great country. Then he promised a
bright new era of bipartisanship and prosperity and, with a fervor that
whipped his sea of supporters into a typhoon of delirious cheering,

vowed that his first act in office would be the introduction, by God, of the Family Matters Bill!

Margaret missed most of the president-elect's acceptance speech because she was crying too loudly, her head buried in August's chest, racked with the kind of sobs she hadn't experienced since she was a little girl. She was grateful in the way a person pulled from a fire is grateful, or in the way a woman who has just pushed through her last contraction is grateful; she was grateful in a full-bodied, gut-wrenching, lie-down-and-die sort of way. To August's chagrin, his parents had remained downstairs to watch the election results; Margaret's sobbing now woke them both where they had been dozing in their chairs.

"Oh, Margaret, dear," said Evelyn, instantly misreading the situation. "I'm so sorry."

But Pastor Vaughn saw things more clearly. There was no mistaking the look of bliss on his son's face as he held his cheesemaker and gently stroked her hair. He was so quiet about matters of the heart, the thought had simply never occurred to Leland: August was in love. He watched his son spin Margaret across the living room floor, in imitation of Adams Brooke and his wife on TV, twirling her into an awkward dip. How happy they all seemed, he thought, with a momentary selfish pang. Before Margaret woke him, he had been dreaming of the Frank children, laid side by side in their shared tiny coffin. It never failed to bewilder him how the Lord could smile on some, while seeming so indifferent to others.

"If only there were some way to thank him," said Margaret, pulling away from August at last and wiping her streaming eyes. "I need to let him know how much this victory means to me."

"Send him a dozen roses," said August. "A singing telegram."

"Make him a cheese," said Evelyn, clapping. "The world's largest cheese!"

"Yes, a cheese." Margaret laughed. "That's what I'll do."

"A Mammoth Cheese," said Leland, abruptly sitting up in his chair. No one had noticed he was awake, and the three started at his sudden proclamation. From his dozing in the leather recliner, the

minister's silvery hair stood on end and a long crease scarred the
length of his cheek. For a moment August thought his father was
talking in his sleep.

"Dad?" said August worriedly.

"You must make him a Mammoth Cheese," Leland continued.
"You must make it and take it to Washington."

"Leland," asked Margaret gently, "what are you talking about?"

"August, tell her the story," ordered his father, now completely
awake and growing more excited by the minute. "Tell her the story
of Jefferson's Mammoth Cheese."

"It's late, Dad," said August slowly.

"Tell it," Leland commanded.

"It's a very funny story from Jefferson's first term," August said
with a sigh, humoring his father. "Some Baptist patriots in Cheshire,
Massachusetts, were so thrilled with Jefferson's election and his promise
of religious freedom that they made him a one-thousand-two-hundred-
thirty-five-pound wheel of cheese and took it to Washington."

He told Margaret that it took a day's milking of nine hundred
Republican cows—no Federalist milk allowed. That it took six
months to make and transport—by sled, by sloop down the Hudson
River, and by cart to the nation's capital. One man joked that by the
time it reached Baltimore, it was strong enough to walk the rest of
the way. Jefferson's friend Charles Wilson Peale had recently discovered the bones of a mastodon, back then thought to be a wooly mammoth, and thus the cheese was immediately dubbed the Mammoth
Cheese by Jefferson's detractors who observed it on its way to
Washington. Ballads were written in its honor, tickets sold for its
viewing, fine speeches delivered. And on New Year's Day 1802, its
instigator, Elder John Leland—now called by some the Mammoth
Priest—delivered as fine an oration on the virtues of Republican-
ism and cheesemaking as August dared say had ever been heard.

"That was Orange County's Elder John Leland," Pastor Vaughn
told Margaret. "The one I'm named for. The one from Leland-
Madison Park."

A small bust and marker off nearby Route 20 commemorated the spot where the same Massachusetts preacher then living in Virginia, had sat under a tree with James Madison in 1788. If Madison would bring an amendment guaranteeing the tenets of religious freedom, Leland would deliver Virginia's Baptist vote to ratify the Constitution. It passed, and Leland had preached for many years in Orange County before retiring home to Cheshire and becoming more famous as the maker of Jefferson's Mammoth Cheese.

"If you want to thank the president," said Leland, "we could stage a reenactment. People love reenactments—just look at how many show up for the battles at Gettysburg and Manassas every year. A new cheese for a new president."

"Leland, that's a lovely idea," said Margaret kindly, "but I could never make a cheese like that."

"Why not?" he asked.

"I don't know how to, for one thing," she answered. "I don't have anything to hold that much milk."

"We could build something," said Leland.

She smiled sympathetically. "A lot goes into making a cheese. I would have to set it and cut the curd. How would I press something so big?"

"How did they do it in Massachusetts?" Pastor Vaughn turned to his son.

"They used a cider press, but—"

"Alan Franklin has a cider press," said the priest. "It's collecting dust in his barn."

Margaret was growing a little annoyed at his insistence. "A twelve-hundred-pound cheese would take over twelve thousand pounds of milk, and I only have two dozen cows."

"But that's what's so beautiful about the original cheese," insisted Leland. "It wasn't about any one farmer. The entire community brought their day's milking. They came together like a family and worked in service of a single ideal," he exclaimed. "Medicine and science have brought nothing but tragedy to this town. But—history. History is something Three Chimneys understands."

"Dad," interposed August, alarmed at his father's perseverance, "a cheese that size would take months, and Margaret doesn't have a lot of time. Her farm is in foreclosure."

"Oh," said Evelyn, blushing on Margaret's behalf. Margaret frowned at August for alluding to her difficulties, especially since Adams Brooke's winning the election would now solve them.

"I didn't know," said Leland soberly. "But all the more reason to pull together. If you file an appeal, you are guaranteed a hundred fifty days before any action is taken."

"That's only five months," said Evelyn.

Margaret had instantly dismissed Leland's wild proposal until August had challenged her by suggesting it couldn't be done. Five months. That gave Brooke three months once he took office in January to pass the Family Matters Act, and with it the amnesty. His birthday was just about five months from now, on April 6, and it would take just about that long to ripen a young Cheshire cheese.

"I could preach a sermon next Sunday to ask for donations," urged Leland. "You'll only bear the cost of your labor. Think about it, Margaret, won't you? Not just for Brooke or yourself, but for Three Chimneys? For us all?"

Margaret's agitated brain spun back on itself, and she couldn't believe she was considering saying yes. A twelve-hundred-pound cheese? She knew larger cheeses had been made, but in factories and by people who knew what they were doing. She was insane to contemplate it, but Leland's shining, hopeful face seemed to be willing her to try. She turned to August, who had grown very quiet.

"Mr. Jefferson, you were the first recipient," Margaret said. "Is this an utterly crazy idea? What do you say about it?"

August could have said many things, for much was in his heart. He could have said that the first Mammoth Cheese became a nationwide joke and Elder Leland went home too depressed to preach for many years afterward. Or that along the way, the cheese generated maggots at its core, and most of it had to be cut away, dumped into the Potomac. Or he might have declared honestly and with great heaviness of heart that this was a country wherein anything was possible, that America loved a large and pointless gesture, and that the orders generated by the publicity might very well save her farm. But then where would that leave him, poor ridiculous farmhand, with his useless proposal of marriage? His opportunity to save her would have passed him by. He could have said all this and more, but how could he, with good conscience, take away her last, long-shot chance to save herself?

"I guess it depends on how grateful you really are," he finally said.

That night, in the bed hewn by her grandfather, under the quilt sewn by her grandmother, Margaret Prickett dreamt not of dancing with the new president at his inaugural ball as she had the night before, but instead of meeting Brooke's long-sought eyes at last, over a giant wheel of cheese.

II

THE CHEESE

"Heaven above looked down, and awakened the
American genius, which has arisen, like a lion,
from the swelling of the Jordon [sic], and roared
like thunder in the states, *We will be free; we will rule
ourselves*."

—Elder John Leland

CHAPTER TWELVE

"Though we rarely think about it," said Pastor Leland Vaughn from his pulpit at St. Barnabas the Sunday after the first Tuesday in November, "a word, like a person, has a life span. Some die having out-lived their use, while others are born to take their place."

Pastor Vaughn looked out over his congregation, who sat in warm wool sweaters and carefully pressed blazers, a wash of color in the pews like a child's paint-by-number. After a few fitful starts, the weather had turned, and a cold November rain beat against the clear panes of glass in the chapel windows. Far off in the distance, he heard morning thunder; not a boom, but rather a long, low rumble like a large herd anxious to get home. The dark gray sky pressed in, serving only to heighten the contrast between the world outside and his bright and welcoming church.

"So, in 1801, when Elder John Leland set out to make his cheese for President Jefferson, he could not have conceived of it as *mammoth*. Large maybe, or imposing, but not mammoth, in the sense we know it, for that word was only just taking its first toddling steps into the world. You see, earlier that year Charles Wilson Peale began displaying the reconstructed skeleton of the woolly mammoth he found in upstate New York. He sold tickets to see her in his museum of curiosities, took her on the road to England, even hosted a dinner party inside her massive rib cage. Single-handedly, he created a craze for all things mammoth.

"Now, when Thomas Jefferson's political enemies, who considered the president's archaeological leanings frivolous, got wind of the enormous cheese in Massachusetts," he continued, "they immediately snatched up the word 'mammoth' and flung it against the Elder Leland's heartfelt gift. The Republican Cheshire became the

Mammoth Cheese; the patriotic John Leland, the Mammoth Priest.
The Federalists meant it as a joke—see how stupid these backwoods
zealots can be? Their gift is as absurd as the reconstruction of a pile
of old bones. And yet the joke was soon to be on them. This homespun, heartfelt, *mammoth* gesture appealed to the populist spirit of
most Americans. The Federalists' elitism foreshadowed their own
inevitable extinction, as must be the case for any group who does
not instinctively understand that this is a country that likes its ges-
tures large."

Pastor Vaughn was gratified to hear the chuckles from his congregation. He had surprised them this morning by calling on their
help to make a 1,235-pound wheel of cheese for transportation to
Washington. He asked them for provisions. He asked them for money.
He asked them for their time and enthusiasm in aid of a neighbor
whose farm was struggling. His parishioners, grateful not to be reminded of the poor Franks, were sitting up straighter and listening
intently. Pastor Vaughn looked down at his sermon notes, and spoke
sincerely.

"Now, friends, it might interest you to know another familiar
word entered the English language only a few years ahead of 'mammoth.' It is one you might imagine had been with us always, and yet
it made its first appearance in the Federalist Papers, which argued our
duty to our country. That word is 'responsibility.' Certainly 'burden'
had been with us a good long while, and we had even been 'responsible' for each other as early as the late sixteenth century, but it wasn't
until 1786, when wrestling with what our nation should become, that
the term 'responsibility' meaning a charge, or a trust, or a sacred
duty—came to be used. Thanks to our neighbor James Madison, we
now have a *sense* of responsibility, a state of being, and a place in
which to dwell.

"I tell you today, friends, we have a mammoth responsibility to
aid one another. I know not all of you voted for Adams Brooke, and
here I am asking you to participate in a project that will magnify him.
But like the Confederate and Union war veterans who donned their

tattered uniforms and re-created Gettysburg, we should understand, as they did, that more important than which side you fought on, are Life's defining battles.

"So I say, let's invite the cameras back! America deserves to see the real soul of Three Chimneys, not weighted down with death and tragedy, but lifted up in celebration of all that is natural and fruitful of the earth."

From the upturned, excited faces, Pastor Vaughn knew he had them. He bowed his head.

"Let us pray," he said.

November 21 was the day set for the cheesemaking, and that morning Polly woke stiff from sleeping curled tightly in a ball. Every winter, her mother promised to get heat upstairs, and every winter they continued to make do with the single oil stove in the living room that exploded on every twenty minutes or so. Polly pinched the tip of her numb nose and tried to visualize her morning routine so that she could get through it with no wasted moments of indecision. Leap from the bed and race to the bathroom. Warm your shins before the space heater—front, then back. Wash your face, but not your hair, (a rule she'd learned after running her brush once too often through crisply frozen locks). One, two, three, go! she told herself. But her body refused to move. Instead, she longed to nestle deeper under the quilt and return to the dream she was having of Mr. March—not even a romantic dream, just the two of them eating breakfast together at a small red table. She was having pancakes and he was eating cantaloupe. Her stomach growled at the memory.

"Polly!" called her mother from downstairs. "Get up!"

Mr. March set down his spoon, and reluctantly, Polly flung off her blankets. She ran to the bathroom, where Margaret had thoughtfully left the space heater running by the sink, but it took her only a moment to realize this was no maternal act of solicitude. Damn it, Polly cursed as she tried first the hot and then the cold tap. The pipes

had frozen. It was her responsibility to keep a lightbulb warm against
the leaders in the pump house, and she had let it burn out. The
morning was not starting well.

"I don't ask that much of you," Margaret said when Polly, unwashed and fully dressed, slunk downstairs. "What are we supposed
to do if someone needs to use the toilet?"

Her mother didn't look up from the cheddar biscuits she was
rolling on the long kitchen table. She slammed the rolling pin, raising a cloud of flour; rolled and dusted, turning as she went. She
punched out twelve perfect circles with an old tin can and slid them
onto a greased pan. The kitchen smelled of melting cheese, which,
so early in the morning, made Polly want to gag.

"I didn't realize it would get so cold last night," she said.

"It's been below freezing for a week now," answered Margaret.
She took the biscuits to the oven and swapped raw for cooked. When
the hot biscuits cooled, they would join the mountain she'd baked
last night; poor recompense, Polly thought, for the farmers donating
an entire milking. She walked to the kitchen pantry and rummaged
for a hundred-watt lightbulb.

"Today of all days," said Margaret.

"Okay, I'm sorry," Polly snapped, and pulling on her boots and
coat, left her mother furiously pounding.

Outside, across the yard, August kindled a fire in the rusted old
oil drum they used to burn their trash, the gristly smoke blending with
the gray dawn and darker gray silhouette of the looming cheese vat
nearby. Within days of Pastor Vaughn's sermon, her mother's Mammoth Cheese had replaced the Frank Eleven as the favorite topic of
conversation at Three Chimneys Junior High. The Pep Club printed
buttons that read "More Cheese Please" (illustrated with a holey slice
that Polly felt compelled to point out was Swiss, not Cheshire), and
even the boys, who had mercilessly ridiculed poor Manda and her
family, were intrigued by the prospect of meeting the president. Anything was possible, they decided among themselves, and maybe, if
they were lucky, they'd be there the day the president took a bullet.
After enduring hours of cheese talk at school, Polly would come home

to find August digging a pit in the side yard, or her mother fielding calls from neighbors: Alan Franklin offered up his large cider press— little good it did him now that the government had gotten so prickly about E. coli; and Speedy Sheet Metal promised a homemade vat and form. Margaret swallowed her pride and took donations of lumber and rope, pulleys, and burlap. Then every night she left Polly to do the dinner dishes while she went to the cheese house, trading in her intuition for the safer methods of science. From the window over the kitchen sink, Polly watched her mother, in her white apron and boots, puzzling like a scientist over the best way to impregnate thirteen thousand pounds of milk.

"Morning," called August.

Polly waved dully as she worked the stiff wooden latch to the lean-to pump house. Inside it was dark and cold as a crypt. August watched her sympathetically.

"Pipes freeze?" he asked. She nodded.

"Yard's frozen, too," he said. "I'm going to lay down some straw."

She watched him head back to the warm barn while she lowered herself to the ground. Above her head ran a circulatory system of lead and copper pipes leading from the ancient mechanical pump into the kitchen and up the wall to the bathroom. She sucked in her breath and shimmied beneath them, catching her hair on bug husks and bits of broken plaster. Her nose brushed the icy pipes; she blinked against sleepy, unseen spiderwebs, feeling rather than seeing the panicked weavers hoist themselves out of reach. Something had died, for the small room smelled like an unwashed meat locker. Gingerly, Polly felt around until she found the socket where the old light had burned out, and screwed in its replacement. Now, in the naked glare, she could see the long shadows of spiderwebs and the mouse carcass in the corner. Sharp, short icicles dripped from the main water lead like a row of teeth. Sometimes she wondered if her mother gave birth to her solely to relieve herself of jobs like this. Adams Brooke got a cheese while she got buried alive.

She quickly slid out at the sound of a truck in the driveway, then brushed the droppings from her coat. The donating farmers weren't expected until after their own milkings, sometime after seven. As she watched, a white van with a corkscrew antenna and side-panel logo pulled up close to the house. She recognized it from the early weeks of the Frank Eleven.

"Mom," Polly called, "someone from Channel 5 is here."

In the kitchen, Margaret was sprinkling homemade cheddar into another batch of biscuits. She had been baking since last night but was afraid to stop, unsure of how many people would show up today. When she heard Polly call, she pulled on her heavy wool jacket and stepped out to join her daughter. Channel 5? What could they possibly want? A tall, bright-toothed man she remembered seeing at Chase Andrew Frank's funeral stepped out from the driver's side. Then the passenger door swung open, and out leapt smiling Pastor Vaughn.

"Look who I brought," he exclaimed, escorting the driver around to meet them. "Margaret, Polly, you know Patrick Lewis, Foster's cousin?"

Patrick Lewis, weatherman and features reporter for the local Fox affiliate, had the same handsome, saturnine features as his first cousin, though years in front of a lens had kept his fleshy physique vertical, in contrast to the newspaper editor's slowly spreading horizontal. He stretched out his hand, and Margaret reluctantly took it.

"Patrick was kind enough to inquire after Manda," Pastor Vaughn explained. "So I told him all about our cheese. He wants to feature us on the nightly news."

"I'm sorry for your town's loss," said Patrick Lewis, gravely. "It's been a difficult autumn." Before Margaret could respond, Patrick directed a cameraman who had followed him out of the van to begin filming. He pointed his camera at the enormous vat in the yard. Margaret pulled the priest aside.

"Leland, what is this all about?" she whispered.

"He wants you to give Channel 5 an exclusive. He'll check in every few weeks, and come along to Washington—he wants to follow this cheese from beginning to end.

"I don't think that's a good idea—," she began.

"Nonsense. Why not let the world see how excited we are about our new president?" exclaimed Leland. Then, leaning in, he conspiratorially added, "And if they find out we have a world-class cheese-maker in our midst, well, that's fine too."

"This is supposed to be a thank-you," Margaret said, "not a publicity stunt."

"I know, I know," the priest assured her. "But why shouldn't you benefit a little? You've worked so hard, and we're proud of you. Anyway, who could we trust more than Patrick? He's practically family."

From across the yard, Margaret watched the reporter warm his hands over the fire August had kindled. Behind him, his cameraman circled the vat, taking in its cedar slats, its reinforced barrel rings, its polished, modified beer tap. He panned her barn and made his way over to her whitewashed stone cheese house. His hand was on the door before Margaret remembered the sign above the door.

"That's just where I keep my supplies," she said quickly, rushing over to stop him from trying the knob. "Please turn the camera off."

The cameraman looked to Patrick, who, with a sigh, gestured for him to comply. The reporter reluctantly left the fire and walked up to Margaret, fixing in place his most winningly apologetic smile, the one he used to announce freezing rain the day of the Christmas Parade or thunderclouds for the Fourth of July.

"Of course we don't want to trouble you," he said. "Leland warned me you might not be so gung-ho about our little idea. It's just that when I heard about your cheese, I thought, This is exactly what our country needs right now. Something wholesome and patriotic after all we've been through. I thought it was the perfect story."

"I appreciate that," said Margaret, relieved to see the red camera light go dark. "But it's important to me that this cheese not be misconstrued. It is merely to thank Adams Brooke for his belief in the small farmer, nothing more."

"Of course, I understand," said Patrick sadly. "It's a shame we didn't even get to meet Mr. Jefferson."

"What do you mean?" she asked.

"I told him about August, too," confided Leland, more subdued now than when he'd bounded out of the news van. "He never thinks about his future, and I thought if he got on TV, he'd surely get booked into every veterans' hall and high school in Virginia."

Margaret stood guiltily before the priest. "I don't think August wants that sort of attention," she said.

"I suppose you're right," said Leland. "You probably know him better than I do."

"Why don't we ask him ourselves," said Patrick, catching sight of August in the barn door, bent under a heavy bale of straw. He beckoned for Leland and his cameraman to follow. "Excuse me, Mr. President! Fox would like to request an interview."

"You're not considering letting this man film us?" asked Polly when she and Margaret found themselves alone.

"Of course not," said Margaret crossly. Through the back door window, she saw the kitchen tap shudder, belching air and rust. A moment later, hot water gushed into the sink.

"Go inside and wash up," Margaret told Polly. "We have a lot to do before everyone arrives."

Polly marched inside and slammed the door, and Margaret turned to August, who held his bale before him like a shield. Every night for the past few weeks, he had worked at the farm until nearly twelve, digging in frozen ground, fashioning tools for Margaret's use. She had to bring him plates of food when he wouldn't break for dinner. He had been against it, but once he saw Margaret was determined to make the Mammoth Cheese, he had stood by her every step of the way. Now Patrick was explaining his idea—Thomas Jefferson would present the new Mammoth Cheese to President Brooke. A passing of the torch, so to speak—August would be half the story. Patrick would see to it, he said, that August became the second most famous president alive today.

"No thank you," said August, shaking his head in embarrassment. "I could never use Jefferson that way. It goes against my philosophy."

"What's a philosophy, son," asked his father, "when you could not only help yourself and Margaret, but bring happiness to an entire town?"

"No, I respect your son's opinion," said Patrick sadly. "It's just a shame. You know congressmen watch a good deal of TV. If they saw how greatly their constituents favored the amnesty, I would imagine they might have a pretty hard time voting against it."

The reporter's words brought August up short. Congress. He hadn't even considered that he and Margaret, so far from power, might somehow affect the outcome of the amnesty. He glanced over at Margaret, who now stared at the reporter with a little of her old campaign intensity. Is this what she wanted? he wondered. If he was with her, was he not with her all the way?

"Your costume is in the truck, isn't it, son?" asked Pastor Vaughn. "Why not put it on. It would be such a help to everyone."

"Margaret?" August asked, willing her to look at him. What do you want from me? he silently asked. But Margaret appeared as confused as he, looking from Patrick Lewis to the ground, to her cheese house, and to the ground again. For a long moment she didn't speak.

"I wouldn't want you to do anything you didn't feel comfortable doing," she said at last.

He couldn't read her expression, but there was no mistaking the look of eagerness on his father's face or the calm assurance on Patrick Lewis's. Who wouldn't want to be on TV, the reporter seemed to be saying. It was every American's dream.

"I suppose it could make a good story," replied August slowly.

"Great!" said Patrick Lewis. "So, Margaret—Mr. Jefferson is on board. Won't you please let us film your cheese?"

August watched her closely. Looking away from them, she gave a curt, miserable nod.

"Well, then, let's have an interview before everyone else arrives," said Patrick, clapping his hands. "America is going to love this!"

It happened so quickly, August could barely comprehend it. He walked back to his pickup truck like a man condemned and retrieved his costume from where it hung, just back from the dry cleaner, in the passenger-side window. *This will be great for him*, he overheard his father tell Patrick Lewis. *The thing about my son is that he never thinks of* himself.

August stepped into the kitchen, where something was burning. With the arrival of the news van, Margaret had forgotten her last batch of biscuits; when he opened the hot oven, their tops were deep golden, but the bottoms had burned black. He slid them from the oven and left them to cool on the counter. Slowly, he made his way up the back staircase to Margaret's bedroom and there undressed before her pier mirror, stepping out of his crusty overalls and into the white hose and buckled shoes of a president. He pulled on his blue silk jacket and draped his cravat around his neck. All that remained was his wig, resting forlornly on the bed. It was silly, he knew, but ever since he'd begun portraying Jefferson, August had felt a nearly mystical connection to his wig. In the breeches and hose, he was still August Vaughn, but once he fit that powdered wig into place, he felt himself, oddly, slipping into the head of his hero. And he continued to be Jefferson until he took it off at the end of his program and reluctantly returned to himself. Now, with a feeling of treachery, he picked it up.

"Knock, knock." Margaret stood in the hall, fearful of barging in on him naked. She inched open the door.

"Come in."

He glanced at her in the mirror. She was wearing his favorite sweater, an olive turtleneck she'd knit herself. He'd been unable to take his eyes off her all morning.

"Are you sure you're all right with this?" she asked.

He smiled weakly. "If it will help you . . ."

"I want it to help *you*," she said. "If I lose the farm, you should have something . . ."

"Don't," he said.

She reached up and gently wrapped his cravat, once, twice around, adjusting the knot as she would have her husband's tie. "You've thrown your lot in with me," said Margaret softly. "You should get something out of it."

He closed his eyes. "I feel weird using my costume this way."

"You shouldn't," Margaret said, smiling at him. "You look very handsome in it."

She took the lightly powered wig from his hand and placed it rakishly on his head. "Come on, Mr. President," she said, raising on tiptoe to kiss his cheek. "Let's go make some cheese."

Farwood Purdy from Hollywell Farm and Sam Abbott from all the way down in Hanover were the next to arrive, their pickup trailers rattling with ten-gallon capped pails like buoys in a storm. Soon after, in a steady stream, came all the stringy farmers of Pastor Vaughn's wide acquaintance, men who still maintained their adolescent habit of chewing Red Man long after everyone else's gums had freckled with cancer. With their prematurely gray crew cuts and pond water eyes, they appeared an entire generation ahead of Margaret, rather than a scant few years. In the seats beside them sat their disapproving wives, only a few of whom helped out physically, most opting instead to manage the books and look after the kids. Some of the kinder wives pitied Margaret her hard existence, left without a father or husband and forced to do all the filthy work herself, while a decided majority thought she got just what she deserved. A woman who didn't own a washing machine and was too proud to microwave a baked potato from time to time was a woman married to her own misery. And now it was up to their overworked husbands to help her out of trouble.

Margaret shook their hands hello, passing out cheese biscuits and coffee like party favors. None of the other wives made cheese, and so they wondered at Margaret's vat, her paddle for stirring, the knife August had rigged from two-by-fours and baling wire. She patiently explained to them how she would heat the milk and add the culture, drain off the whey and transport the cut curd by bucket to the modified cider press in the barn. All the while, she watched the farmers pass pails of milk down a chain like water to a house fire. Over fifteen hundred gallons she needed. By ten o'clock, to her amazement, her neighbors had provided it.

More people arrived, and more press. The *Richmond Times-Dispatch* sent a stringer, and Foster Lewis sent his photographer from the *Three Chimneys Register*. Margaret had borrowed an industrial-sized thermometer from a candy factory in Richmond, and August let her know the milk had reached its proper temperature. The time had come for her to step forward and take over. As the cameramen recorded, Margaret climbed the stepladder and stared down into the deep, white, steaming pool. Who knew what her neighbors fed their livestock? Or with what they were injected? For all that she appreciated and desperately needed their assistance, Margaret couldn't help but worry that this melting pot approach (some of the farmers had provided Guernsey milk, some Brown Swiss, but most had donated thin, insipid Holstein) might be the undoing of her finished cheese. She would do her best with what she had to work with, but perfection, she knew, might very well elude her. An inferior cheese could be her Faustian bargain for having any cheese at all.

It's too late now, she told herself, feeling the camera lens trained on her face. For all her skill, Margaret knew she could only stand back and watch this cheese take shape, stepping in to guide it when she could, urging it along, but ultimately, for all her nurturing, at the mercy of its nature. She took up her sterilized canoe paddle and stirred in her carefully prepared culture. Crouching in his jacket and breeches, August worked a set of bellows to raise the temperature and fed more wood to the fire. Margaret drizzled in a quart of annatto for coloring—another concession to Pastor Vaughn and Patrick Lewis, who swore America would never accept anything but an orange cheese—then stirred in a steady stream of her carefully measured sharp, brown rennet.

Margaret looked across the vat to August, who stood with his wig askew. He studied the steaming pool anxiously, knowing as well as she the prankish property of milk to appear almost unchanged while undergoing its metamorphosis until, without warning, it set in an instant. Had she calculated correctly? Would they be humiliated on the nightly news? Margaret looked for success in August's eyes as he continued to scan the surface of the cheese like a cat after fish. An eternity seemed to pass, magnified by the polite cough or the restless shifting. A smaller batch would have set already, and as the minutes passed, Margaret steeled herself for failure. Forget it, drain the vat, she was about to tell him, when just then a wide smile spread over August's face and, to her infinite relief, Margaret looked down to discover something new and wonderful, fully formed between them.

When Polly was four, her grandfather threw a barbecue for his sixtieth birthday. It was among her earliest memories—neighbors scattered on blankets in the dappled shade, the ladies tucking their bare legs under their skirts. She ran in the hayloft with the older children, sipping lemonade in a can through stray bits of straw that stuck to her lips. Her grandfather had dug a pit in the side yard, just where August excavated his for the cheese, and outfitted it with a heavy iron spit. All morning and into the afternoon, her grandfather turned a whole pig, its bristly hide boiled and shaved, its front and rear hooves nailed to a plank. Throughout the day, until one of her parents would shoo her away, Polly returned to watch the pig roast. In the morning, it was an opaline pink; by late afternoon, a deep charred mahogany, dripping fat onto the glowing coals. As the pig's slanted eyes turned, she would follow it with her head, trying to imagine what it saw. The canopy of trees. A cloud shaped like a smiling crocodile, then the slow devolution to roots, and feet, and budding clover. Polly's father and grandfather lifted the finished pig from its spit and laid it on a wooden picnic table, where oily juice dripped down into the grass. Then the neighbors—those hard-drinking bachelors picking bluegrass by the creek, those boys and girls playing spin the bottle in the dusty hayloft, their tired mothers with late-in-life dozing babies— all gathered around the pig. Its skin had been scored every eight inches or so and peeled back from the flesh as if it were a prickly pineapple. As Polly watched, her grandfather sharpened his carving knife and sawed through layers of skin and fat to reach the succulent white meat below. She stood in line and held out her paper plate like all the rest, but the heavy slice bent her thin wrists backward and her plate fell to the ground.

That barbecue was the last time Polly had seen so many people at Prickett Farm at once. But now Mr. Tinton and Mrs. Larette, the church organist; Coach Emery and Bob Crenshaw all watched in awe as her mother drew her oversized wire knife through the mass of curd, slicing it into a checkerboard of small squares. The curd released its whey and August tapped the vat, siphoning the river into another tub from which Margaret would make whey cheese later. Now instead of lining up for barbecue, her neighbors queued up for the buckets August filled, ferrying the curd like the shuttle run Polly had endured in grammar school. Pick up pails from August, limp it across the frozen yard to Margaret at the mouth of the barn, where she eased it into the massive cheesecloth-lined form donated by Speedy Sheet Metal. Run the empty buckets back to August, where two more neighbors took over, the loop continuing for hours. And always there was the camera. Her mother the purist, who wouldn't let her watch TV, who was so afraid of commercialization she brought her own Band-Aids to Polly's pediatrician rather than risk Mickey Mouse being taped to Polly's butt. Her mother the hypocrite. Polly watched Patrick Lewis pan their farm, instructing his cameraman to zoom in on the cows in the pasture, the rusted pitchfork leaning against the cheese house. He focused on the farmers as they spat their chaw rather than the neighbors who drove up in expensive cars, and took an extensive amount of footage of one of the barn cats intently licking its privates. She overheard him laughing with Bob Crenshaw. *Curd. It even sounds funny, doesn't it?* he said. *Curd?*

Polly wandered away from the crowd, up to her old chimney. From her perch high above, she could watch Mrs. Winston and Mrs. Dickinson, whom she had last seen in a heated argument on School Street over the bill for a fruit basket sent to Manda Frank's hospital room, now race each other with heavy buckets, slipping and falling, and laughing like schoolgirls. Their husbands stood nearby, arms folded, leaning in, sharing a joke at their wives' expense. To Polly, the yard had become a long, chaotic dinner table, anchored at one end by August, doling out his curd like a first course, and by Margaret at the other, emptying plates. But how could Margaret accept favors from these people? Down in the yard, Polly watched more cars arrive, their greens and reds shining through their crusts of road salt like nuggets in a dusty creek bed. She stared dully and only barely registered one smaller car pull in behind a row of mini-vans and pickups. Dressed all in black, its owner moved through the purple and teal parkas of the crowd like a speck of antimatter, carving a channel toward the house. She watched curiously until suddenly she recognized the figure; then Polly was up, and racing down the hill.

"Mr. March!" she cried. "Mr. March!"

"Here you are," he said, when, out of breath, she finally reached him. "I was worried I'd come all this way to find you conveniently absent."

"If only," gasped Polly. "Oh, Mr. March, it's been awful. Much worse than a candlelight vigil."

Her teacher wore a black pea coat over black jeans and a black sweater. His black baseball cap was the only one, she saw, that sported the name of a team rather than a tractor company. She stood help-lessly before him, unable to believe he was here.

"Well, I have braved the hordes," said Mr. March. "Am I to be denied a glimpse of the Mammoth Sleaze?"

Polly collected herself and boldly led the way. Glancing over, she watched him take in her farm—the exfoliated bricks of her house, and the botched operation of her screened porch, where Margaret had attempted to repair the rips with wire and the metal mesh from their fly swatters. She saw his eyes range over the crush of neighbors in the side yard, their bulky, unfashionable clothes and grinning faces. Pastor Vaughn stood by Patrick Lewis, encouraging two of her school-mates who were staggering under the weight of their pails.

"Is that the weatherman from Channel 5?" asked Mr. March.

"Mom's letting him film the cheese. He wants to go with us to Washington."

"Indeed?" Mr. March's raised eyebrow managed to convey all the contempt Polly herself was feeling. She led him to the side yard, where August now hung over the rim of the vat, reaching for the last shovelfuls of curd. All across the yard, spilled steaming whey had cooled into long white finger lakes, which the barn cats lapped eagerly. Here it is, she said, nodding to the vat. Her neighbors had kicked dirt into the pit to kill the fire beneath it.

"I once had a most enjoyable party in a hot tub about that size," said Mr. March blandly.

Polly blushed, imagining herself and Mr. March naked inside the cheese vat. August stood up at that moment, and seeing her, gave her a bright smile.

"And who's that?" Mr. March asked, nodding to August. "I saw him in the schoolyard on Election Day."

"That's just some guy who works for my mom," she said, quickly turning away. "He likes to dress up as Thomas Jefferson."

"Ah, a Founding Father fetish," said Mr. March with a wicked smile. "I've seen the type before. I bet he doesn't know Ho Chi Minh was a Jefferson buff as well."

Mr. March leaned in, and Polly could smell the cigarettes on his wool coat. She felt wildly daring speaking about communist leaders, with her neighbors standing just out of earshot. Her mother had tried to make this day as miserable as possible for her, but now Mr. March was here, and Polly felt reborn. In the doorway to the barn, Polly noticed, Margaret was taking a rest from the marathon curd transfer. Sweating even in the cold, she had stripped down to a thin white T-shirt, and was lifting her wet hair from the back of her neck. Mr. March turned and followed Polly's gaze.

"There's my mother," said Polly, with the sickening realization that Margaret and Mr. March were exactly the same age. Her teacher made no response, but continued to stare as Margaret drew an elastic from the front pocket of her jeans and secured the loose bun she'd made.

"Do you want to meet her?" Polly asked weakly. He turned back to face her.

"I'd rather meet your calves," he said.

He could have made no better answer, and Polly fairly danced to the barn, leading him not past her mother and the crowd by the

press but through the side lot, into the back. The barn was dark after
the bright sun outside and it took a moment for their eyes to adjust.
Beside her, Mr. March breathed deeply, and Polly, so used to the grassy
smell of hay and manure she didn't notice it any longer, quickly apologized. "I'm sorry it stinks in here," she said.

"No, it's nice," he said.

She led him past the wooden stalls and the curious older girls,
past Sultana, who swung her head and pranced away when Polly
reached out to stroke her. The two moon-eyed calves lay curled together in a corner, wedged under their feed trough. Though they
watched warily from the shadows, neither rose as Polly let Mr. March
into their stall. He hesitated, not having touched livestock since the
infant petting zoo at Central Park, and then it had been a goat with
intrusive lips and blank, rapacious eyes that he'd gingerly approached.
Polly told him not to be afraid, they wouldn't bite. He crouched down
before them and slowly stroked their necks.

"They like you," she said.

"So this is what you do when you're not in class?" he said.

"Mostly," she replied, then asked boldly, "What do you do?"

"Wonder about my students." He smiled. "Mostly."

Mr. March scratched the twins behind the ears and squirmed
when the female licked him with her long, velvety tongue. "It was a
good bargain you made," he said. "These calves for Adams Brooke."

Adams Brooke again. Polly scowled at the name. In the doorway of the barn, the bright light of the camera captured the last few
relays of curd. Those in the yard cheered the weatherman as he gamely
joined in the cheesemaking, mugging for the camera and letting the
priest get ahead of him. She looked back to Mr. March, kneeling
before her calves. Mr. March dressed all in black like a partner in
crime. Mr. March, the only person who had thought of her all day.

"Come with me," she said. "I have something else I want to show
you."

She led him through the side lot, skirting her mother, who was
unfurling a sail of filmy cloth and draping it over the face of the cheese.
Everyone in the yard gathered round as August lowered an enormous

wooden disk cut to fit the form. He and Margaret each grasped an end of the screw's handle and tugged, raising a groan from the ancient cider press. Tighter and tighter they screwed, forcing whey from the bottom in a thousand tiny trickles. Polly led her teacher to the old stone cheese house and let them inside, pulling the door behind them.

It was easily ten degrees colder inside the thick-walled building than it was outside, though a slanted beam through the window warmed a single pane on the floor. Polly had been inside the cheese house a hundred times, but never without her mother, and she felt more like a thief here on her own property than she had breaking into Mr. March's car or the empty school. Margaret's glass jars of cheese knives and her hand-labeled specimens of culture gave the room the feel of a mad scientist's laboratory, not helped by the portentously ripe aroma coming from the cellar below. Outside, a muffled cheer rose from the crowd, but inside, all was still and cool, and expectant.

"Do you remember a few weeks ago, you said I was going to have to start making decisions for myself?" Polly asked, leading him farther into the small room. They were up against Margaret's long wooden shelf, upon which stood a tightly clamped Caerphilly. "Take a look," she said.

For as long as Polly had been alive, their motto had hung from a square-headed nail. *Omnis pecuniae pecus fundamentum,* flowed the words in a perfectly fluid antique cursive; indeed, it had been said no one in Three Chimneys could match Polly's great-grandfather for penmanship. If her mother wanted to invite the television cameras, she thought, let them have something to film. Together she and Mr. March would take down this sign and present it to Patrick Lewis in the yard, and Adams Brooke would be exposed, once and for all. Polly turned and swept her arm toward the space above the door, but to her astonishment, all she saw was the iron nail, like an obscene whisker. She glanced swiftly around the room—into the dark corner where the mop was propped, beneath the counter stacked with white plastic buckets and lids, and back to the nail again, as if her eyes had betrayed her and it had been there all along, safely encased in glass, mounted in its prudent black frame.

"What am I looking at?" asked Mr. March softly.

But for the moment, Polly had forgotten her teacher. In two long steps she was at the door, which she flung open so forcefully, it shook the jars on the shelves. Over in the barn, August and Margaret each took hold of a rope August had rigged from the rafters and, on the count of three, heaved the half-ton cheese high above the crowd. They caught their breath and heaved again, tugging it higher on its straining ropes, blinking against the warm white rain.

"Polly," Mr. March repeated. "What am I looking at?"

By the time Margaret and August finished cleaning up, it was long past dark. Their shoulders throbbed from hefting buckets, their faces ached from smiling for the camera. At ten o'clock, August fell limply onto Margaret's battered old sofa, while she pulled the black-and-white TV from the closet. Polly had gone to her room hours ago without speaking to them, and when Margaret crept upstairs to ask if she wouldn't like to watch herself on television, she said no. To August's surprise and delight, when she returned, Margaret threw herself down beside him and settled her head in his lap. August strained not to move a muscle that might cause her to shift, his arms glued to the armrest of the sofa in an attempt to seem casual. She was filthy from the cheesemaking, sticky with dried milk, dusty and sour, but she had never been more beautiful to him than tonight, lit by the vacuum tube glow of the old television set.

"I don't know what I'm going to do with Polly." She sighed. "She's getting more defiant every day."

"She's a teenager," August said. "Remember what you were like back then."

"Not like this."

"I worked here, remember." August smiled. "I recall more than a few slammed doors over the years."

Margaret smiled in acknowledgment and stared up at him. He had long ago stripped off his deep-cuffed jacket and had worked in his waistcoat and breeches, his long cravat slowly unfurling from his neck. His wig lay with his jacket and his own damp, longish hair curled across his forehead.

"I wish men still dressed like this," she said.

"I do too. I kind of like it."

"It suits you," she said.

A double homicide in Lynchburg dominated the headlines and while the newscaster droned, Margaret closed her eyes. The blue light of the old black-and-white television bleached her skin to marble, and her lightly veined lids appeared heavy and serene as an effigy's. A scab of milk dotted her right eyebrow. August moved to brush it away, and she opened her eyes.

"Look, there we are," she said.

Tightly edited, the segment showed a montage of the day, from the milk's arrival to the pressed cheese's ascent. Patrick Lewis explained the project, promising frequent updates on the cheese throughout the winter. He closed with the interview August had given. Too bright and earnest, August thought; he sounded to himself like an eager student trying to please his teacher. *The greatest cheese in America for the greatest man in America*, he heard himself saying. *That's what they called it in my day.*

"I can't watch," he said, turning his face away. "I hate the sound of my voice."

"Don't be silly," she said. "You sound great. Very presidential."

The segment ended, and Patrick moved on to weather. Margaret sat up and gave August a pat on the knee. "I don't know about you," she said, "but I could sure use a cup of coffee."

"If I have the energy to lift it," he said, forcing a smile, not wanting her to leave.

"I'll start the water if you don't mind locking up the barn." She sprung to her feet as though they had not spent a punishing day of lifting and stirring. With great reluctance, he hoisted himself from the springless sofa.

Outside, the temperature had once again plummeted, and he stirred the fire they'd kept burning all day in the argus-eyed old oil drum. August looked back to the kitchen window, where Margaret moved behind a screen of flying sparks. Briskly, she ran her kettle under the spigot, struck a match, and ignited a burner. He watched her take matching coffee cups from the cabinet and gently blow them free of dust. It was in the everyday moments he loved her best, watching her when she was unaware, for she went through her life with such confidence, with the assurance that whatever she was doing at that instant was the one thing in the world that needed to be done, that and nothing else. He yearned for a life of such easy conviction, unclouded by doubt or crippling self-consciousness. In a moment she would fill the cup she had taken down for him and he would drink her hot coffee and then he would have to go home, their perfect day together ended. Another opportunity wasted. When Martha Jefferson lay on her deathbed, she had copied out a line from her husband's favorite book, *Tristram Shandy*.

> *Time wastes too fast:* she wrote, *every letter I trace tells me with what rapidity life follows my pen. The days and hours of it are flying over our heads like clouds of a windy day never to return . . .*

To which, Jefferson finding the incomplete line upon her counterpane, added:

> *. . . And every time I kiss thy hand to bid adieu, every absence which follows it, are preludes to the eternal separation which we are shortly to make!*

Jefferson had burned everything of Martha's—every letter, every likeness, every book—but he kept that one sentence he had finished for her, to remind himself that he and his love had once been the beginning and end of a single thought. Margaret passed from the window into the next room with what somehow seemed the finality of passing from his life altogether. He thought what it would mean to lose her as Jefferson had lost the only woman he had loved.

In the open barn door, August saw the suspended cheese, wedged between the thumbscrews of the cider press, suspended from the rafters like a cow airlifted from a forest fire. Once Jefferson himself had stood before an identical cheese and thought it a joke, but if he had been present at its creation, he too might have been awed by the massive scale of what they had made, its deadweight heft and dripping bottom, its pulsing ferment, as alive as any cell-dividing creature. If August held his breath he could almost hear it devouring itself, swapping liquid atom for solid, hardening into an entity that could crush him like a plinth from Stonehenge. He imagined, with a certain satisfaction, Margaret returning to the barn to find him flattened beneath it.

A bat flew down from the rafters, circled his head, and flew back again. His every sense was on fire tonight; he was keenly aware of the burning wood in the drum outside, the wet hay beneath his feet, the leathery hides of the sleeping cattle in their stalls. All day, he and Margaret had passed the pen between them, composing their cheese like a long, organic poem. Did he now dare ask her to complete the sentence he most longed to speak? Would she give the answer he desired? Under the great orange moon, August felt more hopeful than he ever had before, and in that vulnerable state, his Heart stirred and whispered to his Head, Release me, friend. We will never have a better chance than this.

Margaret stepped into the barn with two steaming cups of coffee. The shadow cast by the megalithic, suspended wheel fell over her face, giving her an almost sibylic countenance. How mysterious and chthonic she appeared to him at this moment, as if, should he ask her to, she might very well pronounce his fate. August did not know what had come over him, what sort of spell had been cast by the interplay of shadow and steam and rich, ripening smell of whey dripping like groundwater in a cave. Yet, even possessed as he was, he could not declare himself directly: I love you, Margaret. Will you be my wife? Instead, he picked his words carefully, and tried his best to sound lighthearted.

"This cheese came along in the nick of time," said August, his voice catching. "If you hadn't come up with a plan, I was going to ask you to marry me."

And then the infinite stretch of silence, more awful than any encounter with Jefferson's Megalonyx whose eyes were two balls of fire ranging in the darkness. Margaret stood motionless, holding her two cups of coffee as if cast in stone. He saw clearly the progression of emotions across her face. Surprise and confusion gave way to distress before resolving itself into what he could only interpret as pained compassion. She took up his pen, as he desired, but with a single, sad stroke, she struck him through.

"Lucky we made the cheese," she said at last, smiling weakly. "How could I have ever lived up to my role as first lady?"

She had meant to be kind, but he felt humored like a fanciful schoolboy. For the first time in his life, he wanted to rip the breeches and jacket from his body and fling them into the fire. He wanted to see the powdered wig go up in a hiss of acrid smoke. Far worse than laughing at him or despising him, she pitied him.

"It's late; I'd better get going," he said, needing to be out of there as fast as possible. She took a step to the side, blocking his exit, wordlessly commanding him to look at her. When he did, her large moist eyes were those of a merciful veterinarian who had just administered a lethal injection.

"Here," she said, holding out not a needle, but a cooling cup of coffee. "Take this for the road. You can bring the mug back tomorrow."

"Okay," he said, ducking past her. "Thanks."

"August——," Margaret called as he made swiftly for the exit. He tried to keep the hope off his face when he turned back to her, tried to damp down the redness in his cheeks.

"Adams Brooke will like this cheese, won't he?" she asked. "He won't think it's ridiculous?"

Ridiculous? Ridiculous? How on earth, thought August, could anything be more ridiculous than he?

CHAPTER THIRTEEN

"I can't believe I forgot to change the oil."

August drove silently down Interstate 64, casting a glance at his distraught father in the passenger seat. Leland was easily as religious about his oil changes as he was about his religion, and he attributed his bus's long life to his fanatical maintenance routine. To have forgotten an oil change amounted to an automotive venial sin.

"Dad, you didn't do any lasting harm. The mechanic said he could take care of it."

"But it's the principle," countered Leland. "It survived going into a ditch."

"We'll pick it up tomorrow. It will be fine."

"I need to keep that bus running long enough to take Margaret's cheese to Washington. She's counting on me."

August winced at the name and looked guiltily at the unreturned coffee mug from last night. It had rolled onto its side and wedged between the dashboard and windshield, where inside it he could see the last slick of undrunk grounds, her own slow-roasted brew, which last night had tasted bitter as hemlock, without the redeeming results. The mug was unreturned because he, himself, was unreturned. He had called Margaret this morning and told her he needed to take his father to the hospital for an MRI. Of course he wouldn't leave her in the lurch—he'd arranged for Glenn Mullins, a high school boy and treasurer of his Future Farmers of America chapter, to fill in for him. No, he didn't know if he would make the afternoon milking either—it depended on what the doctor said. But Glenn was willing to help out for as long as necessary.

After the phone call, he spent his morning lying in bed, listening to the second hour of a documentary on the Founding Fathers on his VCR—listening only, for no amount of will could turn him away from the wall at which he stared, noticing for the first time the uneven texture of its plaster and the thick raised vein that ran from floor to ceiling like an engorged esophagus. It had been years since he'd been in bed at this time of day, when the wan sun nudged through the transom window of the basement apartment and illuminated all the room's imperfections. Most of the spider cracks were covered by the spines of books, but this wall against which his bed rested was a Rosetta stone of nicks and hairline fissures, any one of which might be widened to reveal the room's former brick face. It was a converted cellar, after all, with all the damp, harkenings-back that cellars possess. You could put a skin of plaster over a thing, the very walls seemed to say, but you couldn't change its nature.

As he lay in bed until the extravagant hour of 8 A.M., August was denied even the solace of hating Margaret. No matter how hard he tried, he could not blame her for this numbing inertia, this fixed esophagal staring, this droning on of documentarians reading transcripts of letters in mock-urbane cadence some producer had decided signified "Colonial." August had only himself to blame. All his life he'd known that if he never spoke, he would never receive an unwelcome answer. He had lived by this truism since he was sixteen years old, and in one instant, one unguarded, hypnotic instant, he had thrown it all away.

"You must be awfully pleased to have the whole town take part in one of your Jefferson episodes. To be finally doing something useful with it," said Leland, returning his son's attention to the truck.

"What do you mean by 'useful'?" asked August. "When have I not been useful?"

"Oh, son, you know what I mean," said his father bluffly. "Using your costume and wig to help a neighbor instead of standing up there in the auditorium just talking about things. I'm simply saying it must feel good to get into some action."

August had never imagined his father saw him as so passive. Had he not spent the last eight years of his life educating and instructing his fellow citizens on their civil liberties? Did his father think his lectures had been nothing more than one long dress-up party? For a. moment, August wondered how what he did was so very different from his father's putting on a cassock and every Sunday quoting a man dead these last two thousand years, but then he remembered he was driving the frail person beside him for an MRI.

"It just amazes me I forgot that oil," said his father.

They pulled into University of Virginia Hospital half an hour early so that his father could fill out his paperwork, but Leland insisted on stopping by the pediatric ward first, to check on the Frank children. Of the eight still alive, five had gained considerable weight and been moved to the step-down nursery, but three were still struggling in the NICU. Leland had not spoken to Amanda and Jake in nearly a week, and was surprised to find them at the hospital with five car seats in tow.

"Good to see you, Pastor," said Jake, pumping the cleric's hand. "Can you believe today's the big day?"

August saw the look of confusion pass over his father's face, and then the dawning of embarrassed comprehension. The strongest five children were to go home today, and he had utterly forgotten.

"I'm sorry not to be able to put my bus at your service," said Leland regretfully. "It's in the shop."

"No trouble, no trouble," replied Jake. "You've done so much for us already."

Behind the glass, Manda strapped little Brianna into her donated EvenFlo infant seat, then adjusted the puckered elastic bow that denoted gender for bald female babies. She waved gravely to the priest.

"Manda's a little nervous bringing them home," said Jake. "With the oxygen and monitors and all. I told her the doctors wouldn't release them if they were worried, but you know how mothers are . . ."

"You have help lined up?" Leland asked. "I'm sure I put today's homecoming in the church bulletin."

"Manda's mom and my mom and her sister and a few ladies from the congregation. We'd had a whole lot more sign up, but it's three months later, and, well . . ."

"I'll stop by as soon as I'm done here," assured Leland.

"We couldn't put you through the trouble," said Jake.

"No trouble at all."

"We should see how your appointment goes," August chimed in, herding his father toward the door.

"Just cracked the old noggin." Leland waved off Jake's look of alarm. "Nothing to worry about. I'll see you all this afternoon."

They walked in abstracted silence to the lab, where Leland was handed a thick questionnaire to fill out. August settled himself on one of the interconnected narrow molded bucket seats such as one might find at McDonald's or a domestic airport, and picked up the only magazine in the room. October's cover of *American Child* magazine sported a milky-toothed, blue-eyed girl dressed as a pumpkin or a piece of candy corn, he couldn't tell which. Inside were an article on just how much Halloween candy a three-year-old should be allowed (one carefully chosen piece after dinner, treated as a dessert— even childless August had to chuckle at that one) and one titled, "What Every Parent Should Know About Latex Mask Allergies." On page 89 "Spooky Snackables for Young Ghouls" presented him with photo after photo of mellow orange American cheese dishes: oily rounds cut like jack-o'-lanterns and thin slices rolled into witches' fingers. He wondered how Margaret was getting along with Glenn Mullins, and if he was, even now, helping her tighten the screws on her ripening Cheshire. August gave himself a firm shake. He wasn't going to think about Margaret today. That was the point of not going to work.

"They ask here about glaucoma," Leland said, peering over his reading glasses. "Your great-uncle had glaucoma. Do you think that's relevant?"

"I think they mean mother or father."

"You're probably right," Leland said, nodding, and continued his inky scratching.

The inside back cover of October's *American Child* magazine was devoted to a full-page color photo of three last trick-or-treaters: two eight-year-old boys and a girl dressed as the Spirit of '76. They were freeze-framed as in the old painting, banging their drums and piping their fife, but something was different about this trio, August quickly realized. Their heads were wrapped with oozing bandages, and fake blood trickled from their mouths. A makeup artist had blackened the eyes of the towheaded girl in the middle and traced railroad track scars across the cheeks and foreheads of her two companions, so that they resembled nothing so much as battlefield corpses recalled to life. Who wanted to dress up as a boring old patriot for Halloween when you could be Zombie Liberty, or Rotting Freedom? The casualties of Independence out begging, August thought, and then tossed the issue aside in embarrassment. What was he doing looking at *American Child* magazine anyway? What right did a loveless, rough bachelor have reading a parenting magazine?

Leland shuffled up to the receptionist and handed over his medical history. She made a Xerox of his insurance card and told him to have a seat.

"I can't believe I forgot the Frank children were coming home today," Leland said, settling into the hard chair next to August. "What has gotten into me?"

"You've had a lot on your mind," replied his son.

"No more than usual."

"You're getting older, Dad," said August kindly.

"Look at these youngsters," said Leland, reaching for the magazine August had just discarded. "A couple years ago, you wouldn't have seen anyone dressing patriotically. Makes you feel good, doesn't it?"

But it didn't make August feel good. Any more than having the town rally around the cheese made him feel good. What was wrong with him today?

"Mr. Vaughn." A narrow-hipped nurse dressed in street clothes called the priest to the back. That she looked barely older than Polly did not inspire confidence in August.

"Do you want me to come in with you?" he asked his father.

"Just wait here," Leland answered. "I'll give you the grisly details when I'm done."

August sat with his hands in his lap and his long legs crossed at his bony ankles. He could get used to seeing himself in the kind of khaki, pleated dress pants he wore to the hospital today, letting his body slowly adjust to the newness of them like tender gums to a set of false teeth. He could wear crisp white poly-cotton shirts and rayon ties and thin-ribbed dress socks and shoes with tassels. He could trade in both his farmhand blue jeans and his Jefferson breeches and "join the world," as his father had urged him to do so many times in the past. Would it be so awful to let the horny calluses on his palms soften into kinder keyboard-reddened fingertips? Could he not take any number of office jobs where the most stressful decision he would face was choosing between Choco-Mints and Cheese Nibs from the break room vending machine? Margaret's debt was not his debt, after all; her needs were not his needs. He was a simple man, nothing more, just trying to get through this life with the least amount of pain, and here he had arranged his life to maximize his misery. Margaret Prickett stood for everything he hated: She was uncompromising, she was protectionist, she was positively Federalist in her worldview, and, worst of all, she expected the same level of absolutism from those around her. Why, with all this against her, should he love her?

"Excuse me, are you done with that?"

Lost in thought, August had not noticed the woman sitting opposite him. He hoped his face had not given away his furious internal diatribe.

"That magazine," she repeated. "Are you done?"

"Oh, yes," August apologized. "It's last month's."

"*American Child*?" she noted ruefully. "You'd think a hospital this size could at least afford a *Sports Illustrated* or *Malpractice Digest*."

August smiled at her joke. He could tell she was the sort of woman who had heeded her mother's advice to cultivate her personality, for her looks were quite plain. She was as pale and linear as a sheet of graph paper, with a long square face and shingled bangs, and a shelf of shoulder pads overhanging bony arms. Yet there was something familiarly appealing about her, August thought. She reminded him of his one and only relationship beyond what he'd suffered with Margaret, another Chautauquan, who had portrayed Emily Dickinson and whom he'd befriended years ago at a summer retreat. Letta had been thin like this woman, and soft-spoken, lost in her crinolines and bonnets and as awkward as he throughout their first sexual encounter, which had nearly foundered under the stress of stiff eyelets and too many hooks. They had corresponded for several months after their passionate Chautauquan weekend, but her too-obvious hopefulness and his painful discomfort on the telephone had doomed the relationship to failure.

"I hate to bother you," she said, taking the magazine. "But haven't we met before? You look very familiar."

"I'm from Three Chimneys, over in Orange," August replied politely. "Do you get down that way?"

"Can't say I do," she answered. "Where did you go to school?"

"Georgetown. You?"

"Purdue. So that's not it." She shook her head. "Oh well."

"I must have one of those faces," August said.

"They say the same about me."

The woman opened the magazine and idly flipped through it, automatically plucking out the subscription cards as she went. She looked up to see August watching her. "I hate these things," she said.

"Me too."

"I'm Gillian," she said with a smile.

"August."

"Wait a minute." She laughed. "Now I know. Weren't you on TV last night?"

It hadn't even occurred to August that she might have recognized him from the news. What had come later with Margaret had completely crowded out the memory of Patrick Lewis and the television cameras. "That was me," he mumbled.

"You're out of uniform," she said.

"I only dress that way when I'm presenting a program," said August. "Yesterday was an exception."

"So you make cheese for a living?" she asked.

"I was helping a neighbor. I'm a Chautauquan Living Historian."

"That's quite a mouthful."

August would have given anything for something to hide behind. He glanced nervously around the room, but the only other reading material concerned yearly mammograms and hepatitis B screenings.

"I've always been interested in history myself," said Gillian, not bothering to pretend with the magazine any longer. "British history mostly."

"Then I guess we are mortal enemies." He smiled.

"I can't believe I'm sitting here with an honest-to-God celebrity." Gillian shook her head. "Wait until I tell my mother."

So this was how men met women, August thought. They got themselves on television, then sat in doctors' offices waiting to be recognized. He wasn't sure what to do with this woman's enthusiasm, so he steered the conversation back to her.

"And what do you do?" he asked.

"I'm an assistant librarian at the University. Rare books."

"I'm surprised we haven't met," said August. "'I spend a lot of time in Rare Book rooms. Check your bag. No ink pens. White gloves.'"

"I have a stack of them." She smiled.

"They're always so clammy," said August. "Every time I put them on, I think of Jefferson railing against 'the dead hand of the past.'"

"I'll never look at them the same way again!" When she laughed, her nose crinkled and she looked like a mischievous schoolgirl. "So why Jefferson?"

"Why Jefferson?" August echoed. "Oh, it's a long story."

Gillian glanced around the waiting room. "I'm not going anywhere."

People often asked August "Why Jefferson?" but very few honestly wanted to hear his answer. They asked so that they might interrupt with why *they* had always been interested in Jefferson (or Benjamin Franklin, or King Arthur) or with the news that Jefferson was a moral reprobate and a sham. August had the short get-in-before-their-eyes-glaze-over version, and the slightly longer, invite-them-to-tell-their-story version, but this woman, perched on the edge of her chair, seemed genuinely interested in *him*, a welcome change from last night.

"Well," August said, "Jefferson was cripplingly shy, but when he believed in something he found the courage to speak out, even if it meant standing up before an entire nation. He was cursed with having no ego and an enormous ego at the same time. He was a very flawed man, but he thought America and Americans were infinitely perfectible."

"You don't seem very shy to me," Gillian said, and August realized she was right. It was actually fun talking to Gillian, he thought with surprise. He couldn't remember the last time he'd had fun talking to a woman. Surreptitiously, he checked her finger for a ring.

"So, what are you in for?" he asked. Immediately, he knew he'd said the wrong thing, for Gillian's face fell and she reached once more for the magazine.

"Oh, they've found another lump," she said uncomfortably. "You know."

He understood it now—her thin arms, the boyish flatness of her chest. What kind of monster thinks about picking up women in a doctor's office? He tried not to picture a mold-gray fractal growing beneath the pink silk blouse she covered with *American Child*. He couldn't bear to imagine this nice, plain young woman laid out in a coffin, her hands quiet inside a pair of white gloves. Leland emerged from the doctor's office and Gillian's name was called. She gave August a weak smile good-bye, and he wished her good luck.

"She seemed nice," said Leland, observing the exchange.

"What did the doctor say?" asked August gruffly, brushing aside his father's curiosity.

"He treated me like a drunk," said Leland, with the moral superiority of a man who had never once sat behind the wheel of a car after so much as a sip of brandy. "He made me close my eyes and touch my fingertips to my nose."

"What does that mean?"

"And he made me walk a straight line—heel, toe, heel, toe."